A Sister's Wish

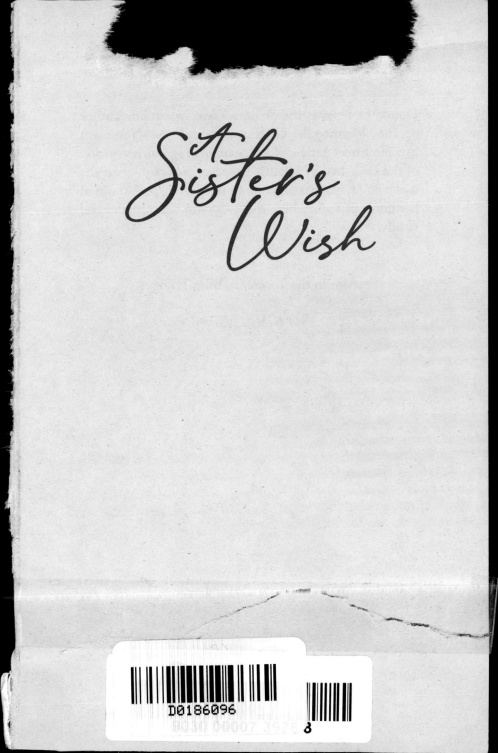

D0186096

9030 00007 3976 8

Donna Douglas is the *Sunday Times* bestselling author of the Nightingale Girls series and the Nurses of Steeple Street series. She began writing stories on top of the coal shed in a south London backyard when she was a child, but has since graduated to a spare room at her home in York, where she lives with her husband and family.

Also in the Yorkshire Blitz Trilogy:

A Mother's Journey

A Sister's Wish

Donna DOUGLAS

ORION

First published in Great Britain in 2021 by Orion Fiction
an imprint of The Orion Publishing Group Ltd
Carmelite House, 50 Victoria Embankment
London EC4Y 0DZ

An Hachette UK Company

1 3 5 7 9 10 8 6 4 2

Copyright © Donna Douglas 2021

The moral right of Donna Douglas to be identified as
the author of this work has been asserted in accordance
with the Copyright, Designs and Patents Act of 1988.

All rights reserved. No part of this publication may be
reproduced, stored in a retrieval system, or transmitted
in any form or by any means, electronic, mechanical,
photocopying, recording, or otherwise, without the
prior permission of both the copyright owner and the
above publisher of this book.

A CIP catalogue record for this book is
available from the British Library.

ISBN (Mass Market Paperback) 978 1 4091 9092 9
ISBN (eBook) 978 1 4091 9093 6

Typeset by Input Data Services Ltd, Somerset

Printed and bound in Great Britain by Clays Ltd, Elcograf S.p.A.

LONDON BOROUGH OF WANDSWORTH	
9030 00007 3976 8	
Askews & Holts	
AF	
	WW20011246

To my family, as always

Chapter One

Saturday 22nd February 1941

Iris Fletcher perched beside her father on his rully, lurching from side to side with the slow, steady plod of the horse. It was a long time since she'd been outside on such a bitterly cold night, and even the heavy blanket gathered around her shoulders couldn't stop her shivering.

'There's another rug in the back if you're nithered?' her father offered.

'I'm all right.'

'Are you sure? I could fetch it for you—'

'I'm all right, Pop, really.'

He gave her a worried sideways glance but said nothing. Iris pulled the blanket tighter around herself, breathing in the faint whiff of horse that rose from it.

They were nearly home. It was some time since they had left the bare trees and country lanes of Cottingham behind them. As they reached the city and headed south towards the Humber, the leafy suburbs gradually gave way to densely packed terraced streets and a skyline of warehouses and wharves and factory chimneys billowing acrid smoke.

A flurry of icy snowflakes stung Iris's cheeks as she looked up at the dark February sky. She dreaded nightfall. Why couldn't Pop have collected her during the daytime? At any moment, the mournful wail of the air raid siren might fill the night and then the planes would come, swooping low, engines droning, raining down their death and destruction.

She looked around, trying not to panic. Where would they hide? They were so exposed out here on the road. She stared at Bertha's gently rolling flanks, willing her to go faster.

'There'll be no raid tonight, lass. Not in this weather.' Her father spoke up, as if he had somehow read her thoughts.

'I in't worried.'

He did not reply. Iris shot a quick look at his craggy profile. Snow was settling on his cloth cap and the shoulders of his old tweed coat.

Dear old Pop. He was sixty years old and still went out with the rully every day, rain or shine, transporting freight to and from the railway yards. But the last few months had aged him. She could see it in his hooded eyes and his sagging, weather-beaten cheeks.

You did that to him. The voice spoke inside her head, sharp and taunting. *You broke them all, one way or another.*

She turned her thoughts away, staring down at the snowflakes melting on her gloved hands. At the convalescent home, the nurses had set up a makeshift ward in the basement to use during air raids. Iris always made sure she was down there well before the siren sounded, in bed with the covers pulled up over her head to shut out the persistent drone of the planes overhead.

She wished she was there now, safe and sound, listening to the whispering squeak of the nurses' rubber-soled shoes and their soft, reassuring voices.

'I'm sorry about this party,' her father spoke up, startling her out of her reverie. 'I told your mother you wouldn't want it, but you know what she's like. Once she gets an idea in her head there's no stopping her.'

'I don't mind.'

'I said to her, it's bound to be a lot for you to take in, seeing everyone again after you've been away so long.'

'I've got to face them sometime, Pop.'

'Aye, I suppose you're right.' Her father fixed his gaze on the road ahead. Then he said, 'Happen it might be for the best to get it over with. You can't hide away for ever, can you?'

Iris turned on him. 'Is that what you think? That I've been hiding?'

'No, lass, I didn't mean that—'

'I've been in hospital, Pop. I nearly died.'

'I know.' Her father retreated into silence and for a while the only sounds were the creak of the wooden rully, the jingling of the reins and the steady clop of Bertha's hooves.

Iris pulled the blanket up around her chin, feeling the scratch of rough wool against her skin.

She could tell Pop didn't believe her. He was just like Miss Billing, the matron at the convalescent home. 'I've been speaking to your doctor, Mrs Fletcher, and he agrees with me that you should go home,' she had said as she stood at the side of Iris's bed a few days earlier. 'The longer you put it off, the more difficult it will be for you.'

As if Iris did not want to go home. She longed to get back to her friends and family in Jubilee Row. She had told Miss Billing as much, but the matron had just smiled and moved on to the next bed.

'Your mother's been busy getting your house ready for you,' Pop was speaking again. 'She and Ruby were down there yesterday, to give everything a good spring clean.' He lowered his voice. 'She left our Lucy's photographs out. Our Ruby thought you might want them put away, but your mother said you'd want to see them?'

Iris kept her gaze fixed on her gloved hands, ignoring his questioning look.

'Anyway, the bains are looking forward to seeing you,' Pop carried on. 'Archie was all for coming with me to collect you, but I told him he should wait.' He sent her another quick sideways look. 'Can't blame him, I suppose. Three months is a long time to go without seeing his mum.'

Iris sensed the criticism in his voice. 'You know why I didn't want them at the hospital. I didn't want to worry them.'

'Aye, so you said.'

Pop did not look at her this time. He was a man of few words – he had to be, married to Big May Maguire. She talked enough for both of them, he always reckoned. But his silence spoke volumes.

As they approached the western end of Hessle Road and the outbuildings of St Andrew's Dock loomed into view, Iris suddenly found it hard to breathe. She clasped her hands tightly together in her lap to stop them shaking.

Once again, her father seemed to guess what she was thinking. 'Sorry, lass. I didn't think,' he said. 'I can turn round and go another way?'

Iris shook her head. 'I want to see where it happened.'

'You don't need to do that. You'll only upset yourself—'

'I want to see it, Pop.'

Her father sighed. 'If that's what you want.' He shook the reins and Bertha lurched forward.

They clopped steadily up Hessle Road, past more outbuildings and warehouses, once a busy, bustling place, standing silent now most of the trawlers had gone over to Fleetwood and Milford Haven. Her father swung the cart left up West Dock Road then pulled on the reins. Bertha slowed to a halt, tossing her shaggy head and snorting her disapproval at the change of direction.

Iris saw the ragged remains of a brick wall where a house had once stood. 'Was it there?' she whispered.

'Aye.' Her father's voice was gruff. 'That's where it came down.'

Iris steadied herself and forced herself to turn towards the spot.

This was it. The place where her baby daughter and her best friend had been killed.

Tears came to her eyes, blurring her vision, but she forced herself to go on staring. She had to do it, to face the pain and let it claw at her heart. No matter how much it hurt, she deserved it.

It should have been you. The voice spoke up inside her head again, soft and insinuating. *You should have been the one holding little Lucy's hand when that bomb went off.*

Inside her gloves, her palms were slick with sweat. But still she went on staring until her eyes dried and the pain in her chest subsided.

She turned back round in her seat.

'I've seen enough,' she said. 'Let's go home.'

Chapter Two

'No, not there. It's hanging too low. Lift your end up a bit, Ruby. No, higher than that. Now you lift your side, Edie. No, no, now it's too high!'

'Make your mind up, Mum!' Ruby sighed. It was turned six o'clock. Pop would be coming home with Iris at any moment, the guests would be arriving and she still had all the food to put out and the cake to fetch from across the road. And there was a meat and potato pie still in the oven. Ruby was sure she could smell it burning from the kitchen.

She caught Edie's eye at the other end of the bunting string. She was looking just as frustrated, balanced precariously on a chair, one eye on the pram in the corner where her baby was beginning to stir.

But Big May Maguire seemed in no hurry as she stepped back and squinted at the bunting they held looped across the window bay.

'It won't do,' she declared finally. 'Put it back over the mantelpiece.'

'But we've just taken it down from there!' Edie protested.

'Then you can stick it back up again, can't you?'

Edie opened her mouth to reply, but Ruby cut in quickly.

'Let's just get it done, shall we?' she pleaded. 'Our Iris will be here before we've had a chance to get everything ready.'

'Aye, well, you'd best get on, then,' Big May grumbled. 'I

don't know why you're both dithering about when there's so much to be done.'

She bustled out of the parlour. Edie stared after her, open-mouthed.

'Did you hear that? As if we haven't been run off our feet all day, following her orders. I've a good mind to go home and leave her to it!'

'Take no notice.' Ruby smiled. 'She's always like this when she's nervous.'

Edie laughed. 'Big May, nervous?'

'You'd be surprised. She's worried about our Iris coming home.'

Edie's smile faded. 'I'm not surprised. I reckon we're all a bit worried about seeing her again.'

Ruby looked over at Edie. 'Even you? But you're such good friends.'

'We were. But I haven't spoken to her for months. I tried writing to her at the convalescent home, but she never replied to any of my letters.'

'Nor mine,' Ruby said. 'She hasn't spoken to anyone but Mum and Pop since ...' She let her voice trail off. Three months after the tragedy happened, she could still hardly bring herself to talk about it. 'Anyway, I wouldn't worry about it,' she said. 'I'm sure you and Iris will be able to pick up where you left off once she's home.'

'I hope so.'

Ruby dragged her chair over to the fireplace. Edie did the same, her expression troubled.

'Do you reckon Iris will have changed much?' she said at last.

Ruby considered the question. 'I don't know. I suppose she's bound to, after everything that's gone on.'

'Imagine losing a child.' Edie shuddered.

'I know.' Ruby's three girls were all grown up now, but she still worried about them as if they were bains.

'I don't even want to think about it.' Edie's gaze strayed to the pram in the corner where her baby son murmured and grumbled, half-asleep. 'If anything happened to my Bobby . . .'

Poor lass, Ruby thought. Edie had already suffered more than her fair share of heartache, losing her husband at Dunkirk last summer. Now she was bringing up their baby by herself and keeping a roof over their heads by braiding nets down at St Andrew's Dock. She was only just turned twenty-one, the same age as Ruby's own twins. She couldn't imagine her Sybil or Maudie going through the hardships Edie had.

They finished pinning up the bunting and climbed down off their chairs.

'Is there much more to do?' Edie said, looking around.

'Only the food to put out. And I've got to go across the road and pick up the cake. Why don't you get off home?' she said to Edie. 'You've done enough.'

'Are you sure? I'd like to give Bobby his last feed and put him to bed, if I can. Mrs Huggins said she'll keep an eye on him tonight so I can come back to the party. But I don't want to leave if there's still work to be done . . .'

She glanced at the door, as if she expected Big May to appear and give her another task to do.

'You go,' Ruby said. 'I'll manage the rest. Go and get yourself dolled up.'

Edie smiled ruefully. 'I don't know about that. It's so long since I got dressed up I think I've forgotten how!' She ran her fingers through her dark curls. Then her smile faded and she said, 'I wish Dolly was here. It will be strange to have Iris here without her.'

'Aye,' Ruby said. The same thought had been on her mind all day. 'I daresay it will be strange for poor Iris, too.'

The Maguire girls, as everyone called Iris and Dolly, had always been inseparable. They were the same age, in their mid-thirties, young mothers with a lively sense of fun. They had been more like sisters, even though Dolly was only a Maguire by marriage. Ruby was married to a Maguire too, but being a few years older at forty-two, she had never shared the same bond with Iris that Dolly did.

But now Dolly was gone, killed by the same bomb that took Iris's three-year-old daughter, Lucy. It was nothing short of a miracle that Iris's nine-year-old son Archie and baby Kitty had been spared.

Ruby couldn't imagine how it would be for Iris, returning home to Jubilee Row knowing her daughter and her best friend would not be there. She pitied her with all her heart.

When Edie had gone home, Ruby took the meat and potato pie out of the oven and set it to cool, then went across the road back to her own house to collect the cake she had baked and iced the day before.

She hurried in through the front door, pausing briefly at the hall mirror to push a stray lock of red hair behind her ear. She would not have time to change out of her old skirt and blouse, but it didn't matter. Everyone was coming to see Iris, not her.

She made her way down the narrow passageway to the kitchen, pushed open the door, and jumped at the sight of a woman smoking a cigarette at her kitchen table.

'About time, too,' she drawled. 'I've been waiting ages for you.'

'Pearl!' Ruby put her hand to her chest. 'Blimey, you nearly gave me a heart attack. What do you think you're doing, sitting here with all the lights blazing? You'll get us fined.'

9

She ran to the window and hastily pulled the thick black-out fabric across the glass.

'I wasn't going to sit in the dark, was I?'

'You could have at least pulled the curtains. That in't too much, even for you.'

'Sorry.' Her sister did not sound in the least bit repentant. She put out her hand and picked off a piece of chocolate icing from the cake in the middle of the table.

'Don't do that!' Ruby slapped her hand away. 'You'll ruin it.' She looked mournfully at the cake she had decorated so beautifully. 'Look at it, it looks like the mice have been at it.'

'You shouldn't have left me waiting so long, should you?'

'I didn't know you were here.'

Pearl tipped back her head and blew out a thin stream of cigarette smoke towards the ceiling. No one looking at them would ever have guessed they were sisters, Ruby thought. There was Pearl, slim and dressed to the nines with her painted lips and carefully waved blonde hair. And then there was Ruby, five years older and sturdily built, her freckled face free of make-up.

'What's all this in aid of, anyway?' Pearl asked, nodding towards the cake.

'Iris is coming home. We're having a party for her.'

Pearl's brows rose. 'Oh, she's decided to come home, at last, has she?'

Ruby ignored her, snatching up a cloth and wiping away the ash her sister had dropped on the kitchen table. 'What do you want, anyway?'

Pearl looked injured. 'Can't I visit my only sister without wanting something?'

Not that I've ever known, Ruby thought. She waited for her sister to speak.

Finally, Pearl threw up her hands and said, 'All right, if you must know, I needed somewhere to hide. The landlady's on the prowl.'

Ruby turned to her, aghast. 'Oh, Pearl! Don't tell me you haven't paid the rent again?'

'I knew you'd give me a lecture if I told you.' Pearl turned away, pouting. 'It's all right for you. You've got a decent husband who sends you money.'

'Your Frank still hasn't sent you anything, then?'

'I've heard nothing from him in a month. Not even a postcard to say he's still alive.' Pearl looked disgusted.

'And you've no idea where he is?'

'Believe me, if I did I'd go and find him and wring his neck for all the worry he's caused me.'

Pearl did not look at her as she said it, and Ruby guessed her sister knew more than she was letting on. Pearl claimed her husband was away on business, but Ruby suspected Frank Tyson was either on the run from the police, or laying low because he was in trouble with one of the shady characters he dealt with.

She stared at her sister's bowed blonde head. She had lost count of the number of times she had tried to steer Pearl out of trouble, but somehow she always managed to get herself in a mess again.

She reached for her bag with a sigh. 'I can let you have a couple of pounds, but that's all I can afford for the rest of the month.'

'I didn't come here for money,' Pearl retorted, 'but I won't say no if you're offering,' she added quickly, as Ruby went to put her purse back in her bag.

You never do, Ruby thought as she counted out three pound notes into her sister's outstretched palm. 'Now promise me you'll pay your rent?' she said. 'You don't want to lose the roof over your head.'

Pearl laughed. 'You're joking, in't you? This won't even cover the arrears!'

'Pearl!'

'It'll be all right, Rube. Don't fuss.' Pearl stuffed the money into her purse and snapped it shut. 'Don't look so worried. Everything will be fine. It always is.'

Ruby thought about arguing, then realised she did not have the time or the breath to waste. 'I hope you're right,' she said. She gathered up the cake and tucked it carefully under her arm. 'Anyway, I've got to go. Mum will go mad if Iris arrives before her cake.'

'You don't want to let your family down, do you?'

Ruby set down the cake and faced her sister, her hands planted on her hips. 'What's that supposed to mean?'

'Nothing.' Pearl looked back at her, all wide-eyed innocence. 'I just envy you, that's all, being part of a big family. Everyone knows how much the Maguires look out for each other.'

'I look out for you, too.'

'I know,' Pearl sighed. 'But sometimes I feel very alone. Especially with Frank away . . .'

Ruby stared at her sister's wistful face. She knew exactly what Pearl was angling for, and she also knew Big May would not like it.

But how could she say no to her own flesh and blood? If she did she would only feel wretched for the rest of the night.

'Do you want to come to the party?' she asked.

'Can I?' Pearl perked up instantly.

'I suppose so. But you've got to promise to behave yourself,' she added.

Pearl's mouth curved into a wicked smile. 'I'm sure I don't know what you mean,' she said.

Chapter Three

Iris stood on the cobbled street, listening to the sound of music and laughter spilling out from the Maguires' house. It seemed unbearably noisy after the soothing hush of the convalescent home. Suddenly she desperately wanted to be back there, safe on the ward, where no one knew her and she didn't have to put on a show.

She started at the sudden pressure of her father's hand on her arm.

'You don't have to do this if you in't ready—'

'I am ready, Pop.' She took a deep breath and squared her shoulders. *As ready as I'll ever be*, she thought.

Everything stopped when she walked in to the parlour. Harry Pearce from the corner shop had been bashing out a joyful tune on the piano, but his hands stilled on the keys as all eyes swivelled in Iris's direction, pinning her where she stood.

Iris looked around at them all. So many faces. Once they had been as familiar to her as her own, but now they seemed like strangers.

She caught sight of Edie Copeland, smiling at her. Iris tried to smile back, but the muscles in her face were too stiff and unyielding to manage more than a grimace.

'Here she is.' Her mother was coming towards her, her hands outstretched. 'We were wondering where you'd got to.'

'We thought you'd changed your mind!' one of the neighbours, Wally Barnitt, called out.

'As if she'd do such a thing.' Her mother beamed at her. 'She knows this is where she belongs. In't that right, lass?'

She moved in quickly before Iris could reply, wrapping her arms around her. Iris allowed herself to be swallowed up in her mother's soft, pillowy embrace. She couldn't remember the last time she had hugged her. May Maguire was a loving mother, but as far as she was concerned, cuddles were only for bains. Being in her arms now just added to Iris's feeling of utter strangeness. If Big May felt the need to hug her then there was truly nothing right in the world.

'You're skin and bone,' her mother declared, releasing her at last. 'Haven't they been feeding you at that hospital? We must get you something to eat.'

'I'm not hungry, Mum.'

'Nonsense, you need feeding up. Ruby, fetch a plate—'

'You heard what the lass said. Leave her be.' Pop was smiling as he said it, but Iris heard the tension in his voice. Her mother must have heard it too. She opened her mouth to argue, then seemed to think better of it.

'I daresay you'll be wanting to see your bains?' She turned, summoning the children. 'Archie, where are you? Come here, lad. Don't be shy now. It's your mum, she in't going to bite you.'

Archie came forward, pulling little Kitty by the hand. He looked like a stranger too, all dressed up in his Sunday best, his hair slicked back and his face scrubbed. And Kitty . . . was this chubby toddler really the baby Iris had left behind? She had changed so much in the three months since Iris had last seen her.

She was aware of everyone watching her, smiling

expectantly. She looked back at Archie. He was staring at her too, his eyes wide and wary.

'Hello, son. Goodness, haven't you grown? You're a proper young man now.'

She wanted to hold her arms out to him but somehow she did not dare. She had the feeling if she tried he would refuse to hug her and she couldn't bear that.

'And here's baby Kitty. Although she in't such a baby any more, as you can see.' Her mother swept up the child and dumped her in Iris's arms.

'Hello, little one.' Iris smiled at her. Kitty took one look at her mother's face and promptly burst into tears.

'Don't cry, pet. It's your mum come home,' May said. But Kitty only screamed and struggled harder, fighting to get out of her arms.

'Here, you'd best take her.' Iris thrust the child back at her mother.

Her mother set the little girl on the floor and she immediately toddled off to hide behind her brother, pressing her face into his jersey.

Out of the corner of her eye Iris could see the neighbours exchanging knowing looks.

'She'll be all right once she gets used to you again,' her mother said.

'I know.' Iris looked at Archie, his arm protectively around his little sister's shoulders.

His silent reproach was even more palpable than Kitty's noisy protests.

Why weren't you there when we needed you?

She could hear the words, almost as clearly as if he had spoken them out loud.

Iris shrank from his steady, questioning gaze. She wanted to tell him how sorry she was. She wanted him to know how much it tore at her that she was not there to hold her little daughter when she was dying.

A burst of laughter from the crowd startled her. Iris looked up and caught a flash of bright blonde hair.

Dolly? She had almost said her name out loud until she realised it was only Ruby's sister, Pearl.

She looked around. Her fear and confusion must have shown on her face because everyone was staring back at her. She pulled herself together quickly and pasted a smile on her face.

'I think I will have something to eat, after all,' she said to her mother.

'Of course. I'll fetch it for you.' Big May hurried off, glad of something to do. Iris turned back to her children but they had disappeared into the crowd.

The party gradually came back to life. Harry Pearce started playing the piano again, and people began talking and laughing. Some of the neighbours came up to Iris, welcomed her home and wished her well. There were so many questions, too, but always the same, over and over again. After a while, Iris found she was answering without even having to think about what she was saying.

'Both legs broken, and my collarbone ... No, I don't really remember what happened that night. One minute I was at our Ada's wedding with everyone else, and the next I was waking up in hospital ... Yes, I have been away a long time, but I'm glad to be home now ...'

Her throat ached from repeating herself. No one talked about Lucy or Dolly, but Iris could see the unspoken questions lingering on their lips as they offered their condolences.

She wondered what they would say if she answered those questions, too.

'No, I wasn't with them when they died ... Dolly was

taking the bains home for me, so I could stay behind with Sam Scuttle. As a matter of fact, we were outside kissing when my little girl was killed . . . Yes, I know. It should have been me with her . . .'

But she kept those thoughts to herself, and instead she made polite conversation and smiled until her face hurt.

Gradually, people seemed to lose interest and left her alone. As all the dancing and the laughter and the chatter went on around her, Iris went to the kitchen to look for her children.

She found her nephews, ten-year-old George and his eight-year-old brother Freddie, helping themselves to cake.

Dolly's boys. There was no mistaking their mother in their fair hair and startling blue eyes.

Her friend had taken such a fierce pride in them. 'Big May had better watch out,' she would always say. 'I've got my own brood of Maguire boys now.'

How ironic that Big May had taken Freddie and George under her wing now, looking after them while their father Jack worked.

Oh God, Jack. Iris hadn't even spoken to her brother yet. She had seen him across the room, but he hadn't approached her.

He probably couldn't face her, she thought. She didn't blame him. Her mother had told her how badly he was grieving.

Guilt lanced her again. Her actions that night had changed so many people's lives, caused so much pain and unhappiness . . .

'Auntie Iris?'

Freddie and George were looking up at her, their innocent faces full of concern. Iris smiled down at them.

'Have you seen Archie?' she asked. They boys shook their heads. 'I thought he might be playing with you.'

They looked at each other. 'He don't play with us any more,' Freddie said.

'I expect he's with Kitty somewhere,' George put in. 'That's where he usually is.'

Iris frowned. Archie and the boys had always been inseparable. They were forever kicking a ball up and down the ten-foot that ran the length of the backs of the terrace, with Lucy at their heels, begging to be allowed to join in.

'Hello, Iris.'

She swung round and found herself nose to nose with Beattie Scuttle. Sam's mother.

Iris took a long, steadying breath. She had known this was coming.

'Hello, Beattie.'

'Your mother's put on a nice welcome for you, I must say.' Beattie looked around. She was a tiny, birdlike woman of sixty, her back hooked from years spent braiding nets. Her sunken features were drawn in a perpetual scowl, whatever her mood.

'Yes. Yes, she has.'

'Our Sam would have come, but he's on duty at the fire station tonight.'

'So Pop said.'

It had been a relief to know he wouldn't be there. Facing him tonight would have been too much for her.

'Mind, we weren't sure if you'd want him here. You didn't reply to any of his letters.' Her beady little eyes searched Iris's face.

'I in't much for writing.'

'Nor is my Sam, but he made the effort.' Beattie looked her up and down, her thin mouth downturned. Then, suddenly, she blurted out, 'He deserves to know where he stands, you know.'

Iris steeled herself. Here it comes, she thought.

'He's still fond of you, although God knows why after the way you've treated him, time and time again,' Beattie went on, the words tumbling out. 'I've warned you before about messing him about, in't I? He in't some puppet you can keep dangling on the end of a string, waiting for you to show an interest.'

'I couldn't help what happened, Beattie.'

'I know that,' Beattie snapped. 'But he's been waiting all this time for you. And if you don't want him then at least have the decency to let him know so he can find someone who does. He deserves that, at least.'

'I'm sorry if I haven't been thinking about your son all this time.' Iris fought to keep her voice steady, even though she was shaking with anger inside. 'But I've had other things on my mind.'

They glared at each other for a moment. Beattie was the first to look away.

'Just let him know where he stands,' she said.

And then she was gone. As she left, she brushed past Edie Copeland in the doorway.

'Someone's in a hurry.' Edie looked over her shoulder. 'Was it something you said?'

'Probably.'

'What did she say to you?'

Nothing I didn't deserve. 'It doesn't matter.' Iris turned to Edie, her smile back in place. 'It's good to see you again.'

'It's good to see you, too. I wanted to come and visit you in the hospital, but Big May said no.'

'I told Mum and Pop I didn't want any visitors. I had to concentrate on getting better.'

'And are you? Better, I mean.'

'I wouldn't be standing here if I wasn't.'

Edie gazed at her, her dark brown eyes warm with concern. She had only moved to Hull the previous summer, but she had become a good friend. For a few months the three of them were inseparable – her, and Edie, and Dolly . . .

Dolly. Why did every memory and every face seem to lead back to her?

'Anyway, never mind me.' Iris changed the subject quickly. 'Tell me about baby Bobby. Mum says he's a little angel.'

'He is.' Edie's face softened into a loving smile.

'Is he here? I'd love to see him.'

She shook her head. 'Mrs Huggins is looking after him tonight.'

'Mrs Huggins?' Iris's mouth fell open. 'Patience Huggins? That old battleaxe?'

Edie grinned. 'Not any more. We're all friends now.'

'Well, I never. Wonders will never cease.'

Patience Huggins was notorious on Jubilee Row as a nasty, snobbish old woman who considered herself above everyone else. She had made poor Edie's life a misery when she had first arrived, trying to get rid of her.

'She's been really good to me since Bobby was born,' Edie said. 'She dotes on him. But I suppose she would, since she helped bring him into the world.'

'Never?'

'Didn't Big May tell you? I went into labour the night of Ada's wedding. The midwife couldn't come out because of bombs coming down. Imagine being born in an air raid!'

It's better than dying in one. Iris bit back the words. It wasn't poor Edie's fault that as her baby was coming into the world, Iris's little girl was being taken from it.

You should have been there.

'You could see him tomorrow?' Edie was speaking again. 'Happen you could come round for a cup of tea?'

20

'And face the dreaded Mrs Huggins?'

Edie pulled a face. 'She really in't that bad when you get to know her.'

'I'll take your word for it.'

'So will you come round?'

'I'll have to see. I daresay there'll be a lot to do in the house, and I'd like to get the bains settled . . .'

From the parlour came the sound of singing. Harry Pearce was pounding out another tune on the piano and everyone was joining in a rousing chorus of the 'Beer Barrel Polka'.

Iris remembered it playing the night of Ada's wedding. She and Dolly were whispering together, and Dolly was egging her on, trying to persuade her to tell Sam Scuttle that she liked him, and everyone was laughing and dancing, and no one knew what horrors were coming for them.

The sound of music filled her head. Iris put her hands to her ears, trying to shut it out, but she could still feel it, the relentless thump of the piano reverberating inside her chest.

'Iris? Iris, are you all right?'

Edie was watching her, her face filled with concern.

'I – I need some fresh air.'

'I'll come with you—'

'No, you stay here, please. I won't be a minute.'

'Don't let the light out!' she heard Edie call after her as she threw open the back door.

Iris stumbled out into the yard, and the back door slammed shut behind her, plunging her into darkness. She stood for a moment, gasping in the sharp night air. The snow had cleared, and above her, the moon was as bright as a new silver penny in the black velvet sky.

A bomber's moon.

She turned to go back inside, but as her hand touched the doorknob she heard the muffled laughter and music from within. The next thing she knew she was picking her way across the yard, ducking under the low-slung washing line, and walking until she reached the back gate.

Chapter Four

Big May approached Edie as soon as she walked back into the parlour.

'Where's our Iris?' she demanded.

'I don't know.'

'Beattie said you were with her in the kitchen just now.'

'We talked for a minute or two, but I in't seen her since.'

'She'd better not have gone home. I'll not be best pleased if she has.' Big May sent Edie a searching look, her eyes narrowing. 'Are you sure you don't know where she is?'

'No, I don't.' Edie dropped her gaze as she said it. It was almost the truth, after all, but she also knew there was no hiding anything from Big May Maguire.

Luckily, at that moment they were distracted by the sound of Pearl screaming with laughter out in the hall.

Big May pulled a disgruntled face. 'Listen to her, making a show of herself. I don't know what our Ruby was thinking, bringing her here. I'm going to have a word.' She looked back at Edie. 'If you see our Iris, tell her I'm looking for her.'

'I will.'

Edie watched her bustle off. She did not like lying to Big May, but she could not forget the desperate look on poor Iris's face as she had darted for the back door.

She didn't blame her for wanting to escape. The room was oppressively hot and the party was getting very loud. Harry Pearce was still thumping out his tunes on the piano and a few of the neighbours were joining in with their tipsy, off-key singing.

There was a time a couple of years back when she would have joined in, dancing and laughing with the rest of them. But now all she really wanted to do was go home to her baby.

She thought of little Bobby, sleeping peacefully in his crib. She could sit for hours watching him while he slept, gazing at his perfect little face, his pudgy nose, rosebud mouth and long lashes curling on his plump cheeks. She would gently touch his hand and smile as his tiny fist closed around her finger.

Her little boy, the most precious thing in her life. When she was not with him, missing him was like a physical ache inside her.

She smiled to herself. *What happened to you, Edie Copeland?*

'What's so funny?'

She turned around to see Jack Maguire watching her, a glass of beer in his hand. Edie shook her head.

'I was just thinking, that's all.'

'I thought it might be Pop's singing.' He nodded to where his father was joining in with a rousing chorus of 'Show Me the Way to Go Home', leaning on the piano while Harry played.

Edie smiled fondly. 'He's having a good time.'

'I expect he's relieved to have my sister home at last.' He turned back to Edie. 'Thanks for not giving her away to Mum, by the way.'

'What do you mean?'

Jack smiled. 'It's all right, I can keep a secret. I saw her sneaking out the back door.'

'I thought she needed some time on her own. This is bound to be a lot for her.'

'Aye,' Jack agreed heavily. 'She looked worn down, poor lass.'

Edie looked at him. He would never say so, but it was a lot for him, too, she could tell. The last three months without Dolly had taken their toll. His grief was there in the hollow of his face and the threads of grey in his thick dark hair.

He had come to the party to support Iris, but she could tell it was a trial for him to smile and pretend to enjoy himself.

'Did you speak to her?'

Jack shook his head. 'I wanted to, but I didn't know what to say,' he admitted. 'I guessed the last thing she needed was to face me.' He shifted his gaze towards the door. 'Whatever we've got to say to each other, it's better if we say it in private.'

Edie looked up into his weary dark eyes. She had never really got to know Jack while Dolly was alive. He had spent much of his time at sea, on board a Royal Naval Patrol Service minesweeper. But after his wife died, he had transferred to a training ship in Immingham so he could be close to his boys. Along with his mother and sisters, Edie often helped out looking after Freddie and George when he was working.

As well as his RNPS work, Jack also volunteered with the ARP as a rescue worker.

'He likes to keep himself busy,' Big May had said. 'I daresay it stops him thinking about Dolly.'

As if that would help, Edie thought. She knew from her own bitter experience that grief could steal into the narrowest cracks, taking hold when you least expected it.

She wished she could tell him it would get better. After nearly a year she still missed Rob desperately. But at least the pain, when it came, did not take her breath away the way it used to.

Harry Pearce changed tempo to a fast Glenn Miller number, and three or four couples began to dance, packing into the tiny front parlour so tightly there was scarcely any room to move. Ruby's sister Pearl swung past in Wally Barnitt's arms, laughing and thoroughly enjoying herself while Wally's wife looked on sourly from the sidelines.

Pearl was taking her life in her hands, Edie thought. She worked with Alice Barnitt at the netting loft, and she was not a woman to be trifled with. Any minute now she would be rolling up her sleeves, ready for a fight.

How Dolly would have laughed, she thought. She would probably be at Alice's side, egging her on.

'Dolly would have loved this.'

She turned to look at Jack, surprised to hear her thought coming from his mouth.

'I was just thinking the same thing. She always enjoyed a party, didn't she?'

He nodded. 'Any excuse to dress up to the nines. And she would have been the first up and dancing, too.'

'Dolly never needed an excuse to dress up. I can still hear her high heels clipping down the street.'

'Mum used to go mad at her. She said she'd break her neck one day.'

They both fell silent for a moment, thinking about Dolly. It was hard to imagine someone so vibrant and full of life had gone from their lives so suddenly.

Edie remembered how nervous she had been when she first moved to the city, pregnant and penniless and feeling as if she did not have a friend in the world. Dolly and Iris had taken her under their wing, found her a job at the netting loft and welcomed her into the extended Maguire clan as if she was one of the family. If it had not been for them, she didn't think she would have survived.

'Jack Maguire!'

They both looked round to see Pearl waving as she whirled

past in Wally Barnitt's arms. 'You're next for a dance,' she called out.

Jack groaned under his breath. 'Not if I can help it.'

Edie looked at Pearl. She was smiling, but her gaze was fixed on Jack like an animal closing in on its prey.

'I don't think she's going to take no for an answer,' she said. 'You'd best get away while you still can.'

'I reckon you're right.' Jack put his glass down and wiped his hand across his upper lip. 'I'll be seeing you.'

'Bye, Jack.'

By the time the music had finished and Pearl had managed to disentangle herself from Wally Barnitt's embrace, Jack had gone.

'Where is he?' Pearl looked around, her red painted mouth turned down in disappointment.

'He had to get home. He's on call with the ARP tonight.'

'But I wanted to dance with him.'

'He'll be sorry he missed you.'

Pearl gazed towards the kitchen. 'Shame,' she said. 'I've been wanting to get my hands on Jack Maguire for a long time. Never had a chance with that wife of his around, though.'

Edie wasn't surprised. Dolly would have scratched out the eyes of any woman who came within ten feet of her handsome husband.

'You wouldn't have had a chance anyway,' she said. 'Jack's devoted to Dolly.'

'Was,' Pearl corrected her. 'She's not here any more, is she? And I've always thought he was a fine man. I mean, I know my sister's husband is good-looking, but Jack's the best of the bunch.' She ran the tip of her tongue over her lips. 'I wonder what Ruby would say if I ended up with her Jimmy's brother?'

Edie fought the urge to slap her. 'In't you already married?' she said tartly. 'What would your Frank say when he comes home, I wonder?'

'Who's talking about marriage?' She roared with laughter. 'I just want a bit of fun.' Then she added, 'Unless you've got your eye on him yourself?'

'No!'

'Are you sure? You looked very cosy when you were talking together.' She nudged her. 'You could do a lot worse.'

'He's my friend's husband.'

'He's a free man now. Best snap him up before someone else does.'

Edie's hands curled at her sides. 'I'd never do that to Dolly. Besides, Jack wouldn't be interested. There'll never be another woman for him.'

'If you believe that, you'll believe anything.' Pearl sent her a pitying look. 'Trust me, once he gets lonely he won't give another thought to his dead wife.'

Edie was saved from replying by Ruby calling out to her sister. Pearl looked over her shoulder.

'Oops, our Ruby's scowling at me again. I'd best go before she sends me home.' She gave Edie a wicked grin. 'Now you remember what I said. If you know what's good for you, you'll snap up Jack Maguire before someone else beats you to it!'

Chapter Five

Iris crossed the street, her footsteps echoing on the cobbles in the silence of the night. With every step, she expected to hear her mother's voice behind her, calling her back, demanding to know why she had left the party.

She ducked down the narrow passageway that led to the ten-foot, the alley that ran along the rear of the terrace. In spite of the bright moon she still had to feel her way along the rough brick wall until she found her back gate.

She let herself in to her backyard and stood for a moment, waiting for her eyes to get used to the gloom. Gradually, the landscape began to take form, outlined in dim silver light. There was the old zinc bath, still hanging on a nail on the wall. The low-slung washing line, an upturned bucket, and her attempt at a vegetable patch. Iris had expected it to be overgrown by now, but the soil felt soft and spongy under her feet. Pop must have been tending to it while she was away, she thought. She should have known he would never have let an inch of ground go to waste, not when he could use it to dig for victory.

She let herself into the house and closed the door behind her, then leaned against it with a sigh of relief. She was home at last. She didn't have to smile and pretend any more, at least not for a while.

Iris's hand was on the light switch before she remembered about the blackout. Something else she would have to get used to. Once again, she thought about the hospital, where everything had been done for her and she had been looked after like a child.

A child.

Guilt stabbed her as she remembered she had left Archie and Kitty behind at the party. How could she forget her own children? She went to open the back door to go out again, then paused. She imagined herself walking back into the party, seeing everyone's faces, having to explain what she had done.

Her mother could look after them for one more night, she thought. Just one night until she got herself sorted.

She stumbled around the house, pulling all the blackout curtains, then switched on the light. The house somehow appeared familiar and strange at the same time. She recognised the furniture, the rugs on the floor, the battered cooking pots on the shelf, and yet they didn't seem to belong to her. She couldn't remember ever buying them, or using them. Even the smell of the house was different. As she tiptoed around, Iris half expected a stranger to appear and demand to know what she was doing in her house.

Her suitcase was at the far end of the hall, just inside the front door. Pop must have dropped it off earlier, while she was at the party. Iris carried it upstairs and stood for a moment on the landing, looking around her. The house seemed eerily silent, and it dawned on her that she had never been completely alone there before. There had always been children's laughter ringing through the house, or their footsteps thundering up and down the stairs as they played. Even at bedtime, she would be able to hear the sound of muffled giggling when they were supposed to be asleep.

Now the door to the children's room stood firmly closed.

Iris set down her suitcase and forced herself to walk across the tiny landing towards it.

What are you afraid of, Iris? It's only a room.

She took a deep breath, grasped the doorknob – then let out a scream as the low moan of the air raid siren filled the air.

No, she begged silently. *No, please, not now.*

She thought about her children. She had to go to them. They needed her . . .

And where have you been these past three months when they needed you? The insinuating voice came into her head, taunting her as she went downstairs and stopping her in her tracks as she reached the back door. Archie and Kitty did not need her. They had learned to do without her all this time. They wouldn't be looking for her now, they would be safe with their grandmother. At least they knew Big May would not abandon them.

No. She screwed her eyes shut and clenched her fists, fighting to silence the voice inside her head. She was home now. She was going to be a mother to her children. Everything was going to be normal again. It had to be.

She threw open the back door, gasping as the icy air rushed in. Planes droned overhead, coming in insistent waves. She had never seen so many in one go before. As fast as one passed, another swept in overhead, caught in the swooping beams of the searchlights.

A flare blossomed high above her, lighting up the sky, and illuminating the dark, stooped figure of a man at the end of the yard, bathed in the strange white light

Iris screamed with shock before she recognised her neighbour Beattie Scuttle's eldest son, Charlie.

'Charlie?' she called out to him, the sound of her voice drowned out by the planes overhead. 'Charlie, go back indoors. It in't safe.'

But Charlie Scuttle ignored her. He stared up at the sky, transfixed.

Incendiaries rained down, clattering on the rooftops opposite and bursting into gouts of fire. Iris flinched back, shielding her face with her arm. But Charlie did not move.

'Charlie!' she cried out again. 'You need to take shelter—'

Her words were drowned out by a whistling scream from overhead, followed by a distant muffled thud.

Iris dived back inside, slamming the back door. She leaned against it, breathing heavily, her heart hammering in terror.

What are you waiting for? The taunting voice whispered inside her head. *Go and get your children, Iris. Prove what a good mother you are.*

Another crash, closer this time. Iris yelped in fear.

'I can't,' she whispered.

A real mother would. A real *mother would never let herself be parted from her bains. She would never leave them to die, alone and afraid . . .*

She slid to the ground, covering her head with her arms, cowering in whimpering terror as the bombs rained down outside.

Chapter Six

'Trust old Hitler to ruin our fun!'

His grandmother was trying her best to sound cheerful but Archie could see the fear behind her smile as she bustled around the kitchen, getting everyone ready to go down to the shelter.

'George and Freddie, get your coats on. Archie, help your sister,' her voice rose against the insistent wail of the air raid siren. 'Ruby, bring the sandwiches and the rest of that pie. We don't know how long we're going to be down there, and it's a shame to let good food go to waste. We can have a feast, eh?'

The rest of the party had dispersed quickly as the neighbours rushed back to their homes to collect what they needed for a night in the shelter.

'Where's Mum?' Archie asked.

'I daresay she's around somewhere.' His grandmother had her broad back turned, wrapping up sandwiches in a damp cloth. But Archie noticed the quick look that passed between her and Auntie Ruby.

'Where is she?' he repeated the question.

'She's gone.' His cousin George piped up behind them. 'Freddie and me were playing out in the yard and she came running past us and went out the back gate.'

He stared at Archie. Once they had been the best of friends, but now George sometimes joined in with the other boys, calling him names in the playground. Just because he no longer collected shrapnel or pretended to be a fighter pilot, running round the playground with his arms outstretched.

Archie turned to his grandmother. 'She went without us,' he said quietly. He hoped George couldn't hear the choke in his voice. He would only be tormented for it when he went back to school.

His grandmother looked blank for a moment, then she quickly pulled herself together.

'She'll turn up, lad, don't you worry. Ruby, will you take Archie and Kitty to the shelter?'

Archie shook his head, his arm around Kitty's shoulders. 'I'm not going without Mum.'

'I daresay she'll be waiting for you there already.'

'Your gran's right,' Auntie Ruby said. Her smile was warm and gentle. 'Let's go and find her, shall we?'

She put out her hand and Kitty moved forward and took it. Archie had no choice but to follow, but all he could think about was that their mother had left them. She didn't even say goodbye.

Auntie Ruby led them all down Jubilee Row to the public shelter on Hessle Road, holding on to Kitty with one hand and clutching a bag of food under the other arm. Archie followed behind, hauling another bag filled with hats, mittens, books, packs of cards and his grandmother's knitting. Bringing up the rear was Auntie Ruby's sister Pearl, a sharp-faced woman with a loud laugh.

'Why did she leave us?' Archie asked.

Auntie Ruby opened her mouth to speak, then closed it again. But she didn't have to say anything; Archie already knew the answer to his question.

Their mother didn't love them any more.

He had seen it in her face when they met again. Her

mouth might have smiled, but her eyes didn't. She couldn't even bring herself to hug him. Kitty sensed her lack of feeling too, which was why she had cried. Archie had seen the relief on his mother's face when their grandmother took them away.

'It'll be all right, Archie.' Auntie Ruby was looking down at him, frowning with concern. 'I daresay all this feels very strange to your mum, after being away for so long. She just needs some time to get used to being home again. You wait and see. She'll be back to her old self soon enough.'

'I know,' Archie mumbled, but he did not believe it. Their mother hated him because of what had happened to Lucy.

He had never really looked after his little sister. Three-year-old Lucy was always getting in the way, hanging around him, wanting to join in his games with Freddie and George. They usually ended up running away and leaving her crying in the street. And then she'd tell their mother, and he would get into trouble for it.

He wished he could turn the clock back. He knew his mother blamed him for Lucy's death because he hadn't looked after her. She probably wished it was him who had died, and not his little sister.

The shelter was around the corner, along Hessle Road. It was a low, brick-built slab of a building with a concrete roof. Auntie Ruby tucked her bag under one arm and held on to Kitty's hand firmly with the other as she led the way down the short flight of steep steps into the gloom of the shelter. Archie followed close behind, with Pearl tottering down after on her high heels.

He hated the shelter, with its flickering light bulbs and bare brick walls. And the smell. Damp and sweat, mingling with something really horrible. The bucket behind the curtain was supposed to be emptied every day, but the reek lingered. Especially if someone had accidentally kicked over the bucket in the rush to get out, which often happened.

Sometimes Archie wished he could be like Mr and Mrs Huggins, who sat under their stairs. But his grandmother would not hear of it.

'I know someone who did that, and the gas meter fell on their head and killed them,' she had said. 'We're safer in the shelter.'

One of the neighbours, Mr Barnitt, had lit a couple of lamps, which threw shadows on the rough brickwork. A few others had set up deckchairs. His grandmother's friend Mrs Scuttle was already there, knitting furiously by the dim light. A couple of others were settling their children to sleep on the long, narrow ledge that ran down one side of the shelter.

But there was no sign of his mother.

'Where is she?' he asked Auntie Ruby.

'She'll be here soon, don't worry.'

'But what if she isn't?'

'She will be, I promise.' His aunt's voice was soothing, but Archie wasn't fooled. 'Here, hold on to your sister while I find somewhere for us to sit . . . How about over here, in the corner?'

She moved away but Archie did not follow. 'We've got to find Mum,' he said.

'I told you, she'll be here.'

'Happen she's decided to stay at home,' Pearl put in. 'I can't say I blame her. I'd rather die than be in this dump.' She wafted her hand in front of her face, grimacing at the stench.

'Pearl!' Auntie Ruby shot her sister a warning look.

'What? I was only saying—'

'Well, don't.'

'I'm surprised you can smell anything, all that cheap perfume you wear.' A squat, angry-looking woman piped up from the corner.

'I'll have you know there's nowt cheap about me, Alice Barnitt!' Pearl retorted.

'That's a laugh!'

'Pearl, please—' Auntie Ruby begged.

While they were arguing, Archie let go of his sister's hand and edged towards the heavy shelter door. But as he reached the steps, his grandmother was already coming down them, her arms full of baskets of food. She was followed by Freddie and George.

'And where do you think you're going?' She eyed him severely, her bulky body blocking the steps.

'I'm going to look for Mum.'

'Oh, you are, are you?' His grandmother set down her baskets and folded her meaty arms across her chest. 'And what good do you reckon you'll do, wandering the streets in the middle of an air raid?'

As if to prove her point, a plane swooped low overhead, followed by the rattle of anti-aircraft fire. Everyone flinched and instinctively ducked their heads.

'I need to find her,' Archie insisted, his voice rising over the noise. Behind him, Kitty picked up on his agitation and started to wail.

'There, love. Don't cry.' His grandmother swept Kitty up. 'Your mum will come when she's ready,' she said to Archie. 'And we'll have no more nonsense about going out looking for her.'

Archie looked at Freddie and George. They stared back at him, their expressions a mixture of contempt and pity.

Auntie Ruby came over, looking flustered. 'I thought you

were supposed to be keeping an eye on him?' his grandmother said.

'Sorry, Mum.' Auntie Ruby shot a look over her shoulder, then back to Archie. 'Why don't you come and play cards with me and the boys?' she said.

He shook his head, his gaze still fixed on the shelter door beyond his grandmother's bulk. He would have made a dash for it, but she gripped him firmly by the shoulders and propelled him round.

'Good idea,' she said briskly. 'We'll get the deckchairs set up and the food out, and we can have a nice little party. How does that sound?'

'I'm worried about him.'

Archie lay on one of the ledges, listening to his grandmother and Auntie Ruby talking. They kept their voices low, but they still carried across the shelter.

Kitty was tucked in beside him, fast asleep. But Archie was wide awake, staring blankly up at the concrete ceiling.

'He's concerned about his mum,' Auntie Ruby said.

'In't we all?'

'Where do you think she's got to?'

'Home, if she's got any sense. But you'd think she'd want to be with her family, wouldn't you?'

Archie thought about his mother's pale, tense face, the smile that did not seem to reach her eyes.

She hates me.

'I don't think she's herself,' Auntie Ruby said.

'You're right, lass. My Iris would never have abandoned her bains.' His grandmother sighed. 'As if that little lad hasn't suffered enough, losing his sister right in front of him. And his aunt, too.'

'Is he still having nightmares?'

'Aye. Terrible they are, screaming and crying out. He sleep-walks, too. Pop found him trying to get out of the back door the other night.'

Archie tensed, his arm tightening around Kitty. He hoped his cousins were not awake to hear.

'He'll be better now his mother's home.' Auntie Ruby's voice was soothing.

'I hope you're right.' The deckchair creaked under his grandmother's weight.

Archie stared up at the ceiling. *I hope so too*, he thought.

Chapter Seven

The insistent drone of the All Clear pierced Iris's troubled dream, dragging her awake.

She opened her eyes, expecting to see a cheery nurse standing over her with a cup of tea, but there was only darkness, so dense it made her eyes ache. Darkness, and cold, and the reek of damp. As if she had been buried alive.

She panicked and tried to sit up, but her head struck something solid inches above her and she cried out in pain until she remembered where she was.

Last night, as the air raid was in full force, she had taken refuge in the cupboard under the stairs. She had curled up in a tight ball in the darkness, and somehow managed to snatch a few hours' sleep as the droning and whistling and crashes and bangs shook the house all around her.

Now, in the deathly silence of the dawn, Iris uncurled her stiff, cramped limbs and fumbled for the door latch to let herself out.

She made her way to the kitchen. It was just after six on Sunday morning, and dawn had not yet broken behind the thick blackout curtains.

Iris went to fill the kettle but no water came out. The mains must have been hit, she thought. She sat down heavily at the kitchen table, trying to force herself to think what to do next.

She should go and fetch the children. She was ashamed to remember how she had abandoned them the previous night.

She had not meant to leave them. She wanted to go back for them, until the raid had trapped her.

Would they understand, she wondered. She thought about Archie's reproachful face. She had let him down once when he needed her, now he would have even more reason not to trust her.

She rested her head in her hands. This would not do. She could not allow herself to give in to the despair that lurked like a dark stranger on the edge of her consciousness. If she let it in it would overwhelm her and then she would be lost.

Think, Iris. Think.

She gazed around the kitchen. She could go shopping, fill those empty cupboards. But the thought of going into Pearce's corner shop filled her with panic. Last night had been bad enough. She wasn't sure she was ready to face everyone again.

The longer you put it off, the more difficult it will be for you. Matron's words came back to her.

She would spring clean, she thought, even though her mother had clearly been looking after the house while she was away. As soon as it was light she would throw open all the doors and windows, let in some fresh air, wash and scrub and polish everything, and then she would fetch the children and make herself feel normal again.

And she would start by freshening herself up. There was still no water in the tap, but she could at least change out of last night's clothes. She looked for her suitcase in the hall, then remembered that she had taken it upstairs last night, just as the air raid siren sounded.

The suitcase was on the landing, sitting outside her bedroom door. Once again, Iris turned to look at the door to the children's room, still firmly closed. She had been about to open it last night when the raid began.

She took a step towards it, then retreated. Later, she

thought. She would go in later, when she was feeling stronger.

She opened the door to her bedroom. Her mother had tidied in here, too. The bed was neatly made, the pillows and eiderdown carefully straightened. The whole room smelled of beeswax polish.

Iris stared at the bed, and her head was instantly filled with a picture of little Lucy, crawling in beside her in the middle of the night as she so often did. She thought about her warm little body huddled into hers, the tickle of her breath against her skin . . .

The next thing she knew she was in the hallway again, leaning against the door, breathing hard as she struggled to collect herself.

Pull yourself together, Iris.

She went back downstairs and tried the tap again. Still no water. She opened the back door and stepped into the yard, breathing in the cold morning air, tainted with smoke and cordite. It made her think about that night at Ada's wedding, the planes roaring overhead, the smell of burning . . .

And then nothing. She had no recollection of anything until she woke up in hospital.

They hadn't told her about Lucy. No one had said anything to her until days after she was buried.

'We thought it was for the best,' her mother had said.

She hadn't been able to say goodbye to her daughter. She hadn't comforted Archie and Kitty, held their hands at the funeral. Even at the very end she had not been there.

'Iris?'

She looked up sharply. Sam Scuttle stood on the other side of the wall, watching her. He must have just come home from his shift, she thought. His burly shoulders were hunched with weariness.

Their eyes met and Iris felt the treacherous quickening of

excitement at the sight of the man she had spent the last three months trying to forget.

'I heard you were back,' he said.

She nodded, not trusting herself to speak. He was so close she could smell the smoke clinging to his fireman's uniform.

'Sorry I couldn't come to your party.'

'Your mum said you had to work.'

'Aye.' He looked down at the tin hat under his arm. There was a heaviness in his voice that made her think it had been a bad night.

She felt her heart go out to him, and it frightened her.

'You've had a busy night?' she said.

He nodded. 'Ellerby Grove and Rowlston Grove got it bad. There was one at the railway crossing at Hawthorn Grove, too, went off before it could be defused—'

Iris winced, her whole body bracing. She didn't want to hear it, she didn't want to think about those bombs dropping, the lives lost . . .

Sam fell silent, as if he understood. 'It was a hard night,' he said quietly.

Iris saw the look in his eyes and knew what he was going to say next.

'I saw your Charlie, standing out in the backyard in the middle of the raid,' she got in quickly. 'I called out to him, but he wouldn't come in.'

Sam shook his head. 'He won't go to the shelter. He doesn't like being underground. It worries Mum senseless, but I suppose you can understand it after what happened to him.'

Iris nodded. Charlie Scuttle had been a young man of seventeen when he joined the Royal Engineers Regiment in the last war. As a sapper, it was his job to dig tunnels towards the enemy lines. But an explosion in no man's land had caused one of the tunnels to collapse, and Charlie and his mates had been buried alive. Charlie was the only one to survive, but it had turned his mind.

She looked at the Anderson shelter in the Scuttles' back yard. She remembered all the time Sam had spent digging it.

'And after you went to all that trouble,' she said.

'I know.'

He smiled at her, and Iris felt panic rising in her chest.

'Anyway, I'm sure you'll be wanting your bed,' she said quickly, retreating behind the door.

'Iris—'

'I'll see you, Sam.'

'Iris,' she heard his plaintive cry as she closed the back door.

Chapter Eight

Monday 24th February 1941

The canteen van lurched clumsily over the rutted road, its wheels skidding on the ice. After a clear night it had started to snow again, and Ruby had to crane forward in the driver's seat to peer through the flurries that pattered against the windscreen. Her hands, curled tightly around the steering wheel, were blue with cold.

The morning sky was dull and leaden, but at least it had brought some peace from the drone of planes and the incessant rattle of anti-aircraft barrage that had terrified them for the past two nights.

Beside her in the passenger seat, Edie Copeland stifled a yawn with the back of her hand.

Ruby smiled. 'You didn't get much sleep last night either?'

'How could I? I don't know which was worse, the bombs coming down or the ack-ack guns firing all night.'

'It was awful, wasn't it?'

The shelter was never comfortable, but it had been terrible last night, with lightbulbs flickering and brick dust showering down from the ceiling. They had stayed awake all night, wondering if there would be anything left when they came out.

As Ruby went to turn the corner, the van hit a patch of ice and slewed sideways. From the rear came the ominous crash of china.

'Sorry.' Ruby wrestled with the steering wheel, her teeth

gritted. She had not long since learned to drive, and she found the van nerve-racking enough without the freezing, snowy weather. 'I hope those cups are all right back there.'

'Never mind the cups. It's us I'm worried about!'

Ruby leaned forward, her nose almost touching the windscreen. 'Thanks for volunteering to come with me this morning,' she said. 'I couldn't have managed without you.'

'I don't know about volunteering,' Edie said ruefully. 'You don't say no to Miss Brekke, do you?'

'That's true.' They had stumbled bleary-eyed out of the shelter when the All Clear sounded, only to be summoned by the WVS District Organiser and instructed to take the mobile refreshments van up to De La Pole Avenue. 'Still, it was worth it, wasn't it?'

Ruby would never forget the desolate scene that had greeted them when they'd arrived just after dawn that morning. Everywhere she looked, there were broken windows, crumpled walls and cracked brickwork. But it was far worse at the end of the street, which was blocked by a broad drift of rubble and fallen masonry. Several men in tin hats and heavy coats were gathered around it, armed with ropes and ladders and shovels, while a couple of policemen and ARP wardens tried to keep back the handful of neighbours who had stayed behind in the street to see what was going on.

In all, ten people had been killed, and twenty-five more were seriously injured.

'I keep thinking of all those poor people waiting at the First Aid Post,' Edie said. 'They looked shattered, didn't they? As if they couldn't quite take it all in.'

'I know what you mean.' Ruby shuddered to think of them, shivering under blankets, staring with blood-smeared faces at the bleak, shattered landscape that had once been their home.

'I wish we could have done more,' Edie said. 'It seems a bit daft, doesn't it? Handing out tea and sandwiches when those poor people have lost everything.'

'It was better than nothing,' Ruby said. 'And it kept the rescue workers going.'

'I know, but—'

'We do what we can,' Ruby said firmly. 'I know it might not seem like much, but if we all do our bit—'

'Look out!'

Ruby jammed her foot on the brake and the van screeched to a halt, followed by an avalanche of falling china from the back.

'Oh God, did I hit something?' She froze, staring straight ahead, too terrified to move.

'I don't think so. It ran off that way.' Edie scrambled out of the van and went to look. Ruby followed her, picking her way over the icy pot holes.

'What was it? Did you see?' she asked.

'I'm not sure. It think it might have been a cat. It went over here . . .' Edie paused, cocking her head. 'Did you hear that?'

Ruby listened. 'I can't hear anything. Was it a rat, do you think?' she shuddered.

'Something's whimpering. It's coming from down here.' Edie dropped to her hands and knees and bent her head to the pavement to look under a heap of broken masonry. A low growl came from the gloom within. 'It's a dog! Poor little thing, it looks terrified.'

'Careful,' Ruby warned, 'it might bite.'

'It's only a little thing.'

'It could still give you a nasty nip. Be careful—'

But Edie ignored her, reaching in to a hollow space in the pile of masonry. 'Come on out, little chap. I in't going to hurt you.'

'Watch it. You don't want it to collapse . . .'

'I've got him.' Edie emerged with a scruffy, quivering bundle in her arms. Ruby caught sight of bright dark eyes like two buttons in a shaggy little face.

'Is it hurt?' she asked anxiously.

'No, it's just scared, I think.' She checked the dog's fur around its neck. 'It doesn't have a collar. It must have escaped from somewhere. I expect it got frightened by the raid and ran away.'

Ruby put her hand out and the little terrier sniffed her fingers with its cold, wet nose. 'It seems friendly enough.'

'What shall we do with it?' Edie asked.

'What do you mean?'

'We can't just leave it here.'

'What else can we do?' Ruby looked around at the broken landscape. 'I'm sure it will find its way home—' she started to say, but Edie shook her head.

'We could take it with us.'

'In the van?' Ruby looked appalled. 'I don't know what Miss Brekke would say about that. It might be against WVS regulations.'

'Miss Brekke doesn't need to know, does she? Anyway, we're supposed to help people when they've lost their homes.'

'Well yes, but I'm not sure that includes dogs—'

'Then I'll walk home with it.'

Ruby stared at her for a moment, then back at the dog. A pair of trusting brown eyes looked back at her. 'I suppose it won't hurt,' she sighed. 'But if the District Organiser has my guts for garters I'll make sure to tell her it was your idea.' She patted the dog. Its fur was coarse with dust and dirt. She relented. 'It is a dear little thing, in't it? What are you going to do with it?'

'I'm not sure. Take it home, I suppose.'

Ruby smiled. 'I'd like to hear what Mrs Huggins has to say about that!'

Chapter Nine

Ruby dropped Edie and the dog off on the corner of Jubilee Row then returned to the WVS centre on Ferensway to finish the stock-taking and accounts.

Her head was full of lists and figures as she hurried into the main room, which was already busy at ten o'clock in the morning.

Ruby paused for a moment, enjoying the quiet buzz of activity. The WVS volunteers were split into various groups, each set to a different task. Some were knitting socks for sailors and jumpers for the RAF, others were sewing badges on to soldiers' tunics, while others were busy making pyjamas and nightgowns for the Infirmary out of old offcuts of flannel that had been sent over from Willis's. Over in another corner, three women were sorting through a pile of donated books that were to be sent off to servicemen.

It was so nice to see everyone hard at work, doing their bit for the war effort. Ruby loved being part of the Women's Voluntary Service, and was very proud of her dark green uniform. She spent her days organising rotas and work parties and salvage drives. She managed stock, raised funds and dealt with accounts – things she'd never dreamed she could have done as a humble housewife.

Everyone leaned on her, especially Miss Brekke, but Ruby didn't mind at all. It was wonderful to feel needed, especially now Jimmy had transferred from the trawlers to the Royal

Naval Patrol Service. He was away for months on end, and the girls were grown up and going their own way.

Her mother-in-law was bickering with Beattie Scuttle in the corner as usual. They had been best friends for nearly all of their sixty years, but that didn't stop them fighting like cats most of the time.

Big May looked up and caught her eye. 'Where have you been?'

'I took the van out to De La Pole Avenue.'

Big May and Beattie exchanged a troubled look. 'Bad, was it?' Beattie asked.

Ruby nodded.

'I daresay you could do with a brew?' Big May said kindly.

'That would be nice.' Ruby ran her hand wearily across her face. She had been so busy serving hot drinks and sandwiches to the ARP men, policemen and firemen that she had not even thought about herself.

Her mother-in-law set down her knitting. 'You sit down, I'll fetch you one.'

'Thanks, Mum.' Ruby looked around. 'Is there anything I should know about?'

'The pipes were frozen when we got in,' Beattie said. 'Someone forgot to wrap rags around them last night. Again.' She twisted round to glare across the room at poor timid little Miss Jeffers.

'We got the fire lit and they've thawed out nicely now,' Big May said. 'I'll go and put the kettle on.' She got to her feet, then remembered something 'Oh, I nearly forgot. There's someone waiting in your office to see you.'

'Who? Not Miss Brekke?' The District Organiser was bound to have another list of tasks for her to do, and even though she was not afraid of hard work, Ruby was befuddled with exhaustion and looking forward to going home to bed.

'Worse than that,' Beattie said. 'It's your sister.'

Ruby glanced towards the closed office door. 'What does she want?'

Big May and Beattie looked at each other. 'I don't know, but I'm sure we can all guess,' Beattie muttered.

Pearl was sitting in the office, her head bent. As soon as Ruby walked in, she leapt to her feet and launched herself at her.

'Oh, Rube, she's thrown me out!' she sobbed.

'All right, all right, calm down.' Ruby held her at arms' length. 'What's all this about?'

'Mrs Dale. I got home and she'd locked me out. I ask you, what kind of a rotten cow throws someone out in the middle of an air raid?' She started crying again, her pretty face contorted.

'Did you give her the money like I told you?'

'Of course I did. But I told you, it don't even cover the arrears.' Pearl wiped her eyes with her sleeve. 'What am I going to do? She says if I don't give her more money by the end of the day she's going to chuck all my stuff out on the street!'

'It won't come to that, I'm sure. How much do you owe?'

'Six pounds.'

'Six pounds?' Ruby stared at her, dumbfounded.

'It in't my fault!' Pearl wailed. 'You know I'm no good at managing money. I let all the bills get on top of me and now I'm going to lose everything!'

'There now, don't upset yourself.' Ruby put her arms around her sister, comforting her. 'I'm sure we can sort it out.'

'How? Where am I supposed to get hold of that sort of money?'

You should have thought about that weeks ago, Ruby thought. But there was no point in lecturing her now.

'I've got a few pounds in my post office account,' she said quietly. 'I was saving for a new winter coat.'

Pearl shook her head. 'I can't take it.'

'You've got to.'

'But your new coat—'

'It doesn't matter. I'm sure I can find something in the salvage. Or if not, there's still plenty of wear left in my old one. It's more important we keep a roof over your head.'

'I suppose so.' Pearl sniffed back her tears.

'I'll go to the post office when I've finished here.'

'Can't you get it now?' Pearl snapped, then seemed to think better of it. 'I'm just worried the landlady will throw my stuff out,' she said meekly. 'She's capable of anything, I reckon.'

'I'll go as soon as I can,' Ruby promised.

'Will you talk to Mrs Dale for me? I got into a bit of a shouting match with her before I walked out. I don't think I did matters much good.'

'Oh, Pearl.' Ruby sighed. 'You've got to stop letting your temper get the better of you.'

'I know.' Pearl pulled a face. It made her look very young, and Ruby was instantly transported to when they were children.

She patted Pearl's arm. 'It will be all right, honestly.'

'Thanks, Rube.' Pearl gave her a watery smile. 'I'm sorry I've made a mess of everything,' she said. 'I'm just not very good at all this sort of thing. Frank always took care of the bills before he left. I'm not as good at managing things as you are.'

As they left the office, Ruby said, 'You know, if Frank's not coming back soon, it might be a good idea for you to start finding a way to look after yourself.'

Pearl looked round sharply. 'What do you mean?'

'They're crying out for women workers. It says in the paper

we're all going to have to start registering for war work—'

'I'm not going into a munitions factory, if that's what you mean!'

'You could get some shop work?'

'And stand on my feet for hours on end? No, thank you.'

'Well, you should do something.'

'I'll think about it.' Pearl stopped to adjust her felt hat to a stylish angle. 'But I can't make any promises. I in't like you, Ruby. I'm not one for do-gooding.'

She looked around the centre as she said it. Ruby cringed, seeing the looks some of the women were sending their way.

It was too much to hope her mother-in-law had not heard. As Ruby returned, Big May said, 'It wouldn't hurt her to do a bit of good for a change.'

'She didn't mean anything by it.'

'You want to stop sticking up for her, Ruby. She'll never do the same for you.' Big May handed her a cup of tea. 'How much did she want this time?' she asked in a low voice.

Ruby felt her cheeks colour. She was about to deny it, then she caught Big May's shrewd expression.

'Not much.'

'You know you won't see that money again?'

'She'll pay it back.'

'Like she did the last lot you lent her?'

Ruby turned to her mother-in-law helplessly. 'What else can I do, Mum? I can't let her go short.'

'She's a grown woman. She in't your problem, lass.'

That's where you're wrong, Ruby thought. She had been taking care of her sister for as long as she could remember.

God knows, their mother had never bothered with either of them. Right from the moment Pearl came into the world, five-year-old Ruby had looked after her. She kept her clean and fed, played with her and sang to her, and did her best to shield her from the harsh realities of the life into which they had both been born.

Elsie Finch was no mother to her girls. She was too busy getting drunk or chasing men. Theirs was a precarious sort of existence, hiding from the landlord or the tally man, in constant peril of being turned out on to the streets. Ruby would never forget the shame of seeing their belongings on the pavement, or being sent to the pawn shop, or to beg for food on tick from the corner shop – 'You do it, Ruby, he'll not say no to a bain.'

Ruby tried to protect her sister from the worst of it by turning it all into a big game. They played hide-and-seek when the bailiffs knocked on the door, and pretended they were explorers setting off on their next big adventure when they had to do yet another moonlight flit.

She protected Pearl from their mother's moods, too. She knew how quickly Elsie could switch from laughing one minute to tearful and maudlin the next.

'I could have made something of my life if it weren't for you,' she would sob. 'I could have been a big star, just like Marie Lloyd or Vesta Tilley. But I had to go and get saddled with a pair of kids, didn't I? You ruined everything for me.'

But it was her quickfire rages that Ruby feared the most. Elsie didn't care who she lashed out at, and all Ruby could do was put herself between her mother and the baby and take the blows until the storm had passed.

And she had been shielding her sister from life's blows ever since.

'Old habits die hard, Mum,' she sighed.

Chapter Ten

'I should think not! I'm not having that filthy animal running around this house. I don't know what possessed you to bring it home in the first place.'

'It was lost. I couldn't leave it wandering the streets.'

'I daresay it would have found its way home if you'd let it be.'

'And what if it doesn't have a home any more?' Edie hugged the little dog closer, feeling the tickle of its rough fur against her cheek. 'You didn't see the state of the street, Mrs Huggins. There was scarcely a house left standing.'

Patience Huggins pursed her lips. 'All the same, it can't stay here,' she said. 'Look at it. It's probably crawling with fleas.'

As if it knew it was being discussed, the dog started whimpering and huddled against Edie.

'It is in a bit of a state,' Horace Huggins remarked. 'How about we give it a wash?'

Edie smiled gratefully at him, but his wife was not to be moved.

'You could polish it with Brasso but it's still not staying here,' she said, folding her bony arms across her chest. 'And you'd best not think about using my wash tub to bathe it in . . .' Her voice followed Edie and Horace out into the yard.

'She's right, you know,' Horace whispered, as they lifted Edie's galvanised tub down from its hook on the brick wall. 'It can't stay here. It's against the tenancy agreement.'

'I know,' Edie sighed. 'But what else can I do?'

'Happen it's not such a bad idea to take it back where you found it? Its owner's probably searching high and low for it.'

'If they're still alive,' Edie said quietly.

They were interrupted by Patience coming out with a pan of hot water. 'If you're going to wash it, you might as well do it properly.' She glared at the dog, who trembled under her stony gaze.

'I'll tell you something, that dog in't daft,' Horace chuckled. 'He knows who's boss!'

They set to washing the dog, but the little creature had other ideas. As they tried to rinse the thick dust from its coat it wriggled and squirmed, splashing water everywhere.

'Looks like you're the one getting the bath, Missus!' George piped up from over the fence as Edie wiped her face with her sleeve. He and Freddie had been watching them avidly ever since they began bathing the dog.

Edie looked over at them. 'Shouldn't you be at school?'

'Day off. There's an unexploded mine next door,' George said.

'They wouldn't even let us go and look at it,' his brother added mournfully.

The dog took advantage of Edie's distraction and shook itself, spraying her with water. The boys roared with laughter.

'Why don't you come and help, if you think you can do better?' she said.

They did not need telling twice. They disappeared from behind the fence and appeared a moment later at the back gate. But as the gate creaked open the little terrier suddenly leapt from the tub and bolted between their legs.

'Quick, he's getting away!' Freddie cried. The boys scampered after him and by the time Edie had scrambled to her feet they had returned, George carrying him triumphantly.

'We got him just before he went into Pearce's shop!' Freddie laughed.

'Come on, then. Let's get him washed before this water goes cold,' Edie said.

The boys started through the gate then both stopped, casting nervous glances towards the house.

'It's all right,' Horace smiled. 'Mrs Huggins won't chase you off this time.'

The boys' presence made the little dog even more animated. He splashed around, and kept trying to jump at them with his soapy paws, much to their amusement.

'I thought many hands were supposed to make light work?' Horace muttered, as he tried to rinse the wriggling animal. But even he had to smile at the boys' squeals of laughter.

'Is it your dog, Missus?' George asked.

Edie glanced at Horace. 'No,' she said. 'It's a stray. I found him wandering the streets.'

'What's he called?'

'Lucky.'

'Lucky?' Horace raised an eyebrow. 'So he's got a name now, has he?'

'I couldn't keep calling him dog, could I?' Edie blushed.

'I like the name Lucky,' Freddie said.

'So do I.' Edie looked defiantly at Horace, who shook his head.

Finally, they managed to get all the dirt and dust out of Lucky's fur, revealing the pale, sandy colour beneath. He looked a pathetic sight, his body so thin under his bedraggled coat.

'What are you going to do with him, if he don't belong to you?' George asked, as they dried him on a scrap of old towel.

'Good question, lad,' Horace muttered.

'I was going to look after him until I found his owner,' Edie said.

'And what if you don't find them?'

Edie looked at Horace. 'I suppose we'll find somewhere else for him to live.'

'He could live with us,' George said. 'We've always wanted a dog, eh, Fred?'

'I'll say!' Freddie reached out his hand to stroke the little dog, and Lucky licked his fingers enthusiastically.

'Look, he likes us,' George said. He turned pleading eyes to Edie. 'Can we have him, Missus? Please?'

'That's not up to me,' Edie said. 'You'd need to ask your father.'

'Ask me what?'

Jack stood in the open gateway. He had just returned from a night of rescue work. He looked exhausted and his clothes were caked in filth.

The boys jumped to their feet and rushed to greet him, both gabbling at once.

'The dog's got no home, Dad. Can we have him?'

'He's got nowhere else to go.'

'Hang on a minute, let me get in the gate first.' He laid his hand on his eldest son's shoulder. 'Why in't you with your Granny May if you in't in school?'

'She said we could lark out as long as we didn't get in trouble.'

'We'll take good care of him,' George joined in. 'He'll be no bother.'

'Can we, Dad?'

'Shush a minute, both of you.' Jack held up his hands to silence them. 'I can't think when you're both shouting at once.' He looked down at the dog, which had escaped from Edie's arms and was now sitting at his feet, looking plaintively up at him. 'Where did he come from?'

'Mrs Copeland got him off a bomb site.'

'We found him near De La Pole Avenue,' Edie explained. 'I didn't know what else to do so I brought him home.'

'I told her she would have done better to leave it to find its own way home,' Horace put in.

'It was chaos up there. His owner might have been evacuated already.'

Or they might be dead. Edie's eyes met Jack's, and saw his look of understanding. She had spotted him up there this morning, among the other ARP rescue workers. He knew what it had been like.

'His name's Lucky,' Freddie said.

'Lucky, eh?' Jack bent down to pick up the dog. 'He's a handsome little lad, I'll say that. And you don't want him for yourself?' he asked Edie.

'Well . . .'

'I daresay she would,' Horace said. 'And if it were up to me he'd be more than welcome. But if I know my missus, she'll be writing a letter of complaint to the landlady as we speak.' He grimaced apologetically.

'Can we have him, Dad?' George asked.

'I don't know, lad. There's a lot to looking after a dog. You'll have to take him for walks and such. And with me working all hours I don't reckon I'd be able to do it . . .'

'We'd do it,' Freddie said eagerly. 'We'd love to take him for walks.'

'And I'd help out,' Edie said.

Jack frowned at her. 'Whose side are you on?'

'I just want him to have a good home. Look, he likes you already.'

Jack gazed down at Lucky, who was enthusiastically licking his hand. 'He's just trying to get round me.'

'And is it working?'

Once again their eyes met, and Jack smiled reluctantly. 'I suppose so. But only for a while, mind,' he said. 'Just until we can find his real owner. So I don't want you two getting too attached. He don't really belong to us.'

From the way the boys were grinning, it was clear they had not listened to a word their father had said.

'We won't, we promise. Can we take him for a walk?' They looked at Edie.

'Don't ask me. He's your dog now.'

'You'll have to find a lead for him,' Jack said. 'I think we've got a bit of string in one of the drawers. That'll have to do until we find something better.'

'Come on, Lucky!' The boys ran out of the gate, back to their house. Jack set the dog down and it scampered after them.

Jack and Edie watched them go. 'I suppose I'd best go after them, make sure the three of them don't get into any trouble,' he sighed.

'Thank you for taking the dog,' Edie said.

'I couldn't see him without a home, could I?' He looked rueful. 'Anyway, happen he'll cheer us all up a bit.'

Edie glanced sideways at him. He was smiling, but there was no hiding the lost expression in his eyes.

It would take more than a pet to make him happy again, she thought.

Chapter Eleven

Thursday 27th February 1941

'When are you going to go and see little Lucy, then?'

Iris froze where she stood at the sink. Her mother's question was asked lightly enough, but there was a world of weight behind her words.

She glanced over her shoulder. Her mother was standing at the stove, stirring a pot, as if she had not spoken at all.

Everyone else in the kitchen had fallen silent. Iris's sister Florence kept her attention fixed on laying the table, while Pop hid behind his newspaper. None of them met her eye, but Iris knew they were listening.

She turned back to the potatoes she was peeling. 'I don't know, I haven't had time to think about it.'

'You've been home nearly a week.'

'I've had a lot to do.' Iris plunged her hands back into the cold water, rummaging for her knife. 'I'll go soon.'

'When?'

'Soon, I said. When I'm ready.'

'And when will that be?'

Mind your own business and leave me alone! Iris gritted her teeth to stop herself shouting the words. She could feel the muscles in her shoulders growing rigid with tension.

Did her mother not understand how difficult this was for her? Even now, standing here, she was aware of what she had lost.

Dolly should have been here. They always peeled the

vegetables together, standing side by side at the sink, watching their children playing in the yard. They would have been nudging each other, whispering and giggling. Dolly would probably have been making fun of Florence as usual. She worked for the corporation and volunteered as an ARP warden and was very full of herself.

She stared out of the window. Dolly's sons were playing with their new dog, while her Archie sat on an upturned bucket, watching Kitty toddling around the yard. They did not speak or even look at each other.

'I usually go up there on a Friday, if you want to come with me.' Her mother interrupted her thoughts.

'I'll think about it.'

May opened her mouth to speak again but Pop got in first.

'Leave the lass alone,' he said quietly. 'She said she'll think about it, and that's that.'

'Yes, but what is there to think about? That's what I want to know.' Her mother put down her spoon. 'She's been home all this time, and she still hasn't been to see her daughter . . .'

'What difference does it make if I'm there or not?' The words burst out of her. 'Lucy won't know, will she? She's gone.'

'You should still pay your respects. You owe them that.'

You owe them. There it was, the unspoken accusation, out at last. Iris looked at the others. Florence had stopped, a fork in her hand. She was glancing anxiously between Iris and their mother.

'What's that supposed to mean?' Iris fought to keep her voice level.

'Nowt,' Pop put in. 'She meant nowt by it. Did you, May?'

'Yes, she did.' Iris kept her gaze fixed on her mother's turned back. 'She blames me. She thinks it's my fault they're dead. In't that right?'

'I never said that.'

'You didn't need to. It's written all over your face.' Iris put down her knife, dried her hands on her apron and went to the back door. 'Fetch your sister,' she called out to Archie. 'We're going home.'

'Don't be like that, Iris.'

'You don't have to go.'

Her father and her sister started to talk at once, but her mother stayed stubbornly silent, still stirring the pot.

'What about the bains' tea?' Florence said.

'I'm capable of feeding my own children, thank you very much!'

'No one's saying you in't, love,' Pop joined in quietly. 'We just don't want you to go. Not like this. In't that right, May?'

Iris looked at her mother. 'Let her go, if that's what she wants,' May muttered, her back still turned.

'What were you and Granny May arguing about?' Archie wanted to know.

'Nothing that need concern you,' Iris muttered under her breath. She charged down Jubilee Row, pushing Kitty's pram ahead of her like a battering ram. Archie trailed miserably behind, scuffing his boots on the cobbles. For once, Iris was too angry to tell him off about it.

How dare her mother talk to her like that? She didn't understand at all. She had no idea how hard it was for Iris. She was barely holding on as it was. Over the past week she had struggled to get her life together. She shopped and cooked and cleaned and looked after the house and the children, even though every day required a force of effort that left her utterly exhausted.

But no matter how tired she was, by the time she went to bed sleep would elude her, and she would spend all night tossing and turning and reliving that night, over and over again, thinking of how she could have made things different.

Her mother made it sound as if Iris had forgotten Lucy somehow. How could she when her little face was there every time Iris closed her eyes? Sometimes she could almost hear Lucy's plaintive cries in the yard, calling out for Archie to come and play with her.

'Was it about Lucy?'

Iris turned to look at Archie sharply. 'Why do you say that?'

'I heard you shouting.' Archie's cheeks turned a guilty red. 'I tried not to listen, but I couldn't help it.'

'Yes, well, it needn't concern you.'

As Iris fumbled with her front door key, Archie said, 'Granny May took me and Kitty to see the grave. It weren't too bad, honestly.' He hesitated a moment, then said, 'Happen we could go and see her?'

'I don't want to talk about it, all right?'

Iris saw her son's forlorn expression and immediately felt wretched for snapping.

She did not want to tell anyone, least of all her mother, but she had tried to go to the graveyard. A couple of times while Archie was at school she had set off with Kitty in the pram, determined to walk up to the cemetery. The last time she had got to the gates, but then she had looked through and seen all the rows of headstones, and she just couldn't bring herself to do it.

She wanted to remember Lucy as she was, a happy, laughing little girl, not as a name on a slab of stone.

And if she was honest, she was afraid to let herself mourn. She was scared that if she allowed herself to give in to the grief inside her, it would overwhelm her and send her into madness. It was better to turn her back on it, to pretend it wasn't there.

They let themselves into the house and Iris pulled the

blackout curtains. There had not been many air raids since the bad one the previous weekend, but nightfall still made her nervous.

'What are we going to have for tea now?' Archie asked.

'Why don't I go out for fish and chips?'

Archie looked towards the window. 'It's getting dark.'

'I've got my torch.'

'But what if there's an air raid?'

'There won't be.'

'But what if there is?'

'I'll be back before you know it.'

'I wish we could have stayed at Granny May's.'

'And I wish Granny May would learn to mind her own business!'

Archie flinched and once again Iris felt a stab of guilt.

'It'll be all right,' she said, more gently. 'Granny May and I fall out all the time. We'll make it up sooner or later. We always do.'

No sooner had she said it than there was a knock on the back door.

Archie looked hopeful. 'That might be her now, come to say sorry.'

Not if I know your gran, Iris thought. *More likely she's come to have the last word.*

She threw open the back door, braced for another fight. 'Look, if you've come to—' she started to say, but it wasn't her mother on the doorstep.

Chapter Twelve

Sam Scuttle stood in the yard, clutching his cap between his hands. His unruly sandy hair was combed flat, his collar was clean and he was wearing a tie.

He looks like he's come courting, Iris thought. It gave her an unsettled feeling.

'What do you want?' The question came out abruptly.

'Good evening to you, too.' Sam grinned. 'I wanted to talk, if you've got a minute?'

'I was just going out for fish and chips—'

'I'll walk with you.'

Iris glanced back over her shoulder towards the safety of the kitchen, fighting the urge to dart back inside.

As if he could guess what she was thinking, Sam said, 'You can't avoid me forever, you know.'

'I in't avoiding you!'

'In't you?' He sent her a shrewd look. Iris felt her face colouring.

'Give me a minute to fetch a coat,' she muttered.

She took her time getting ready, gathering her thoughts. She knew why Sam had come. There was unfinished business between them, and it needed to be sorted out.

Beattie Scuttle's words came back to her. *Let him know where he stands. He deserves that.*

She was right, Iris thought. Sam did deserve to know how she felt.

She only wished she knew herself.

He was waiting in the yard when she came out. He fell into step beside Iris as she headed for the back gate. It had been fine all day, but now a chill wind whistled down the alley and she pulled her coat tighter around her.

'You see?' Sam said, as they emerged on to Jubilee Row, opposite Pearce's shop. 'This in't so bad, is it?'

'I wasn't avoiding you,' Iris repeated sullenly.

'Course you weren't. You always dart in and out of your door like a rabbit disappearing down a hole.'

Iris ducked her head, smiling in spite of herself. 'All right, maybe I was,' she admitted. 'But only because I didn't know what to say to you.'

'"I've missed you" might have been nice.'

Iris fell silent. How could she say she had missed him when she had spent the last three months doing her best to forget him?

They walked on, turning their feet at the same time towards Hessle Road. Ahead of them she could see a line of people outside the fish and chip shop, waiting for their tea.

'You don't have to wait with me,' Iris said, as they joined the end of the queue.

'I've nowhere else to go. I'm not due on duty until half past. Besides, we've not finished talking. And if I let you go now you might go to ground for another month.'

They shuffled forward towards the door. Iris willed the line to move faster as the silence stretched between them.

'I wanted to come and see you at the hospital,' Sam said finally.

'I didn't want any visitors, except Mum and Pop.'

'You didn't answer my letters, either.'

Iris kept her gaze fixed on the door. Another couple of

minutes and she would be inside, and this conversation would be over.

'When you didn't write back I thought there was something you were trying not to tell me.'

He was looking at her, waiting for her to speak.

Tell him, her inner voice urged. She willed herself to say the words but they would not come.

'Happen I was right?' Sam murmured.

She left him outside on the pavement and went into the fish and chip shop. Being alone for a moment gave her the chance to think.

She'd had a long time to think about this moment, while she was in the hospital. She had wondered how she would feel when she finally saw him again. After three months of telling herself she had no feelings for him, she was dismayed to find that dangerous tug of attraction was still there.

It was hard not to want him. Even now, as she waited for her order, Iris could see a couple of the other women in the queue giving him the eye. She didn't blame them. He was a handsome man – tall, broad shouldered, with sandy fair hair and a wicked glint in his sea-green eyes.

For years there had been an unspoken attraction between them. It might have stayed that way, if it had not been for Dolly, egging her on to tell Sam how she felt. Now she wished she had never taken the plunge. If she hadn't, they could have stayed friends and she wouldn't be in this position now.

And perhaps Lucy would still be alive.

She paid for her fish and chips and tucked the newspaper-wrapped bundle under her arm. She came out of the shop to where Sam was leaning against a lamp post, waiting for her. She took a deep breath. It was now or never.

'You're right,' she said. 'I haven't been fair to you. You deserve to know where you stand.'

Sam's eyes narrowed warily. 'Go on.'

'We've always been really good friends, haven't we? Right from when we were bains.'

He sighed. 'Why do I feel a "but" coming?'

'But things have changed. I've just come home, and I've been away so long. I've got to get myself back on my feet before I think about doing anything else. And I've got Archie and Kitty to think about, too. They've been so unsettled, what with – everything that's happened.' She picked her way through the words. 'I owe it to them to put them first . . .'

'I understand.'

She risked a glance at Sam. He was gazing back at her with so much love and compassion, it nearly broke her heart. 'Do you?'

'Of course. Like you said, you've got a lot on your mind. The last thing you need is me hanging around, distracting you.'

'I'm sorry.'

'Don't be. I can't say I in't disappointed, but I understand. Anyway,' he smiled ruefully, 'I've waited for you this long, I don't mind waiting a bit longer if that's what it takes.'

What if you have to wait forever? Iris thought. But she kept silent.

'Mind, I don't think my mother will be best pleased,' he added.

Iris smiled reluctantly. 'I know. I've already had one warning about messing you about.'

'She wants to see me married off before I end up on the shelf.'

'That will never happen!'

'I hope not.' Their eyes met. Iris looked away first.

'I'd best get these chips home before they go cold,' she mumbled.

'Do you want me to walk you back? I've still got a while before my shift.'

She shook her head. 'No, you go to work.'

'Are you sure? I thought you might still be a bit wary after dark—'

'I've got to get used to it.' Iris cut him off. Why did he have to be so kind? It just made it even harder for her to resist him. 'It's only a couple of minutes back to Jubilee Row.'

He smiled. 'I'll be seeing you, then. Unless you decide to go on avoiding me?'

'I wasn't—' Iris started to say, then she saw him grin. 'Go and put out a fire,' she said.

'Let's hope I don't have to. We could do with a couple more quiet nights.' He winked. 'I don't suppose I could have a kiss before I go?'

'Definitely not.'

She started to walk away, but Sam called after her: 'I in't giving up on you, Iris Fletcher!'

Iris watched him striding down the street.

You should, she thought. She had given up on herself a long time ago.

Chapter Thirteen

Saturday 15th March 1941

It was four o'clock in the morning, less than an hour since the last All Clear, and the Emergency Reception Centre was already packed.

They had been coming in since two o'clock, after the bomb fell near St Andrew's Dock. Ruby had felt the force of the explosion as she dozed in front of the fire at home. She was on call for WVS duty, so she did not go to the shelter with the rest of the Maguire family when the first siren sounded. She woke up to the house trembling around her and a shower of plaster dust falling from the ceiling on to her upturned face.

She was still brushing dust out of her hair when the telephone rang.

'Bean Street's been hit,' Miss Brekke had said.

Ruby gripped the telephone receiver, her hand suddenly slippery with sweat. 'Is it bad?'

'It seems like it. Can you open up the Emergency Centre on Boulevard?'

'Not Anlaby Road?'

There was a silence on the other end of the line, before Miss Brekke said, 'Anlaby Road has been hit, too.'

Ruby immediately thought of all the shops she visited, the shopkeepers she passed the time of day with. Mr and Mrs Huggins's daughter Joyce owned the hardware shop on the corner of Anlaby Road and Bean Street . . .

'Are you there, Mrs Maguire?' The District Organiser's sharp tone brought her back to the present.

'Yes. Yes, I'm here.'

'I'm putting you in charge. I think we're going to be in for another night of it and I need someone who can keep their head.'

Ruby straightened her shoulders. 'I'll do my best.'

'I know you will, Mrs Maguire. I can always count on you, can't I?'

The sky was alight as Ruby cycled west down Hessle Road towards Boulevard. To her right, fire engine bells clanged, smoke billowed and flames licked the sky. The air was thick with it, smoke mingling with the smell of burning wood.

But she did not know how bad it was until she reached the church hall that was serving as the Emergency Centre. One of the other volunteers, Ann Peachey, was there waiting for her, shivering in her heavy green coat.

She rushed to greet Ruby as she got off her bicycle.

'Have you heard the news? The public shelter in Bean Street has been hit.'

'No!' Ruby let her bicycle drop to the ground with a crash.

'The warden's just telephoned. All gone, so they say.'

Ruby turned to look back at the smoke rising over the rooftops. She thought of all those poor people, hurrying down the steps to the shelter when the siren sounded, trusting they would be safe there . . .

Then she thought about her own family, taking refuge in their shelter on Hessle Road. It could so easily have been them. She felt sick with terror, and for a moment all she wanted to do was to get back on her bicycle and hurry back to Jubilee Row to make sure they were all right.

She looked down at the bunch of keys in her hand. Miss Brekke was relying on her to do her duty.

I can always count on you, can't I?

'Come on,' she said. 'Let's get this place open. I have a feeling we're going to be busy.'

She was right. Ruby and the other women barely had time to get the tables and chairs laid out before the first people began to arrive. Families who had been bombed out of their homes, who had nowhere else to go.

Since then, they had been rushed off their feet, serving tea and sandwiches, and organising the mobile canteen vans to go out to the rescue workers and the volunteers on the First Aid Posts. They helped find emergency billets, sorted out clothes, ration books and nappies and milk for the babies. Some of the people who came to them had nothing left, only the clothes they stood up in.

They also tracked down missing relatives, filled in endless paperwork and answered telegrams from worried friends and families. As fast as one thing got done, there seemed to be another three jobs to take its place.

And all the while the telephone rang and rang with yet more problems, more queries, more people needing help. Ruby did not think she would ever stop hearing the insistent jangling in her head.

Outside, dawn broke and Ruby hardly noticed. Her limbs felt heavy with weariness and her eyes stung from lack of sleep. It took her three attempts to fill in a form for a woman who had lost all her week's rations when her ceiling collapsed in her kitchen.

'I'm sorry,' she sighed, screwing up the paper.

'You take your time, love,' the woman said as she sat before her, a baby under one arm and a canary in a cage perched on her lap. 'Happen you should have a rest? I've been watching you running about.'

Ruby smiled ruefully. 'No time for that, I'm afraid.' Not when people kept coming, bringing with them their troubles and their heartache.

Her heart lurched with pity as she looked at the rows in front of her. Some were weeping while others tried to comfort them. Families huddled together, while others sat alone, their eyes wide in shocked, soot-blackened faces. Many had come straight from being treated at First Aid Posts, their limbs and faces bandaged.

By nine o'clock in the morning, their supplies were depleted and they were all exhausted. Even the WVS women were beginning to snap at each other, and it took all Ruby's efforts to stay calm and keep up their spirits.

She knew her attempts to rally the troops did not go down well with everyone.

'Do you have to be so cheerful all the time?' Wyn Johnson snapped at her when she caught Ruby humming in the kitchen. 'There are people out there in real trouble, in case you hadn't noticed.'

'I know that, Wyn. That's why we're here, to help them.'

'Much good we can do. A cup of tea and a sandwich isn't going to bring their home or their husband back, is it?'

'No, but it might make them feel better. And I'm sure they'd rather see a smiling face than a miserable one.'

'Yes, well, I can do without another lecture from you, thank you very much!'

As Wyn left, slamming the door behind her, Ann Peachey said, 'You mustn't mind her. She's just worried.'

'Worried?'

'Her sister was in the Bean Street shelter.'

'Oh lord.' Ruby stared at the door. 'Has she heard anything?'

Ann shook her head. 'Nothing so far. I daresay she's thinking the worst, though. I know I would be.'

'I wonder why she came in, then.'

'She told me she needed to keep busy.'

Ruby bit her lip. 'I wish she'd said something.'

'Perhaps she just wants to put it out of her mind. Shall I take the tea trolley through?'

'What? Oh, yes. Please. But be careful with the urn, it's starting to leak.'

Ruby stood in the kitchen for a while after Ann had taken the trolley out to the waiting room, absently folding tea towels.

Poor Wyn. Ruby could not even begin to imagine how she was feeling. She wondered if she could have turned up for duty if anything had happened to Pearl, or one of her girls.

She jumped as the door opened, and Ann stuck her head round.

'You need to come,' she said. 'We're having a bit of trouble.'

'Is it the urn? I did warn you—'

Ann shook her head. 'Someone's refusing to wait her turn and she's being quite nasty about it. Poor Miss Jeffers is in tears.'

'We can't have that.' Ruby hung the tea towel back over the rack and followed Ann out of the kitchen.

At the far end of the hall a woman in a musquash fur coat and felt hat stood over the table, bearing down on elderly Miss Jeffers, who had been given the job of helping to sort out the emergency billets. The poor old dear sat behind the table, her pen trembling in her hand.

'What do you mean, wait my turn?' the woman was screeching. 'What do you think I've been doing all this time? I've been here hours. No, I won't sit down and be quiet. Don't you dare try to shut me up. Who do you think you are, anyway? Sitting there in your daft uniform. You think you're so important, don't you? But you don't scare me. I've dealt with old busybodies like you before, trying to tell me what to do—'

Miss Jeffers caught sight of Ruby, relief flooding her face. 'Oh, thank goodness,' she said. 'Mrs Maguire, can you help?'

The woman swung round. 'Oh, here comes another one. And who are you, when you're at home?'

But Ruby could not answer. She was too stunned to speak as she found herself face to face with the last person in the world she had ever expected to see.

Chapter Fourteen

'I asked you a question. Are you in charge here?'

Ruby stared at the woman. The years had not been kind to her. Age had taken the flesh from her face, leaving it sunken, lined and bitter. Under her felt hat, her dyed blonde hair was as dry and brittle as straw. But her thin lips were still outlined in the scarlet lipstick Ruby remembered so well.

She would have known her anywhere. But there was no spark of recognition in the woman's cold grey eyes as she looked back at Ruby.

'I've been bombed out,' she snapped. 'I was told to come here, they said you'd sort me out, but I've been sitting here ages and no one's lifted a finger to help me. And every time I try to get someone to listen, they just tell me to sit down and wait.' She jabbed her bony finger at Ruby. 'What are you going to do about it, that's what I want to—'

'Elsie Finch?'

The woman stopped, her eyes narrowing. 'What?'

'Oh no, Mrs Maguire. This is Miss Duvall,' Miss Jeffers put in timidly.

So that's what she's calling herself now. She had been through at least half a dozen names that Ruby knew about.

The woman stared at Ruby. 'Do I know you?'

'You should. I'm your daughter.'

She heard the whispers of the women behind her, but she kept her gaze fixed on her mother's face. Elsie's expression was rigid, her crimson lips rimmed with tense white. Looking into her eyes, Ruby could almost see her mind working as her eyes flicked back and forth.

Then, suddenly, she clutched her hand to her heart and let out a cry.

'Ruby? My darling girl, is it really you?'

Before Ruby could react, Elsie had thrown her arms around her, enveloping her in mothball-scented fur. 'Oh, Ruby, I can't believe it. It's a miracle.'

Over her mother's shoulder, Ruby could see the other women gawping in astonishment. Even the rows of people waiting to be seen were smiling and nudging each other.

'You don't know how often I've thought about you, wondered where you were,' Elsie was saying, loud enough for all of them to hear. 'I used to dream about finding you again, but I didn't know where to look.'

Ruby carefully detached herself from her mother's embrace. 'Happen you should have tried the orphanage where you left us?' she said flatly.

She caught the fleeting look of panic in her mother's eyes. Then Elsie started sobbing. She made a great show of fumbling for her handkerchief until Miss Jeffers handed over her own.

'Thank you,' Elsie whispered. 'You're very kind. I'm sorry, this has all been so much for me ...'

'Don't worry about it, my dear,' Miss Jeffers said kindly.

Ruby watched her, unmoved. She could feel the other women looking at her expectantly, but she did not trust her mother's tears; she had seen her turn them on too often.

'Why don't you take your mother into the office?' Ann suggested quietly.

Ruby turned to look at her. 'Why?'

'I – I just thought you might prefer to talk in private?'

79

'There's no need. Miss Jeffers is in charge of emergency billeting. I'm sure she can sort out the necessary paperwork.'

'But—' Ann looked around uneasily. 'It's your mother,' she whispered.

'It's all right,' her mother sniffed back her tears. 'I can't blame her for not wanting owt to do with me. I've not been much of a mother to her.' Her lips trembled and she dabbed at her eyes. 'Happen this nice lady could help me?' she managed a brave smile at Miss Jeffers. 'All I want is to find somewhere to lay my head. I'm so tired . . .'

She started sobbing again. 'I'm sorry,' she mumbled into her borrowed handkerchief, as the other women fussed around her. 'I'm such a nuisance . . .'

Ruby caught Ann Peachey's accusing look.

'You'd best come with me,' she sighed.

'I still can't believe it,' Elsie was saying as Ruby closed the office door behind them. 'My Ruby, all grown up and in charge.' She looked around, impressed. 'Mind, I always knew you'd do well for yourself. You've got your head screwed on straight.'

Ruby took her seat behind the desk and opened up the file, ready to begin the paperwork.

'How is Pearl?'

'She's fine.'

'You're still in touch, then?'

'Of course.' Ruby carried on going through the papers in front of her, looking for the right one.

'Did you own the house?' she asked.

'What?'

'The house that was bombed. Were you the owner?'

'Me, own a house?' Elsie snorted. 'Chance would be a fine thing. I was lodging there, if you must know.'

Ruby selected the correct form and picked up her pen.

'So you stayed together, then? At the—'

'The orphanage?' Ruby said, as Elsie hesitated over the word. 'Yes, we did.'

'I'm surprised. I really thought Pearl would be adopted. She was such a pretty little thing.'

Unlike you. The insult hung unspoken in the air between them.

'No one adopted either of us. We stayed in the orphanage until I was old enough to go out to work, and then I found lodgings and took Pearl to live with me.'

That silenced her for a moment. But then she smiled and said, 'I knew you'd look after her.'

'I had no choice. Someone had to do it.' Ruby stared at her mother across the desk until Elsie's gaze slid away.

'My jewels,' she said. 'That's what I used to call you. Ruby and Pearl. My precious little jewels.'

So precious you dumped us on the steps of an orphanage in the middle of the night and left without a backward glance.

'It's all right,' Ruby said. 'There's only us here. You don't have to pretend to care.'

'Of course I care!' Her mother looked shocked. 'Do you think I wanted to do what I did? I had no choice. I wanted to give you what I never had, the chance of a fresh start . . .'

Ruby watched her mother fumbling with her handkerchief again. Did she think Ruby had forgotten what really happened? Or perhaps after this time she had started to believe her own lies.

Either way, she did not want to argue with her. She looked down at the blank form in front of her. 'Let's just get this done, shall we?' she said wearily. She consulted the form and started to fill it in. 'Name, Elsie Finch . . .'

'Elise Duvall. That's the name I'm going by these days.'

Ruby raised her eyebrows but said nothing. 'Address?'

'I in't got one. Why do you think I'm here?'

'Where were you living?'

She gave the address of a seedy boarding house north of Anlaby Road. Ruby felt a twinge of compassion. It wasn't the kind of place an elderly lady should have ended up, no matter who they were.

'We'll find you somewhere else to live,' she said kindly. 'And we'll sort out an emergency ration book so you can get some shopping—'

'What about money?'

'What do you mean?'

'I should be compensated for my loss, surely? I had jewellery, antiques, lots of things. I've lost everything.'

Ruby blinked at her. This was not usually the first question she was asked. 'That will have to be covered by insurance,' she said.

'Insurance!' Elsie's thin mouth curled. 'As if I've got insurance. How am I supposed to afford the payments?'

Then how can you afford jewellery and antiques?

Ruby and her mother faced each other across the desk. She had been eight years old when Elsie left them, but she still remembered all her tricks. She was constantly on the lookout for a way to make money, or to take advantage of someone else's good nature.

She turned back to the form. The sooner she filled it in, the sooner her mother would be gone.

'Let's see if we can find you somewhere to live, shall we?'

'I don't want to go too far away.'

'We'll have to see what emergency billets are available.' Ruby reached for the ledger. 'I'll telephone around the hostels . . .'

'Hostels?' Her mother bridled.

'It's all we have.'

Her mother regarded her thoughtfully. 'They called you Mrs Maguire. You're married, then?' Ruby nodded. 'What does he do, your old man?'

'He's on the minesweepers.'

'Any bains?'

'Three girls.'

'Very nice.' Elsie sighed. 'I daresay you've got a nice home, too. It must be lovely to have people to look after you. That's what families do, in't it? They look after each other.'

There was no mistaking her meaning as she looked at Ruby across the table.

'I'll start telephoning around those hostels,' Ruby said.

Chapter Fifteen

It was clear the other women had been talking about them. As they emerged from the office, all eyes swivelled in their direction.

'Thank you for your help,' Elsie said. 'I'm sure I'll be very comfortable in the hostel. It won't be the same as a home, but at least I'll have a roof over my head.' She sighed and looked around at the other women as she said it.

'That's what we're here for,' Ruby said stiffly. All she wanted to do was get away, but Elsie had other ideas. She dived at Ruby, enveloping her in another mothball-scented embrace.

Ruby tried to pull away but her mother held on to her, her bony fingers biting into Ruby's arms.

'I'm so proud of you,' Elsie said in a choked voice. 'My Ruby. My little jewel.'

Ruby glanced over to where Miss Jeffers was wiping away a tear with her sleeve.

Finally Elsie left, and Ruby was able to escape to the kitchen. She set about making sandwiches to restock the refreshments van, but her hands were shaking so much she could barely hold the knife.

The last hour had been such a shock for her. The whole time she had been talking to her mother, she felt as if she was in some kind of strange dream. Even now, she could hardly believe that she had been there at all. Was that really Elsie Finch who had stood before her, after all these years?

'Well, I call it strange.' Ruby lifted her head at the sound of Olive Oxley's voice outside the kitchen. 'The way she spoke to her own mother! I've never heard anything like it. It's as if they were strangers.'

'It has been a long time,' she heard Ann Peachey say.

'All the more reason to welcome her, I'd say. She didn't look pleased to see her, did she?'

'I daresay Ruby has her reasons. We know nothing about it.'

'It's very odd, that's all I'm saying.'

'And you'd think she would have offered her a place to stay, wouldn't you?' Another woman, Maggie Cornell, put in.

'That's what I thought,' Olive said. 'I never thought Ruby Maguire of all people would be so hard-hearted. When you think about how much time she puts in helping strangers. And yet she turns her back on her own mother.'

'And they say charity begins at home!'

Ruby fixed her attention on the bread she was spreading with margarine. She could not blame them. Anyone would have been surprised at the way she treated her mother.

But they did not know Elsie Finch.

The last time Ruby had seen her was thirty-four years ago, just after her eighth birthday. It was a cold November night when her mother had dragged her from her bed.

'Get your sister dressed,' she had said curtly. 'And hurry up, we in't got much time.'

Ruby knew better than to ask questions. There had been too many moonlight flits from lodgings to be surprised.

She roused three-year-old Pearl, lifting her warm, sleepy body from the mattress they shared. She dressed her, wrapping her up in lots of layers to keep out the cold. There was already a thin layer of frost on the inside of the window pane.

'Where are we going?' Pearl mumbled sleepily as Ruby bundled her into her coat.

'We're off on another adventure.'

'I don't want to go.'

Neither do I. Ruby eyed her mother, who was busy stuffing belongings into an old carpet bag. Their belongings, she noticed, not her own.

'You'll enjoy it when we get there,' she said.

Their mother did not speak to them as she led the way through the darkened streets. Only the sound of her clipping heels broke the deadly silence. They walked for a long time and Pearl's little legs got tired so Ruby had to carry her to stop her whining.

They walked north, away from the Humber, to an area Ruby did not know. Here the streets were wider, lined with trees, and there were no houses to be seen.

'Are we in the country?' she whispered.

Her mother ignored her, walking purposefully ahead until she suddenly stopped outside a pair of high, wrought-iron gates.

Ruby peered through but could see nothing but the shapes of tall, dark trees. She could hear leaves rustling in the cold wind. They sounded like the whispers of the dead.

She was horrified when her mother started to push open the gate. It squeaked on its rusty hinges. 'We can't go in there!' she cried fearfully. 'It's haunted.'

'Don't be daft. Come on.' She picked up the carpet bag and started through the gates, but Ruby hung back.

'Who lives here?' she asked.

'Some friends of mine.'

Ruby hesitated. Even at eight years old, she knew her mother well enough to know when she was lying.

A short distance from the gates, the dark shape of a large

house loomed ahead of them. Elsie stopped and set down the bag.

'This is as far as I go. You'll have to walk the rest of the way by yourself.'

'I can't!' Ruby froze in terror.

'Don't be a baby, it isn't far.' Her mother grabbed her by the shoulders, shaking her. 'Stop crying. You must be brave for Pearl. You'll set her off if you make a fuss.'

She wheeled Ruby around to face the house. 'You're to go up to the door but don't knock. Sit on the steps and they'll find you.'

'Who? Who will find us?'

'Don't mention my name,' her mother went on, ignoring the question. 'You can tell them you're called Ruby and Pearl, but don't say anything else. And for Christ's sake, don't tell them where we live. Understood?'

'But I thought they were your friends—'

'Is that understood?' Elsie cut her off. Ruby saw the panic in her mother's face and she began to panic too.

'I'm scared,' she whimpered.

'I told you, don't start crying.' Her mother sighed. 'Look, it won't be for long,' she said. 'I'll come and fetch you and we'll all be together again.'

'When will you fetch us?'

'A few days, not long.' Her mother was already distracted, looking off back towards the gates. 'Now mind you look after your sister.'

'Mum—'

'I'll come back for you, I promise.'

She was already walking away from them. Ruby stood there, holding Pearl's hand in hers, listening as the clipping sound of her heels faded away. She had to bite her lip to stop herself crying.

'Where are we?' Pearl's voice sounded small in the darkness.

'I told you, we're on an adventure.' Ruby bent to pick up the old carpet bag her mother had dumped. 'Come on.'

The house rose up before them, very large and very old, a big gothic slab of sharply pointed gables and sinister-looking mullioned windows. The ivy-covered walls rustled and shivered in the wind like a hundred whispers in the darkness.

Ruby set the bag down on the worn stone steps that led up to the heavy wooden door.

'In't we going to knock?' Pearl whispered.

Ruby shook her head. 'Mum said not to.' She eyed the vast iron knocker apprehensively. She was in no hurry to find out what was behind that door.

'I'm cold,' Pearl whispered.

'Here.' Ruby took off her coat and wrapped it around her sister's shoulders. 'This should keep you warm.' She wrapped her arms around Pearl, hugging her little body close.

'I want Mum,' Pearl said.

'She'll be back.'

'When?'

'Soon.' But even as she said the word, Ruby knew their mother would not be returning.

Look after your sister.

It was all up to her now. She squared her shoulders, mentally preparing herself for what lay ahead.

'Ruby?' Pearl whispered.

'What?'

'I don't like this adventure.'

Ruby looked around her and shivered.

'Nor do I, Pearl,' she murmured. 'Nor do I.'

Chapter Sixteen

Tuesday 18th March 1941

'It was a good thing we called in to the Co-op first thing, wasn't it?'

It was a chilly March morning, and Edie had been out shopping with Iris. Now they were heading home, side by side down Anlaby Road. Edie pushed baby Bobby in his pram while Iris was loaded down with their shopping. Kitty trotted on a few paces ahead of them.

'I mean, imagine if we'd gone there last?' Edie went on. 'Those onions would have sold out. There weren't that many left when we got there, and the shop had only been open ten minutes. I'll bet they're all gone now, mind.' She bumped her pram down the kerb, but Bobby slept on soundly. 'Lucky they weren't just keeping them for registered customers, too. You know what some shops are like, hiding the best stuff under the counter for their regulars. Not that anyone can blame them, I suppose.' She smiled. 'Your mum will be pleased. She was only saying the other day, she can't remember the last time she saw an onion—'

'Blimey, Edie, have you heard yourself?' Iris interrupted her. 'Honest to God, I've never heard anyone so excited about a bit of fruit and veg before!'

Iris laughed, and Edie joined in. 'Sorry, I am going on a bit, in't I? What's my life come to if the sight of an onion can make my day?'

'I reckon you should get out more!'

'Chance would be a fine thing.'

They were still laughing as they made their way up Anlaby Road. But they quickly sobered as they passed Colton Street and saw the damage that lay ahead of them. Two days after the raid, the road was still blocked by drifts of rubble and shattered masonry.

'Look, there's Charlie Scuttle.' Edie stopped to wave to him. He was perched precariously on top of a jagged wall which had once formed part of Shelby's ironmongery. The shop was still standing, but a high explosive that landed nearby had taken away most of the workshop attached to it.

'Beattie said he was working here,' Edie said. 'Poor Charlie, he was beside himself when the workshop got hit. Lucky the builders were all looking for an extra pair of hands . . .'

She looked around for Iris but she had hurried on, her head down and face averted. Edie could have kicked herself. Poor lass, the last thing she probably wanted to do was to stop and gawp at bomb damage.

Iris was waiting for Edie on the corner, Kitty at her side. 'Hurry up,' she called out to her. 'Mum will be waiting for her onion!'

She was smiling, but her smile did not seem to reach her eyes. But that was how Iris was these days, Edie thought.

On the outside, she seemed to have settled back to life in Jubilee Row. She was bright, cheerful, and she laughed and joked nearly as much as she did before. But from time to time Edie would catch her smile faltering, or an unguarded look of desolation in her eyes, and she would know that there was something missing.

Or someone.

Neither of them ever talked about Lucy or Dolly any more. Edie had mentioned their friend's name a few times but Iris always pretended not to hear, or changed the subject. It was as if she wanted to pretend that neither of them had ever existed.

It felt strange, not talking about Dolly. She had been such a big part of both their lives. And it brought Edie comfort to talk about her, just as it did to talk about Rob.

But it was plain Iris did not see it that way, and Edie did not want to push it.

As they approached Big May's house along the ten-foot, there were voices coming from the open back door.

'Sounds like your mum's got a visitor,' Edie said, but Iris had already picked up her pace, hurrying towards the sound.

The back door was open. As she parked Bobby's pram in the yard, Edie could see a young man in a Merchant Navy uniform sitting at the kitchen table, his kitbag at his feet.

'Well, I never,' Iris said. 'Look what the tide washed in.'

John looked over his shoulder. 'Hello, Sis,' he grinned. 'Long time, no see.'

Edie stared at him. This must be the famous John, the youngest of May Maguire's children. He had been away at sea since Edie moved in so they had never met, but she had heard a lot about him.

He had already caused a stir, by the look of things. Big May and her eldest daughter Florence were at the stove, bickering over who was going to make him a cup of tea.

He was very handsome, Edie thought. He was twenty-one, the same age as her, with the same dark hair and warm brown eyes as his older brothers. But unlike Jimmy and Jack, who wore their good looks lightly, John carried himself like a film star. His dark hair was slicked back and his smile was all practised charm.

'I'll say,' Iris said. 'When did you get home?'

'We docked at Immingham a couple of hours ago.'

'I wish you'd told us you were coming,' Big May grumbled.

'I didn't know my ship was going to be brought in for repairs, did I? Anyway, you know me. I like to keep people guessing.' He looked at Edie. 'Who's this?'

'This is Edie,' Iris introduced them. 'She lives up the road, next door to our Jack.'

'Pleased to meet you, Edie.' John stood up, his hand held out. He was as tall and well-built as the other Maguire men, too. 'I'm John, Mum's favourite son. But I daresay you know that already, since she probably never stops bragging about me.'

'Stop that!' Big May laughed. 'You know I don't have favourites.'

'That's what she tells the others!' John winked at Edie.

'I don't know about bragging,' Edie said, 'but she's certainly warned me about you.'

'Warned?'

'She said you were a terrible flirt, with a girl in every port.' John laughed. 'Now there's a reputation to live up to!'

'Sounds like she's got the measure of you already, John!' Florence laughed. Edie stared at her in astonishment. Florence Maguire was usually such a sober, serious sort of woman. Edie had never seen her so giddy. Clearly she had a soft spot for her youngest brother.

'There's only one girl in my life. Eh, sweetheart?' John bent down and scooped Kitty into his arms, sweeping her high in the air so she squealed and chuckled with delight.

'How long are you staying?' Iris asked.

'Hear that?' John said to Kitty. 'First Granny May tells me I shouldn't have come, then your mum asks me when I'm leaving. Talk about making a fellow feel welcome!'

'That in't what I meant and you know it,' Iris said.

'It's hard to say how long I'll stay.' John set Kitty down on the floor. 'I've got to wait for another ship. It could be days or it might be weeks.' He looked at Edie. 'Happen I might enjoy spending a bit of time at home.'

Edie felt herself blushing. But before she could say anything, the back door opened and Pop came in.

'So the prodigal son returns,' he said to John.

'All right, Pop?' John greeted him. 'You don't seem surprised to see me.'

'I met a mate of yours in the street who told me you were here.' Pop looked over his shoulder. 'It's all right, lad, you can come in. We in't going to bite.'

The man stood framed in the open doorway. He was dressed in a Merchant Navy uniform like John, but there the similarity ended. He looked to be a few years older, as slightly built as her brother was muscular, his hair fine and light brown. Pale lashes framed ice-blue eyes.

'There you are,' John said. 'I thought you'd got lost.'

'I forgot which number you told me.' He spoke softly, his voice deep and low.

'He were wandering in the street,' Pop explained to his wife.

Big May frowned at the new arrival. 'And does he have a name?'

'This is Matthew, a mate of mine from the ship,' John introduced them casually. 'He had nowhere to stay so I told him he could bunk here.'

'Oh you did, did you? And where are we supposed to put you all?'

Matthew looked uneasily from one to the other. 'I could always go down to the Mission, if it's not convenient . . .'

'Take no notice of her,' John dismissed. 'Mum would never turn anyone away. In't that right, Mum?'

'I wouldn't hear of it,' May said. 'Any friend of John's is welcome here, as long as you don't mind sleeping on the floor.'

'We're used to roughing it,' John said. 'The merchant ships are hardly floating palaces.'

'Thank you, that's very kind of you,' Matthew said.

Big May smiled. 'Listen to him! In't he got a lovely speaking voice? You in't from round here, are you, lad?'

'I'm from London.'

'They've had it bad down there,' Pop remarked. 'With the bombing and all that. I read about it in the paper.'

'Yes,' Matthew said. 'Yes, they have.'

'Take your bags upstairs for now,' May said. 'We can sort out the sleeping arrangements later.'

'And then happen we could go for a pint down at the Fishermen's Rest?' Pop suggested.

'I don't know about that.' John looked at Edie. 'Happen I might stay and get to know our new neighbour?'

'Oh, I in't staying. I've got to get the baby home for his feed.'

'Baby?'

Edie pointed to the pram in the yard. 'That's my Bobby. He's asleep at the moment but you wait. He'll be roaring for his food in a minute.'

John stared out of the window for a moment, then turned back to his father. 'Happen I will come for a pint,' he said.

Ten minutes later they were gone. Florence looked quite put out about it. 'It in't fair of Pop to take our John away when he's only just got back,' she complained.

'Stop mithering,' Big May said. 'The lad's been away at sea for months, he deserves a drink on dry land. You don't want to smother the lad.'

Florence glared back at her but said nothing.

Just at that moment the back door flew open and Ruby's daughter Sybil came hurtling in.

'And what do you want?' Big May asked.

'I heard our John was home. I thought I'd come and say hello.'

Edie and Iris exchanged shrewd looks. 'You've just missed him,' Edie said.

'And his friend,' Iris added.

'Oh. Did he have a friend with him?' Sybil feigned indifference, twisting a curl around her finger.

'You know very well he did. You wouldn't be here otherwise!' Iris laughed.

Sybil opened her mouth, then thought better of it. 'All right, I might have seen Pop with someone,' she admitted reluctantly.

Edie and Iris looked at each other. 'Our Sybil can sniff out an eligible young man a mile off,' Iris whispered with a smile.

'Never mind, love,' Big May laughed at her granddaughter's crestfallen expression. 'They'll be staying for a while, so I daresay you'll have plenty of chances to work your charms on him.'

'She in't the only one working her charm,' Iris said. 'Our John seems very taken by Edie.'

Edie laughed. 'And did you see how quick he lost interest when he found out about Bobby?'

Big May and Iris looked at her sympathetically. 'Happen he'll change his mind?' Iris said.

'Oh, it doesn't bother me,' Edie shrugged. 'I in't interested. Bobby's the only man in my life, and that's exactly how I want it.'

Iris and Big May glanced at each other. Edie did not understand the look that passed between them.

'One thing's for sure,' May said. 'We're in for some fun and games. There's never a dull moment when our John's around!'

Chapter Seventeen

Tuesday 18th March 1941

'Never!'

'It's true.'

'And it was really her? Our mother?'

'As large as life.'

After much debate with herself, Ruby had decided to tell Pearl about Elsie. Her first instinct was to say nothing about it and to pretend it had never happened. Bringing Elsie Finch into their lives felt too much like trouble.

But the more she thought about it, the more uneasy she felt. She had never hidden anything from her sister, and she wasn't about to start being dishonest now. Pearl deserved to know the truth.

It was Kitchen Front Week and they were on their way to Bladons to watch a demonstration of haybox cookery. As usual, Ruby had had to drag her sister along.

'What do I want to watch a cookery lesson for?' Pearl had whined like a child all the way there. 'You know I can't even boil an egg.'

'All the more reason to go, surely?' Ruby had reasoned, but Pearl had just pulled a face.

She was still sulking when Ruby told her about her unexpected encounter with Elsie. That soon made her forget her bad mood.

'I still can't believe it.' Pearl shook her head.

'I know.'

'What was she like?'

Ruby pictured Elsie's gaunt, thin-lipped face, her watchful eyes darting around. 'Older, of course. But much the same as I remembered.'

'I wish I remembered her,' Pearl sighed. 'I always think of her as being very glamorous, as she was on the stage.'

'She was in the back row of the chorus, Pearl. She was hardly Florrie Forde.'

'All the same, she must have led quite a life, don't you think?'

Ruby thought about all the moonlight flits, the men, the catfights with the other chorus girls, the tears and the tantrums. She thought about putting her mother to bed after yet another drunken night out, carefully pulling off her shoes, trying not to wake her, knowing she would get a clip if she did.

Pearl should be glad she was too young to remember.

'You could say that,' she said.

Most of the rows of seats were full by the time they arrived at Bladons. At the front of the room, a woman in a starched apron was stuffing a box with straw.

'I told you we should have got here earlier,' Ruby said.

'And sit through even more of this? No, thank you.' Pearl grimaced. 'Look, why don't we stand over there, at the back? Then we can sneak out if it gets too boring.'

Ruby found it anything but boring. She sat fascinated as the demonstrator explained how the contents of a pot buried in a haybox could go on cooking without the need for wasteful gas.

But as she listened, she was aware of Pearl shifting restlessly beside her. From the faraway look on her face, her mind was wandering.

No prizes for guessing where, Ruby thought.

Sure enough, as they were leaving the store, Pearl said, 'You've got to feel sorry for her, haven't you?'

'Who?' Ruby asked, as if she did not know.

'Our mother. It's such a shame for her, losing her home.'

'A lot of people lost their homes that night.'

'Yes, but she's our mother.'

'She stopped being my mother the day she dumped us.'

It started to rain. As Ruby stopped to put up her umbrella, Pearl said, 'You really don't like her, do you?'

'I don't care about her any more than she's ever cared about me.'

She settled her umbrella over her shoulder and hurried across Jameson Street, Pearl following behind.

'You know, she might have had her reasons for what she did.'

'Oh, she had her reasons, all right.' Ruby gritted her teeth grimly against the rain that spattered her face.

His name was Julius St George. At least that was his stage name – if he had a real one, Ruby never knew it. He was a magician, and quite a successful one, too. He certainly had enough money to shower her mother with gifts and take her out on the town.

He was kind to them, too, unlike so many of her other men. He bought them toys, and entertained them with his magic tricks. Sometimes they would all go to the park and Julius would treat them to an ice cream. The sun would shine and her mother would be in a good mood, and all would be well with the world.

But, inevitably, the arguments started. Ruby would lay awake at night, her arm around sleeping Pearl, listening to the raised voices and slamming doors. She could not make out what was said, but she knew it would not be long before Julius would be gone, just like all the others.

Or so she had thought.

It made her sad, because out of all the men her mother had entertained, she liked Julius the best.

'Why do you and Julius argue?' she had asked her mother one night, as she sat sewing a button onto her stage dress. It was Ruby's job to keep Elsie's costumes cleaned, pressed and mended.

'It's because of you,' her mother replied bluntly. She sat at her mirror, patting powder on to her face with a big puff. 'He doesn't want children.'

Ruby stared at her mother, the face powder rising in fine, scented clouds around her blonde head. 'But I thought he liked us?'

'He puts up with you. But he says he'd marry me if it weren't for you.'

Ruby bent her head and went back to her sewing.

'I suppose it won't be long before he's gone, then,' she said. Her mother said nothing. 'That's a shame. I like him.'

'So do I,' Elsie said.

A week later, she and Pearl were on the steps of the orphanage, trying to pluck up the courage to knock on the door.

'I want to see her.'

Pearl's sudden declaration shocked Ruby out of her reverie. She turned to face her sister in astonishment. 'Why?'

'I'm just curious, that's all.' Pearl shrugged.

Ruby felt the blood beating in her ears. This was what she had dreaded and feared all along. 'It in't a good idea, Pearl.'

'Why not?'

'Because . . . because she's trouble.'

'She might have changed.'

Ruby remembered that night at the centre, how Elsie had pushed and whined and demanded. 'She hasn't.'

'Anyway, she's our mother.'

'I told you, she's no mother of mine. Have you forgotten what she did to us, Pearl? How she abandoned us? She walked away from us without a backwards glance. And in all these years she's never contacted us, never bothered to try and find us, to make sure we were all right—' she stopped, taking a deep breath. 'What kind of a mother does that to her bains?'

'I don't know, do I? I just want to meet her, that's all.' Pearl sounded defensive. 'You might have all these bad memories of her, but I don't remember anything about her. The only things I know are what you've told me.' She sent Ruby an accusing look. 'It's all right for you,' she muttered. 'You've got a family. You're a Maguire. I've got no one.'

'You've got me. We've always had each other, haven't we?'

But Pearl wasn't listening. 'All the same, I want to meet her,' she said stubbornly. 'Where is she staying?'

'I'm not telling you.'

'Ruby!'

'I mean it, Pearl. I don't want to get involved with her.'

'You don't have to.' Pearl pouted. 'And anyway, if you won't help me I'll go down to the corporation office and find out for myself.'

Ruby sighed. 'All right, I'll give you the address. But I'm warning you, Pearl, you're making a big mistake. She's trouble.'

'I reckon we'll have a lot in common, then!' Pearl laughed.

'Don't say that.' Ruby shuddered.

'I'm only joking. Look, it'll be all right, I promise.' Pearl slung her arm around Ruby's hunched shoulders. 'If she's anything like as bad as you say she is, I won't be taken in by her. I in't daft, Ruby.'

Ruby looked into her sister's face. She did not like to admit it, but sometimes she could see their mother in Pearl's blonde good looks and carefree manner.

'I hope not,' she said quietly.

Chapter Eighteen

Wednesday 19th March 1941

'I don't know what you think, mate, but I reckon we chose the wrong time to come for a visit!'

John laughed when he said it, but Iris could see the tension beneath his broad grin. He was doing his best to lighten the atmosphere, but underneath he was as frightened as everyone else in the shelter.

It was the worst raid they'd had. Just after nine o'clock the warning siren had sounded. They'd all trooped down into the shelter with their books and their knitting and their sandwiches, expecting the usual to and fro that went on every evening.

But three hours later they were still there, listening to the relentless crash of the bombs and the rattle of anti-aircraft fire, feeling the walls shuddering around them and the clatter of shrapnel raining down on the concrete roof.

It was nearly midnight but no one was sleeping. In the dim light, Iris could make out rows of exhausted, fearful faces. Books lay unopened on laps, knitting needles were idle in hands. A few people tried to keep up conversation with their friends and neighbours, all the while looking around them, jumping at every crash and bang from outside.

Iris had managed to settle the children on one of the narrow benches. But while Kitty slumbered peacefully, Archie thrashed and whimpered in his sleep.

Another one of his nightmares, Iris thought. She put out

her hand to let him know she was there, then drew it back again when he flinched at her touch.

She tried to concentrate on the darning she had brought, half an ear cocked to what was going on around her. To one side, John and his friend Matthew were chatting to Sybil, while to the other her mother and Beattie Scuttle were talking about anything but what was going on outside the shelter. Pop was trying to do his crossword, but his pencil had not moved for as long as Iris had been watching him.

Beside them, Edie was teaching George and Freddie to play chess. She held her baby in the crook of one arm, while the other was wrapped around Jack's scruffy little terrier, trying to comfort it as it whimpered and trembled.

They all jumped as the door opened and Florence came hurrying down the steps. She looked shaken, her tin ARP helmet askew.

'What's up, lass?' Pop asked.

'Three bombs have dropped on Lister Street, next to the stables.'

'The stables?' Even in the dim light, Iris saw the colour drain from her father's face.

He jumped to his feet, but her mother put out a hand to stop him.

'Albert Maguire, don't you even think about going out there,' she growled.

'But my Bertha—'

'You won't do that horse any good if you get yourself killed, will you?'

'Mum's right, Pop,' Florence said. 'You don't want to be going out there.'

Pop looked from one to the other, then slowly sank back down into his seat. Iris could tell he was still fretful as he picked up his newspaper. Poor Pop, that old horse had been part of his life for as long as she could remember. They depended on each other.

A plane roared low overhead and Iris tensed, ducking her head. When she looked up, Matthew was watching her intently from the other side of the shelter. Iris looked away quickly, glad that the dim light hid her blushing face.

When she looked again, he had turned back to Sybil, who was chattering away, barely pausing for breath as usual.

Iris watched him out of the corner of her eye. He wasn't the tall, handsome film star type Sybil usually went for, but she could understand why her niece was so taken with him. There was something oddly compelling about him, an intensity that drew her attention beyond his ordinary appearance.

'Is everyone all right?' Florence flashed her torch around the shelter.

'We were till you started shining that thing in our eyes!' her mother grumbled. But Florence ignored her, settling the beam on Edie.

'What's that thing doing in here?' she wanted to know.

As if it could understand what she meant, the terrier started squirming and trembling under Edie's coat.

'You know dogs in't allowed in the public shelter,' Florence said.

'I couldn't leave him behind,' Edie pleaded. 'He gets so frightened during air raids, especially after what happened to him.'

'I can't do anything about that,' Florence sniffed. 'Rules are rules.'

'Yes, well, you know what you can do with your rules,' May muttered, as Freddie and George cried out in protest. But Florence stood firm, her hands planted on her hips.

'It's got to go,' she insisted.

'Have a heart, Flo,' John said. 'Can't you see the poor thing's terrified?'

Florence hesitated for a moment, her gaze flicking from her brother to the dog and back again. Then her shoulders slumped and she said, 'All right, it can stay this once. But mind you don't bring it down here again, all right?' she warned.

'You're an angel, Sis.' John grinned. Iris shook her head in wonder. Her sister Florence was a stickler for the rules, except where their little brother was concerned. John had always been able to get round her when no one else could.

'Thanks,' Edie said, when Florence had left the shelter. 'I didn't want to have to take him home. Jack was so worried about leaving him.'

'That's all right. Couldn't leave the poor little lad on his own, could we?' John moved across to sit beside her on the pretext of petting the dog. Iris smiled to herself. She wasn't surprised Edie Copeland had caught his eye – John always sought out the pretty girls. But he was wasting his time with her.

'Care to share the joke?'

Iris looked round, startled to see Matthew had moved his chair across to sit beside her.

'I was just thinking, our John doesn't have a hope with Edie.'

'What makes you say that?'

Iris looked across at her friend. Edie was listening politely to John, but she could tell she wasn't impressed by his chatter.

'She's not interested in him,' she said. 'The only man in her life is baby Bobby.'

'You underestimate your brother's charm,' Matthew said.

Iris shrugged. 'Happen I do. But I'd be very surprised. Anyway, I hope she doesn't get taken in by him,' she said. 'Edie's been through too much to get messed about.'

'What makes you think he'd mess her about?'

'Because that's just how he is. Our John's never been one to settle down. A lot of girls have tried to tame him, and they've all ended up with broken hearts.'

'Perhaps they would have been better off just enjoying his company while it lasted, and not looking to the future?' he said.

'You've got to make plans, in't you?'

'Why? What's wrong with just taking life every day as it happens, and not thinking about the future? Or the past, come to that.'

He stared at her as he said it, and Iris had the strange feeling he was looking straight into her soul.

'It's hard not to think about the past,' she mumbled. 'Especially when it's all around you.'

'You're right,' Matthew said. 'Sometimes you need to get away.'

'Is that why you joined the Merchant Navy?'

He looked at her sharply. 'What makes you ask that?'

'Nothing. I was just making conversation, that's all. Our John says a lot of men he meets on the ships are running away from something.'

He looked away, releasing her from the intensity of his gaze. 'I suppose he's right,' he said in a low voice. 'I was running away too.'

'Away from what?'

'From everything I'd lost.' His voice was flat. 'My fiancée and my parents were killed in the London Blitz last year. And my brother's Spitfire was shot down over the south coast two months ago.'

'Oh God.' Iris was aghast. 'I'm so sorry.'

His mouth twisted. 'Why do people always say that?'

'I don't know. Happen they don't know what else to say.'

'Then better to say nothing.'

They fell silent for a moment. Iris watched him out of the corner of her eye, fascinated. He seemed so calm and self-possessed, she thought. Was it really possible to go through so much pain and heartache, and come out the other side?

'How do you cope?' The words came out before she could stop them.

Matthew turned to face her. He did not seem surprised by the question. 'I don't think about it,' he said.

She frowned, not sure if he was teasing her or not. 'It in't that easy, is it?'

'It is if you want it to be.'

'But you can't just forget—'

'Why not?'

She paused, thinking about it. 'It don't seem right,' she said finally. 'It feels – oh, I don't know. Like you're letting them down, somehow.'

'What difference does it make to them? Mourning for them and living in misery won't bring anyone back. And neither will torturing yourself with guilt.'

Their eyes met, and once again Iris had the uncomfortable feeling he could read her thoughts.

'That's what I said to Mum,' she murmured. 'She keeps wanting me to go and visit Lucy's grave, but—'

'But you don't see how it would help you?'

She nodded. 'I wish I could escape all the memories,' she sighed.

'You can.'

'How? I can't exactly join the Merchant Navy, can I?'

He smiled wryly. 'You'd certainly brighten up life on board!'

Iris laughed. But then she looked away and caught Beattie Scuttle's accusing stare from across the shelter. Her eyes were hard as iron.

Yet another part of her past she could not escape from, she thought.

Just then John came over. 'Is this a private conversation, or can anyone join in?' he asked.

Iris shifted her seat to make room for him. 'Your charm didn't work on Edie, then?' she said.

John lifted his chin. 'She's just taking a bit of time to warm to me, that's all.'

'What did I tell you?' Iris said to Matthew. 'Happen you're losing your touch.'

'I doubt it!' John looked offended.

'Why have you lot all abandoned me?' Sybil stood over them, eating an apple. 'One minute we were having a laugh, the next you've all sidled over here.'

'Happen we're tired of your company?' John said.

Sybil stuck out her tongue at him. They were more like brother and sister than uncle and niece, with only six months between them.

'Where's Maudie tonight?' Iris asked, changing the subject.

'Fire watching.'

'She's picked a fine night for it,' John said.

'I know. Mum's going mad, what with Maudie on Hammond's roof and our Ada at the Infirmary.' Sybil took another bite of her apple. 'But I quite envy her. I bet her shift is a lot more exciting than mine usually is. Sometimes I sit there for hours, just longing for a basket of incendiaries to relieve the boredom.'

Matthew smiled, and Iris saw the way he looked at Sybil. It was hard not to admire her, with her pretty face and lush mane of strawberry blonde hair.

'What were you talking to Edie Copeland about?' Sybil asked John. 'You looked very cosy together just now.'

'Not as cosy as he'd like to be,' Iris said.

Sybil stared blankly at her uncle. 'What? You mean – you like Edie?' she looked stunned. 'Why?'

'Why not?' Iris said.

'She doesn't seem your type,' Sybil said. 'Anyway, in't she too old for you?'

'She's the same age as you,' Iris pointed out.

'Is she? She seems older.' Sybil crunched on her apple. 'Anyway, she seems so—' she searched for the word. 'Homely,' she said finally.

Iris bridled. 'That in't a very nice thing to say.'

'It's true, though. I can't imagine her ever going out.'

'That's because she's got a baby to think about.'

'Exactly. She's homely.'

'Well, I like her,' John said.

'It's a shame she don't like you.' Iris smiled.

'I'll soon change her mind, don't you worry.' John looked confident.

'Happen we should all go dancing one night?' Sybil suggested. 'You and Edie, and me and—' she trailed off, looking thoughtfully at Matthew.

Iris looked at him, too. But either he did not understand Sybil's meaning, or he was deliberately ignoring it.

'Looks like I'm not the only one losing my touch!' John whispered to Iris.

'Not for long.' Iris shook her head. 'You know our Syb. She always gets her man!'

Chapter Nineteen

Wednesday 19th March 1941

'Fetch, Lucky. Fetch the ball.'

The little dog's tail wagged at the sound of his name, but he paid no attention to George and Freddie's calls. He was too preoccupied with the tabby cat that was taunting him from the top of the coal shed.

'Looks like he's got other things on his mind,' Edie commented from where she sat on Jack Maguire's back doorstep, Bobby in her arms. The baby was watching the boys play, smiling in fascination at them darting about.

It was a bitterly cold, foggy day, but it still felt good to be in the fresh air again, after a long night in the shelter. The raid had lasted nine hours, and it wasn't until after four in the morning that the All Clear finally sounded and they emerged, groggy from lack of sleep and quaking with fear about what they would find.

Jubilee Row was still standing, thank God. But other places had not been so lucky. The centre of the city and the north had taken a terrible battering. Sissons varnish works had gone up in flames, and bombs had fallen on the gas works and the electricity generating station, putting them out of action.

Mr Huggins had gone down after breakfast to look at the casualty lists posted and come back to say that Gladstone Street just north of Anlaby Road had taken a hit, along with several streets either side of the river up near Wincolmlee. Smoke still mingled with the fog, reeking of cordite.

And Jack Maguire had not come home.

Edie had volunteered to look after the boys so Big May could get some much-needed sleep.

'Let me know as soon as our Jack gets back,' was her last instruction to Edie as she shuffled back to her house at the end of the row. 'I need to know he's safe.'

'It could be hours yet,' Edie said. 'I daresay there's a lot to be done.'

But even so, she couldn't help her gaze straying to the back gate as she watched the boys play. She feared for Jack, too. She had seen the rescue parties at work when she and Ruby went out with the mobile canteen, and she knew about the risks they sometimes took to save people buried under the rubble of their homes.

She looked at the boys, waving their arms at the cat to chase it off. She prayed Jack would not put himself in danger. Freddie and George had already lost their mother, they could not lose their father too.

'Shoo! Go away!' George shouted at the cat, but it did not move. It lay safely out of reach on the corrugated iron roof, sending him disdainful looks through half-closed eyes.

'I hope you in't talking to me?'

John Maguire grinned from the open back gateway that led from the ten-foot.

'Uncle John!' the boys ran to him.

He ruffled their hair. 'All right, lads?'

'Have you got anything for us?'

John winked at Edie. 'And there was me, thinking you were just excited to see me.'

'But you always bring us a present,' Freddie said.

'So I do.' John delved in his pocket and pulled out a crumpled twist of brown paper. 'Here you are. Don't eat them all at once.'

'Humbugs!' The boys fell on them happily.

Edie smiled at John. 'They've not had sweets for weeks. How did you get them?'

'You can get anything if you've got my charm and good looks.'

'Not to mention your modesty!' Edie laughed.

Big May was right, there was never a dull moment when John Maguire was around. He was so much fun, always laughing and messing about. Even last night in the shelter, grim as it was, John had managed to keep their spirits up.

'If you're looking for Jack he in't home yet.' Edie looked past him towards the gate.

'As a matter of fact, I was looking for you.'

'Me? What for?'

'It's your lucky day.'

'Oh, yes? Why's that?' Edie smiled, expecting another joke.

'There's a dance on at the Metropole the week after next, and I've decided to take you.'

'Oh, you have, have you? And what if I don't want to go?'

'How could you not want to go dancing with the most eligible bachelor in Hessle Road?'

'I know, I'll probably look back and kick myself.'

John's smile faltered. 'You really mean it? You're turning me down?'

'Don't look so surprised. I'm sure I in't the first lass to reject you.'

'I can't say I recall any others.'

'John!'

'Seriously, you've got to come,' he said. 'We'll have fun.'

Edie looked down at Bobby, propped in her arms. 'And what about this one?'

'In't he a bit young for tripping the light fantastic?'

'Daft beggar!' she smiled. 'I mean, who's going to look after him?'

'Mrs Huggins watches him when you're at the WVS, doesn't she?'

She looked up at him sharply. 'How did you know that?'

'I might have been asking around about you.'

'Have you now? I suppose I should be flattered.'

'Does that mean you'll come?' John looked hopeful.

'You're persistent, in't you?' Edie laughed.

'You know what they say. Faint heart never won fair lady.'

'Neither did being too forward.'

'It's always worked for me in the past.' He leaned against the fence, his hands in his pockets. 'So how about it, then?'

'I told you, I can't.'

'No such word as can't.'

'Won't, then.'

'Won't what?'

Jack Maguire stood in the gateway, and it was all Edie could do not to cry out in relief.

He looked weary. His whole body was slumped, as if it was an effort to hold himself up. His clothes were filthy, and thick grey dust had settled in his hair and the creases of his face.

John hardly seemed to notice as he rolled his eyes. 'Talk about bad timing! Can't you make yourself scarce for a minute? I'm trying to work my charm on Edie here.'

'Oh, aye?' Jack sent her a questioning look.

'Take no notice of him,' Edie said. 'Come inside and sit down. You looked exhausted.'

'I'm all right.' Jack smiled wearily.

'You're dead on your feet.' Edie put Bobby in his pram and followed Jack into the house. John trailed after them.

'Well this is charming,' he said. 'I've come here to invite you out, and you ignore me for my brother!'

Jack looked at Edie. 'What's this?'

'Nothing,' Edie said, reaching up to help him off with his coat. He smelt of smoke and dust. 'Just John being daft.'

'I've asked her to go dancing with me,' John said.

'And I told him no. Now, can I get you something to eat? Your mum gave me a couple of sandwiches left over from last night. I'd make you a cup of tea, but the gas in't working—'

'Excuse me?' John interrupted them. 'I'm still here, waiting for my answer.'

'I've already given it to you.'

John shook his head regretfully. 'You do realise you're missing a once-in-a-lifetime chance?'

Edie caught Jack's amused look. 'I know.'

'You know where I am if you change your mind?'

'I thought it was a once-in-a-lifetime chance?'

John frowned. 'You're a hard woman, Edie Copeland!'

'You do realise he won't give up?' Jack said when his brother had gone.

'Never mind him,' Edie said. She watched as Jack sank down on a kitchen chair with a groan. 'Are you all right? You look like you're in pain?'

'Just a bit stiff, that's all.' He bent to take off his boots, wincing with the effort.

'Here, let me.'

'You don't have to do that—'

'I want to help.' She knelt down, unlacing his boots. They were thick with mud. 'Bad night, was it?'

'It was bad for all of us.' He suddenly seemed to remember and looked around. 'Where are the boys?'

'They're fine. They've gone off to play.' She pulled off his other boot and stood up. 'They'll be glad to see you back. I'll go and call them—'

'In a minute. Let me get myself right first.' Jack ran a hand over his face. Edie caught the unguarded look in his eyes and saw so much wretchedness and pain there, she could almost feel it herself.

She wanted to ask him what it had been like out there. How many people he had rescued from the rubble and the wreckage, and how many he was unable to save.

Those were the ones he would remember, she thought. When he closed his eyes to sleep, they were the faces he would see. Not the ones he had saved, but the ones who had perished, and the awful tragic loss of them.

'How can you do it?' The words came out before she could stop herself. 'Those awful things you must see . . . It must be unbearable.'

'I do it for Dolly.' He raised his gaze slowly to meet hers. 'I wasn't there when she needed me. I couldn't save her.'

'So you try to save everyone else?'

'Every time I manage to pull someone out of a bombed-out building, I tell myself it's her.' His mouth twisted. 'I suppose that sounds daft to you?'

'No,' Edie said. 'No, it doesn't sound daft at all.'

Chapter Twenty

Saturday 22nd March 1941

'You know, I quite fancy being a Wren.' Sybil twirled her tea-spoon between her fingers. 'I've always looked good in blue. And I think I'd suit that little hat they wear. What do you think, Mum? Mum?'

'Sorry, what did you say?' Ruby looked around at her daughter. 'I was miles away.'

'She's probably thinking about work, as usual!' Maudie laughed.

Ruby smiled, but her daughter wasn't wrong. 'I was just thinking about how they're managing at the new café.'

The municipal café, or communal feeding station, had opened on Prospect Street two days earlier, in what had once been Jordan and Son's motorcycle shop. Several of the WVS volunteers had been recruited to work there. Ruby had put her name forward, but Miss Brekke reckoned she could not do without her at the centre.

'Your talents are needed elsewhere, Mrs Maguire,' she had told her on the telephone.

Ruby was flattered, but she would have liked to make herself useful. And the communal feeding station could not have opened at a better time, what with the gas still out over much of the city.

'Happen we should have gone there for lunch instead?' Maudie suggested.

'Oh no, I daresay they've got enough customers to deal

with at the moment,' Ruby said. 'Besides, we'd probably have to wait a long while, and you two have got to get back to work.' She looked around her. 'Anyway, I'm quite happy here.'

It was a real treat to go to the Octagon Café in the city centre, especially with her girls.

Sybil gave an exaggerated sigh. 'Is anyone listening to me? I was saying I quite fancy being a Wren.'

'They're fussy about who they take, so I've heard,' Maudie said, helping herself to a forkful of cake from her sister's plate.

Sybil's chin lifted. 'What's that supposed to mean?'

'I mean you have to be posh.'

'I can be posh. You should hear me, talking to the customers at Hammond's. I can be right plummy when I try.'

'I mean really posh. They're all debs, not shop girls.' Maudie forked the cake into her mouth. 'And you'd be hopeless at taking orders.'

'Well, I hope neither of you will have to sign up,' Ruby said shortly.

'Of course we will,' Sybil said. 'The twenty- and twenty-one-year-olds are already being asked to register. We're bound to be called next.'

'Yes, well, we'll think about it when it happens,' Ruby said.

Maudie frowned. 'I thought you said we all have to do our bit?'

Ruby pushed her plate away, her appetite gone. *Not my girls*, she thought. She knew it was wrong, but she had seen enough anguish among her friends at the WVS whose sons had been conscripted.

And Ruby had enough to worry about with her husband Jimmy out at sea. They never talked about the dangers he faced, but Ruby was all too aware of them.

She looked across the table at her daughters, sitting side by side, Maudie teasing Sybil as usual. They might be twenty-one but they were still her babies. They were so carefree, so full of life, and she wanted them to stay that way for as long as she could.

It was one thing for her to support the war effort with her salvage drives and mobile catering vans and collecting comforts for the forces. But she did not want to see her daughters sent off to war.

'Anyway, my friend Ellen says we should volunteer before we're called up because otherwise we'll have to take what we're given,' Sybil was saying. 'That could mean the Land Army or the ATS. Imagine, those awful khaki uniforms!' She pulled a face.

'It could be worse,' Maudie said. 'They could send you to a munitions factory.'

'Anything but that!' Sybil shuddered. 'I've heard all about munitions work from Edie Copeland and I don't fancy it at all. All that horrible yellow dust getting everywhere. She said people used to laugh and point at the factory girls on the street because they looked like canaries. Can you imagine . . .'

But Ruby was no longer listening to her daughter. She was staring at the two women who had just walked in to the cafe.

'Mum?' Maudie's voice invaded her thoughts. 'What is it? You've gone pale.'

'Ooh, look, it's Auntie Pearl,' Sybil looked towards the door. 'Coo-ee! Auntie Pearl!'

'Don't—' Ruby hissed, but Pearl had already spotted them and was making her way over.

'Who's that with her?' Maudie asked.

Before Ruby had a chance to speak, Pearl was at their table.

'Fancy seeing you in here.' She looked a bit wary, as well she might.

'I could say the same to you.' Ruby looked past her to the

woman at her side. Elsie was still dressed up in her ratty fur coat and heels, but she was carrying one of Pearl's handbags, Ruby noticed. She was smiling like the cat that got the cream.

'Well, this is a nice surprise.' Elsie turned to the girls. 'You must be Sybil and Maudie? Your auntie's been telling me all about you.' She smiled. 'I daresay your mother's been telling you all about me, too?'

The girls turned to look questioningly at Ruby. 'Mum?' Maudie prompted.

Ruby caught the vindictive glint in her mother's eye.

'This is your grandmother,' she muttered.

She stared down at her plate. She could not bring herself to look at her daughters, to see the shock on their faces.

'What?'

'Our grandmother?'

'We thought you were dead,' Sybil said bluntly.

'As you can see, I'm alive and well.'

'We should go to the counter, while it's quiet,' Pearl interrupted. She looked as uncomfortable as Ruby felt.

'You go and order, love. I'll find us somewhere to sit. Oh, look, these people on the next table are leaving. That's a bit of luck, in't it?'

Elsie plonked herself down at the table next to theirs.

'Well, in't this lovely?' she smiled around at Ruby and the girls. 'You know, I was only saying to Pearl this morning that we should all meet up. Give me a chance to get to know my new-found family.' She smiled at the twins, who stared back at her uneasily. Ruby stared down into her teacup, wishing she was a million miles away.

It was Maudie who spoke up first. 'I don't understand . . . how did you two meet again?'

'Will you tell her, or shall I?' Elsie said. Then, before Ruby could answer, she went on, 'I were bombed out in the last bad

118

raid. I ended up at the Emergency Centre, and your mum helped me.' She smiled fondly. 'As I said, it were like a miracle to see my little Ruby there, like an angel . . .'

Ruby remembered her mother's blank expression when she first saw her, the lack of recognition in her eyes.

'Why didn't you tell us, Mum?' Sybil asked.

'I daresay she had her reasons.'

Ruby looked at Elsie's smirking face. 'Yes, I did,' she said.

'I'm sorry you lost your house,' Maudie filled the awkward silence.

'Oh, it were no loss, love, believe you me. That awful old boarding house was nearly coming down around our ears. If the Luftwaffe hadn't got it, the dry rot would have!' Elsie shrugged her skinny shoulders under her heavy fur. 'Anyway, I in't a stranger to hardship. I'm used to being knocked down and having to start all over again. Your mother will tell you that. In't that right, Ruby?'

Before Ruby could reply, Pearl reappeared carrying a tea tray laden with tea and cake.

'They didn't have any jam for the scones,' she said. 'I hope that's all right?'

'I suppose it'll have to be, won't it?' Ruby caught the flash of dissatisfaction in her mother's face, before it was quickly masked behind a smile. 'Lord knows, I in't one to complain,' she said to the girls. 'I count my blessings every day. And I've got a lot to be thankful for.'

Spare me, Ruby thought. She remembered her mother's whining voice, demanding attention at the Emergency Centre.

Pearl sat down and poured the tea, and Elsie watched her, beaming with pride. 'Look at her,' she said. 'She really looks after me. She's an angel.'

'Stop it.' Pearl blushed as she passed her mother's cup over. But she looked pleased at the compliment.

'You are, love. You certainly came to my rescue when I needed you. When I think about that horrible billet the corporation tried to put me in when I lost my house. No offence,' she said to Ruby. 'I know you did your best. But you ought to check those places before you send people to live there. Honestly, they're not fit for pigs to live in.' She looked smug. 'Anyway, I don't have to put up with it now our Pearl's brought me to live with her.'

Ruby looked sharply at her sister. Pearl kept her head down, pouring her tea. She didn't meet Ruby's eye, but her cheeks were stained pink.

'Has she?'

'Oh, hasn't she told you? Yes, once she saw the place she insisted I should pack my bags and move in with her. Wouldn't hear of me staying there a minute longer.'

Ruby was scarcely listening. She stared at her sister but Pearl still couldn't look at her.

'Anyway, I'm much better off living with Pearl,' Elsie went on happily. 'I can't tell you how lovely it is to be part of a family again . . .' She nibbled on the edge of her scone and pulled a face. 'This is a bit dry. Are you sure they've got no jam?'

'I did ask them.'

'Happen you should ask again?'

Ruby looked from her mother and her sister and back again. She waited for Pearl to make some snappish reply, but to her surprise, her sister stood up and went back to the counter.

Ruby followed her.

'Don't start,' Pearl warned over her shoulder. 'Whatever you've got to say, I don't want to hear it.'

'Do you mind telling me what's going on?'

'You heard.'

'You've asked her to move in?'

'I was going to tell you.' Pearl stood at the counter, trying to catch the eye of the women hurrying back and forth.

'Why, Pearl? Why did you do it? After everything I said—'

'I had no choice. Honestly, Ruby, you didn't see the state of that hostel. It was so dark and depressing. And damp, too. It was doing her arthritis no good.'

Ruby looked over to where Elsie was talking to Sybil and Maudie. 'I'd be surprised if she even had arthritis.'

'It in't like you to be so unkind.'

'I was afraid something like this would happen,' Ruby said. 'I told you what she was like, didn't I? I warned you she'd try to get round you.'

'I don't know what you're talking about.'

'Can't you see what's going on? She's playing you like an accordion. And you've fallen for it.'

Pearl's chin lifted. 'Are you saying I'm stupid?'

'You are if you believe a word that comes out of her mouth. Can't you see she's using you, Pearl? She used to do it all the time when we were little. You're too young to remember, but she was forever spinning stories to people, getting them to feel sorry for her. She'd take what she could get from them and then she'd dump them when they stopped being useful to her. She'll do the same to you, too—'

'You don't know that.' Pearl looked reproachful. 'I'm surprised at you, being so hard-hearted.'

They were interrupted by the sound of Sybil laughing. Ruby turned to look back over her shoulder. Elsie was holding court and the twins were listening avidly.

'Your girls seem to like her,' Pearl said.

'Yes, well, they don't know her. And neither do you,' Ruby muttered.

'Neither do you,' Pearl said. 'People can change, you know.

Honestly, she's a different person now. She knows she's made mistakes and she wants to make amends. You'd realise that if only you got to know her . . .'

'I don't want to.'

'Please, Ruby, just give her a chance? She's a frail old lady, she needs her family around her. Families should stick together. In't that what you're always saying?'

'It's a pity she didn't think of that when she abandoned us.'

Pearl sighed. 'Look, I don't want to fall out with you,' she said. 'Just try to get to know her, that's all I'm asking. If you don't think she's changed then I won't ask you again.' She tilted her head to one side. 'Please, Ruby?'

Ruby looked back at her mother. The girls were chattering away to her, but as if she knew she was being watched, Elsie suddenly lifted her gaze to meet Ruby's. There was something almost taunting about her smile.

Look at me, she seemed to say. *I'm part of your family now and there's nothing you can do about it.*

'It doesn't look as if I've got much choice, does it?' she said.

Chapter Twenty-One

Saturday 22nd March 1941

An icy drop fell on the back of Iris's neck and she straightened up, plunging her spade into the earth. She looked up at the leaden sky and sighed as the rain began to fall. Just what she needed.

'You need to get your onions and your early potatoes in before the month's out,' Pop had warned her. 'And don't let those weeds take over, or you'll make extra work for yourself.'

Iris looked down at the sorry-looking little patch of weed-strewn earth at her feet. Pop would have a fit if he could see how she had neglected it, especially when he had tended it so carefully over the winter while she had been in hospital. But she just could not seem to find the energy or the enthusiasm to deal with it.

John had sworn he would come round and help her. But as usual, her brother had forgotten his promise. Either that, or he'd had a better offer. So now Iris was left to do it on her own.

'I'll swing for you, John Maguire!' she muttered under her breath as she plunged her spade back into the earth.

'You know, they say that's the first sign of madness.'

She looked over her shoulder. Sam Scuttle was watching her over the garden fence.

Seeing him gave her a start. They had not spoken for three weeks, not since their conversation outside the fish and chip shop. Iris had seen him coming and going a couple of times, and she had certainly heard enough about him from Beattie and her mother. They never seemed to stop talking about him at the net loft where they all worked.

But coming face to face with him made her instantly wary. It took her a moment to gain control of herself enough to sound casual.

'What?'

'Talking to yourself. They say it's the first sign of madness. Although I'd say digging in the rain might be a close second,' he grinned.

'It's our John that's meant to be digging,' Iris said, going back to her work.

'Let me guess. He found something better to do?'

'I don't know what he's doing. All I know is he in't here helping me.'

'Can I give you a hand?'

Iris kept her back to him, turning the earth. 'There's no need. I'm sure our John will turn up soon.'

'I wouldn't bet on it.' Sam squinted up at the rainy sky. 'Anyway, we'll get it done quicker if there's two of us. And to be honest you're hardly putting your back into it.'

'Charming!' Iris held out the spade. 'Go on, then, if you reckon you can do better.'

'I couldn't do much worse,' Sam said as he hopped over the fence and took the spade from her.

Iris looked over her shoulder at him as he started to dig. The rain was already soaking through his shirt and the cotton fabric clung to his body, outlining his powerful muscles. Iris went to the far end of the patch and started wrenching up fistfuls of weeds but her gaze kept straying back to him.

'I dunno about digging for victory,' she muttered. 'I wish I'd never started the ruddy allotment. I only did it because Pop nagged me into it.'

'You'll change your mind when you're pulling up carrots and potatoes,' Sam said. He straightened up and looked towards the fence. 'I'm wondering if I should dig up our shelter and do some planting instead, since no one bothers with it any more.'

'I thought your mother was dead set on an Anderson shelter?'

'She was, but now she's decided she prefers the public one. She likes the company, she says. Anyway, she only wanted the Anderson because she thought our Charlie might go down there.'

Iris caught the worried look on his face. 'He still won't go near it?'

Sam shook his head. 'It scares Ma to death. But I've told her there's no sense in trying to push someone into doing something they don't want.'

He sent her a long, steady look. Iris went back to her weeding, her face flaming.

'What's this I hear about you being a hero?' She changed the subject.

'Who told you that?'

'Your mother's been telling all the girls in the net loft how you went into a burning house to rescue someone?'

'Oh, that.' Sam turned back and started digging. 'Ma exaggerates sometimes.'

'She says you were a hero. I'm surprised you didn't get your name in the paper for it.'

'I'm glad I didn't. I've had enough ribbing from the lads at the fire station over it already.'

'Why? What happened?'

Sam looked rueful. 'It was an incendiary fire, just off Spring Bank. There was this old lady standing on the pavement, sobbing and screaming. "My poor Joey's trapped inside," she kept saying. Making a hell of a fuss, she was. I couldn't get any sense out of her. The way she was carrying on, naturally I assumed it was her old man, or her son, so I rushed inside to get him out. And do you know who I found? A budgie.'

'No!'

'Aye. Bad-tempered little thing it was, too. It gave me a nasty bite. It let loose with a few choice swear words, as well.'

'Your mum didn't tell us that.'

'She wouldn't, would she?'

'No wonder you didn't want your name in the paper.'

'I can see the headlines now, can't you? "Budgie tells fireman to bugger off".'

'Oh, Sam!' Iris laughed.

'I'm glad you find it funny,' Sam said, the picture of injured pride. Then he caught her eye and started laughing too. Soon they were both doubled up, helpless with mirth.

'Sorry, am I interrupting?'

Matthew stood in the open back doorway, watching them. 'I knocked, but the door was open,' he said, his gaze moving from Iris to Sam and back again.

Iris straightened up quickly, brushing the dirt from her hands. 'Is John not with you?'

Matthew shook his head. 'He had to go into town with your mother, so I thought I'd come and help you with the allotment instead.' He kept his gaze fixed on Sam as he said it.

'We've nearly finished,' Sam said.

'There's still a bit to do. I might as well get on with it, since I'm here.' He was already shrugging off his coat.

'But we don't need you.'

'That's up to Iris, surely?'

They both turned to face her. Iris looked uneasily from one

to the other. There was more going on than a struggle over a spade, she thought. But she did not want to be in the middle of it.

'I suppose he might as well make himself useful.' She shrugged. 'Anyway, you've already done more than enough.'

Sam looked from one to the other, his expression darkening. Then he thrust the spade into Matthew's hand without a word.

'Thank you for your help,' Iris said to him, as he vaulted over the fence. But Sam did not even look back at her as he slammed into the house.

'I hope I didn't offend him?' Matthew said. He was leaning on the spade, watching the scene with interest, the slightest of smiles playing on his lips.

'He's fine. He was only lending a hand till John got here.'

'You two didn't look as if you were getting much gardening done.'

She felt the heat rising in her face. 'We were only messing about.'

'Your mother says you were courting.'

'You don't want to pay any attention to what my mother says. I was just about to put the kettle on, if you'd like a brew?' Iris changed the subject abruptly.

'Thank you.'

When she returned with the tea, Matthew was hard at work digging, his head down. He barely seemed aware of Iris as she set the cup down on the front step. But as she turned to go back into the house he suddenly spoke.

'So what is going on between you two?'

'Who?'

'You and him.' He nodded towards the fence. 'Are you courting, or not?'

'No.' She caught his level look. 'There was – something

– once,' she admitted slowly. 'But it was over before it even started. We're just friends now.'

'Not as far as he's concerned.'

'What do you mean?'

'He still likes you, I can tell.'

Iris bristled. 'And what business is it of yours?'

'I just like to know where I stand. I don't want to step on anyone's toes.'

'In what way?'

'I wanted to ask if you'd go dancing with me on Friday night?'

Iris stared at him. 'What?'

'This dance next week, at the Metropole. I wondered if you'd like to go with me?'

'Why can't Sybil go with you?'

'I haven't asked her.'

'But she likes you.'

Matthew smiled. 'I like her, too. But I want to go dancing with you.'

'But why?'

'Does there have to be a reason?'

'I suppose not.' Iris looked down at her hands. Her finger-nails were still ingrained with soil. She couldn't imagine what a sight she must look, in a mouth-eaten jersey and a pair of Pop's old trousers, two sizes too big for her.

'You don't want to go out with me,' she said.

'I know what I want. The question is, what do *you* want?'

Iris met his gaze. There was something compelling about the way he spoke in that low, deep voice.

A cry from inside the house distracted her, breaking the spell.

'That'll be Kitty, waking up from her nap. I'd best go and see to her.' Iris darted inside the house, relieved to escape.

She gathered her thoughts while she was upstairs. Matthew's offer had come out of nowhere and set her reeling. It was such a bizarre notion, she wondered if she had imagined it.

Matthew had finished digging the allotment and was putting on his jacket when she returned with Kitty a few minutes later. The yard smelt of rich, turned earth.

'There wasn't much to do,' he said. 'I've put the spade over there—'

'Why do you want to go out with me?' she blurted out the question.

He frowned. 'Why?'

'You have to have a reason. I want to know what it is.'

He thought for a moment. 'I thought you might enjoy it.'

Iris narrowed her eyes. 'So you feel sorry for me?'

'No!' He looked shocked at the idea. 'Believe me, I'd never do anything out of pity.' He paused. 'You interest me,' he said at last.

'Me?'

'The other day, when we talked . . . I don't know, I felt as if we understood each other.' He regarded her thoughtfully. 'But perhaps I was wrong,' he said. 'Perhaps you've got someone else on your mind?' He glanced towards the fence.

'I told you,' Iris muttered. 'It's over between me and Sam.'

'Is it?'

She glanced away, afraid her feelings were written too plainly across her face. She thought about earlier, the heady rush of sensation she had felt when Sam was near her. It was too easy, too dangerous.

It had been a mistake. She had encouraged Sam, given him a reason to hope. And she had ignited a spark inside herself that she had spent months trying to put out.

'I want it to be,' she said quietly.

Matthew's mouth curved. 'I can't think of a better way of sending a message than to go out with another man?' he said softly.

Iris looked at him. It would be too cruel, she thought. It would break Sam's heart. But surely it was better to make a clean break than to slowly allow it to wither and crumble on false hope?

'You're right,' she said.

'So you'll go dancing with me?'

Iris met his gaze. There were no tangled emotions or painful memories of her past with him. He was a clean slate on which she could write her future.

'Yes,' she said. 'I'll go dancing.'

Chapter Twenty-Two

Friday 28th March 1941

'Am I making a terrible mistake?'

Iris's face was furrowed with worry as she met Edie's gaze in the dressing table mirror. 'What do you think? Should I be going?'

'It's a bit late for doubts now.' Edie passed her the pot of rouge. 'Here, put some of this on. You're as white as a sheet.'

Iris dabbed it half-heartedly on her cheeks and Edie went back to combing out her friend's newly set curls. It wasn't an easy task; Iris was so agitated she could hardly keep still.

'I never should have said yes,' she muttered. 'It was a daft thing to do. What was I thinking?'

'For goodness' sake, calm down. You're only going dancing, you in't promised to marry him!' Edie put down her comb and stepped back to admire her handiwork. 'There, you're all done. What do you think?'

'Very nice.' Iris hardly spared herself a glance in the mirror, Edie noticed.

'Right, now let's find you something to wear. I've brought a couple of frocks for you to try . . .' She spread out the dresses on the bed. 'I'm sorry there in't much to choose from,' she said, seeing Iris's downcast expression. 'I sold most of my good clothes when I moved here. But these were my favourites, so I couldn't bear to get rid of them.'

'They're lovely,' Iris said quietly.

'How about this one?' Edie held up the blue flowery one.

'It will really suit your dark colouring, I think.'

Iris shrugged her shoulders. 'If you like.'

'Try it on, anyway. Although you might have been better off borrowing a frock from Sybil? She's got lots of fancy clothes.'

Iris's mouth twisted. 'I don't think she's in the mood to do me any favours at the moment.'

'She in't still sulking, surely?'

'She told Mum yesterday I'll be lucky if she ever speaks to me again.'

'She'll calm down in a couple of days. You'll see, by next week she'll have a new boyfriend and she'll forget all about it.' Edie fiddled with the mother of pearl button at the nape of Iris's neck. 'Anyway, it's hardly your fault if Matthew prefers you.'

'Yes, but why does he? Sybil's so lively and pretty, she's far more his type than I am.' She looked back at her reflection in the long mirror. 'What have I got to offer?'

Poor Iris, Edie thought. She couldn't see what the rest of the world did. She had more than her fair share of the Maguire good looks, with her glossy dark hair and warm brown eyes. 'You're beautiful,' she said.

Iris laughed. 'I'm thirty-three and a mother! Syb's right, I shouldn't even be thinking about going dancing with a younger man.'

'He's closer to your age than he is to Sybil's,' Edie pointed out, but she could tell Iris wasn't listening.

'What do you think of him?' she asked, as she put on her shoes.

'I hardly know him.' Edie chose her words carefully. She had only met Matthew a couple of times, but he unnerved her slightly and she did not know why. He was charming and pleasant enough, but like an iceberg, Edie had the feeling there was something darker lurking beneath the surface.

'Mum doesn't like him,' Iris said. 'She doesn't approve of me going out with him either.'

'Only because he's not Sam Scuttle.'

She knew straight away it was the wrong thing to say, as Iris turned on her. 'Why does everyone keep trying to push me and Sam together?' she demanded.

Because you're made for each other, Edie thought. But she knew she had already said too much.

'Sam and I just aren't meant to be, and that's all there is to it,' Iris said. 'The sooner people accept it, the better.'

Edie said nothing.

'Anyway, I don't know why everyone's so against Matthew,' Iris went on. 'I like him. He's not like any man I've ever met. He understands me.'

'You know your own mind,' Edie said. 'Besides, who cares what anyone thinks, as long as you're happy?'

'You're right.' But Iris still looked doubtful as she gazed back at her reflection, biting her lip.

'So what do you think of the dress?' Edie asked. 'Will it do?'

'It's lovely.' Iris twirled, looking at herself properly for the first time. 'Are you sure you don't mind lending it to me?'

'You might as well get some use out of it. I'm hardly going to go anywhere to wear it, am I?' she said ruefully.

Iris looked over her shoulder at her. 'You could still come with us, you know. I'm sure our John would be delighted . . .'

Edie shook her head. 'Thanks, but I've already told him it in't for me.'

'I'm not sure it's for me, either.'

Edie saw her friend's nerve failing again and stepped in quickly. 'You'll have a wonderful time,' she said. 'It's a long time since you've had a night out.'

Just then there was a knock on the door.

Iris looked at her with panic-stricken eyes. 'He's here!'

Edie glanced at the clock. 'Right on time, too. He must be keen.'

'Do you think so?' Iris did not look happy at the thought. She looked as if she would have bolted, given half a chance.

Edie gripped her by the shoulders. 'Listen to me, Iris Fletcher. You're going to go out and you're going to have a good time. And tomorrow I'll come round for a cup of tea and you can tell me all the details. That way I'll feel as if I've had a night out too.'

Iris looked towards the door, then back at her reflection. She seemed to make up her mind.

'You're right,' she said. 'Why shouldn't I have a good time?' She looked at Edie. 'You've got to grab your happiness while you can, don't you? Life's too short.'

There was another knock on the door, louder this time. 'Go on,' Edie said, shoving her towards the bedroom door. 'Before he changes his mind!'

Edie watched them from the bedroom window. Whatever crisis of confidence Iris had felt earlier seemed to have passed now. She was walking proudly at Matthew's side, her arm linked through his, laughing at something he had said.

She looked happy, Edie thought with relief. If anyone deserved to have a good time, it was Iris.

She started to tidy away the curlers and the make-up. The dress Iris had not chosen was laid out on the bed. Edie picked it up to fold it but at the last moment she held it up against herself and gazed wistfully at her reflection in the mirror.

It was her favourite, cream cotton with a pattern of red cherries. She had been wearing it the night she first met Rob. Seeing it now, she could almost remember her nerves as she descended the stairs down to Betty's basement bar. Her heart had been hammering so hard she was surprised it didn't burst the bodice buttons.

The dress brought back so many other happy memories, too. The sixpenny dances at the Rowntree's factory or the Folk Hall at New Earswick, where she and her friends Mollie and Jen would dance all night. Was that really only a couple of years ago? It felt like a lifetime. Looking at herself in the mirror now, she no longer recognised the giddy girl who had laughed and danced and flirted.

You've got to grab your happiness while you can. Life's too short.

Iris's words came back to her. Had she been too hasty, she wondered, saying no to John Maguire? Perhaps she should have been like Iris and taken a chance.

'Auntie Edie? Bobby's just been sick.'

Archie's voice, calling out from the foot of the stairs, broke her train of thought.

'I'll be there in a minute.' Edie took one last wistful look at herself in the mirror, then put the dress away and went downstairs.

Chapter Twenty-Three

If Matthew had not been holding her hand so firmly, Iris might have fled long before they reached the Metropole.

The band was already playing a lively swing number when they arrived. The sound of trumpets and pianos drifted down the stairs as they lined up at the cloakroom to hand in their coats.

Iris looked around her at the other women, done up in their finery, their ears and throats glittering with jewels. Suddenly she wished she had made more of an effort.

'You look beautiful.' Matthew seemed to guess what she was thinking.

'I don't know about that.' She touched her hair uncertainly. The curls were already beginning to turn limp in the warmth of the room, even though Edie had done her best with no setting lotion.

'I'm telling you, you're the most beautiful woman here.' He squeezed her hand. 'Don't look so scared. We're going to have a good night.'

Iris smiled back at him weakly. She appreciated his confidence, as hers was beginning to fail her.

'Here's John,' Matthew said. Iris turned to look over her shoulder and the smile froze on her face as she saw who was with him.

'Hello, Auntie Iris,' said Sybil.

She was dressed up to the nines as usual, in a beautiful

cornflower blue dress that matched her eyes perfectly. The bias-cut satin skimmed over her slender curves. She looked so glamorous, Iris was even more conscious of her simple cotton dress.

'Hello, Syb. Fancy seeing you here.' Iris looked accusingly at her brother as she said it.

'She wanted to come.' John spread his hands, as if he'd had no say in the matter. 'And I had a spare ticket and no one to go with, so . . .'

He didn't look particularly sorry about it. Typical John, Iris thought, always out to cause mischief.

'Why did he have to bring her?' she hissed to Matthew as John and Sybil went off to check in their coats. 'He knows full well she's furious with me.'

'He probably meant it as a joke.'

'I in't laughing.'

'Don't let it ruin our night. We're here to have fun, remember?'

'That's all right for you to say. You in't the one she'll be looking daggers at all night.'

'Come and dance, then you won't have to look at her.'

Iris wanted to say no, but Matthew was already guiding her towards the staircase that led up to the dance floor.

Upstairs, the dance floor was surrounded by tables of people chatting and laughing together under the sparkling chandeliers. Several couples were already gliding around the floor. Iris hesitated, but Matthew grabbed her hand.

'Oh, no you don't,' he said. 'We've come here to dance, remember?'

'I'm not sure I remember how,' Iris protested, as he led her on to the dance floor.

They ended up staying on the dance floor, stepping and swinging their way through one song after another. Iris was surprised to find that not only did she remember how to dance, she actually enjoyed it. Matthew was an excellent partner, too, guiding her expertly around the floor. Iris felt her confidence returning as she whirled round in his arms.

'You see?' Matthew grinned, as they finished a lively quick-step. 'I told you you'd have fun, didn't I?'

'I am, thank you.' Iris smiled back. 'But can we sit down now? My feet are starting to kill me.'

As soon as they walked off the dance floor, Sybil appeared out of nowhere to claim Matthew.

'My turn,' she said, leading him back in to the whirl of dancers.

They made a handsome couple, Iris thought as she watched them in each other's arms. They seemed to belong together. Sybil was a wonderful dancer, and she matched Matthew's fancy footwork with expert ease.

'You've got nowt to worry about,' John said behind her. 'He's only got eyes for you.'

Iris looked away. 'I'm sure I'm not bothered.' She slipped off her shoe and massaged her aching foot. But then her curiosity got the better of her and she said, 'What makes you so sure?'

'I know Matthew. Once he sets his sights on someone, that's it.'

'And does he often set his sights on someone?'

John laughed. 'Not as often as me, if that's what you mean! Speaking of which . . .'

His gaze strayed over to a group of young women two tables away. A couple of them were boldly giving him the eye while their friends giggled and nudged each other.

'So now you're abandoning me too?' Iris said. 'That's nice of you, I must say.'

'Be fair, Sis. I've been at sea for months!' John laughed.

Iris watched her younger brother as he sauntered towards the girls' table. She saw their faces brighten with hope, settling in to coy smiles as he approached.

She looked around, back towards the dance floor and caught Matthew's eye. He was still dancing with Sybil but he was staring straight at Iris, his gaze never leaving her face. There was something so intense about him, it excited and unnerved her.

Once he sets his sights on someone . . .

John's words came into her head.

She went off to the cloakroom to rearrange her hair and powder her face. When she returned, Matthew was alone at their table.

'Where's Sybil?' Iris asked, looking around.

'I don't know.'

'You could have carried on dancing with her, you know. I wouldn't have minded.'

'No, but I would. I wanted to be with you.'

'Yes, but Syb—'

'Why should I waste my time doing something I don't want to do, just to please someone else?' Matthew looked genuinely perplexed.

Iris stared at him, lost for words.

'Anyway, it looks as if your niece has found someone else to entertain her.' Matthew nodded towards the dance floor, where Sybil was in the arms of a handsome young RAF officer.

'I don't think she's pining for me, do you?' Matthew said dryly.

He held out his hands. 'Dance with me again?'

It was a question, and yet somehow it wasn't. Iris looked up into his icy-blue gaze.

Once he's set his sights on you . . .

She took his hand.

'If you like,' she said.

By ten o'clock, Iris was ready to go home, but the others were not so keen.

'What are you talking about? The night is young!' John said. He was having the time of his life, taking to the dance floor with a different partner every time.

'Not for me,' Iris said. 'Besides, I promised Edie I wouldn't be late home.'

'I'm sure she won't mind,' Matthew said.

'All the same, it in't fair to take advantage.'

'Please stay,' he said quietly. 'I don't want the evening to end just yet.'

'You can stay if you want to?'

'But I don't want to stay without you.'

Their eyes met in challenge. Iris could already feel herself giving in but just at that moment the band stopped playing and the band leader announced there was an air raid, to a chorus of groans and jeers and cat calls.

'Well that's that, then,' John said. 'It looks like the evening's over anyway.'

As they were ushered down to the basement, Iris looked around and said, 'Where's Syb?'

John shrugged. 'Last time I saw her she was having a fine old time with that pilot fellow.'

'We should look for her—'

'Leave her be,' Matthew said. 'She'll be fine. I don't suppose she's worrying about you, wherever she is.'

He led the way over to one of the narrow benches that lined the walls, and they squeezed into a tiny space between two other couples. Everyone looked so strange, hunched in the drab, gloomy cellar in all their glittering finery.

John had already drifted over to join the young women he had been dancing with earlier, but Iris could not stop scanning the benches, looking for Sybil.

'I can't see her anywhere. What if she's gone? What if she's caught in the middle of the air raid?'

'She's an adult, she can take care of herself.' Matthew cut her off, an edge of irritation in his voice. 'Why do you have to think of everyone else all the time?'

'I don't.'

'Yes, you do. First we have to go home early so we don't upset Edie, now you're fretting over Sybil . . . you're always worrying about other people.'

Not always, Iris thought. The one time she hadn't worried about someone else, she had ended up losing them. She was terrified of making the same mistake again.

Within an hour the All Clear had sounded. To Iris's relief, Matthew seemed to have changed his mind about staying at the dance and offered to walk her home. John decided to stay behind.

'Someone's got to keep an eye on Syb,' he said, but Iris knew he was more interested in making the most of his freedom. Especially since one of the young women was proving to be very keen on him.

The buses had stopped running so they had to walk back to Hessle Road. Iris hurried, but Matthew dawdled, looking up at the velvety black sky sprinkled with stars.

'Look at it,' he marvelled. 'There are so many stars out, I can't count them all. And that full moon . . .'

'A bomber's moon,' Iris said. 'That's what they call it,' she explained, as Matthew turned to look at her. 'When it's clear and bright enough to light the way for the German planes.'

'I know what it is.' He shook his head. 'I just feel sorry for you, that's all.'

'Me? Why?'

'When I look up at the sky I see a wonderful array of stars, and all you see is a pathway for bombers.'

Iris gazed up at the sky. 'You're right,' she said. The thought made her sad. When had she stopped seeing the wonder in the world, and started to see only the danger and the darkness?

She turned to look at him. 'How do you do it?' she asked. 'How do you still manage to see the world as a beautiful place, even after everything that's happened to you?'

He smiled. 'I'll have to show you, won't I?'

She looked away. 'I'm not sure I ever will.'

'Of course you will.' He reached for her hand. 'You stick with me and I'll show you the stars, Iris.'

She looked down at his hand, then back at his face. He was so certain of himself, Iris thought. She was so lacking in assurance, she couldn't help being attracted to it.

But at the same time it made her feel uneasy. She had the feeling that if she said yes to him she would be taking a step towards a future she might not like.

But she would also be taking a step away from her past.

She made up her mind and grasped his hand.

'I'd like that,' she said.

Chapter Twenty-Four

Monday 31st March 1941

Ruby paused at the corner of her sister's road to shake the rain off her umbrella. She had visited her sister's house a hundred times, but as she stared down the narrow terraced street, it was all she could do to make her feet walk towards it.

She could not face it, not after last night. Last night's raid had been another bad one, strafing along Hedon Road, Ferensway and Prospect Street. She had been out with the mobile canteen on Boulevard when she heard the Infirmary had been hit and her heart was instantly in her mouth, knowing her Ada was on night duty. She could scarcely carry on until the news came through that all the staff and patients were safe.

And then, just as she was reeling from one shock, they found out the bomb on Ferensway had hit the Shell Mex building, destroying the WVS centre.

By the time Ruby had returned with the mobile canteen just after dawn, several of the other women had gathered outside what was left of the centre. They were all in tears to see the building reduced to rubble. Ruby was supposed to go off duty, but of course she had volunteered to stay and help, and they had spent all day moving what they could into a temporary new office at the Guildhall, borrowing typewriters and trying to get themselves sorted.

Ruby had tried to keep her chin up but after a night and day without rest, she was exhausted, getting by on nervous energy and in no mood for another meeting with her mother. But she had promised her sister she would come, and so here she was.

As she let herself in she heard the sound of laughter coming from upstairs.

'Pearl?' she called out.

'We're up here.'

She followed the sound up to her sister's bedroom. As she pushed open the door Pearl and their mother both turned to greet her.

'What do you think?' Pearl giggled.

Ruby looked from one to the other, scarcely able to believe her eyes. Pearl and Elsie were dressed in matching green striped frocks, and Elsie had styled her bleached hair to match Pearl's fair curls.

'It was Mum's idea,' Pearl said. 'She thought it would be a lark.' She twirled, admiring her reflection. 'We look like sisters, don't we?'

Ruby saw the smile that passed between them and felt a twinge of jealousy.

'Very nice, I'm sure,' she muttered.

Pearl looked at her, as if noticing her for the first time. 'You look tired,' she said.

'I haven't slept in two days.'

'I thought about you last night,' Pearl said. 'We walked into town this morning, and there wasn't a single window left in the Infirmary. Your Ada was all right though, wasn't she?'

Ruby nodded. 'She's safe, thank God.'

'And Ferensway, too.' Pearl looked at her sympathetically. 'That must have been a terrible blow.'

'We lost everything.' A lump came to her throat, blocking the words. She had been smiling all day, putting on a brave face for the other women, but now she felt weak from it all.

Elsie laughed, breaking the sombre mood. 'Don't be so melodramatic, it was only an office. When you've lost the roof over your head like me, then you can start complaining.' She turned to Pearl, taking charge briskly. 'But what are we thinking, standing here gossiping when your sister's shivering in that wet coat? Take it downstairs and dry it in front of the fire, will you, love? And put the kettle on while you're at it.' She turned to Ruby. 'We'll go down to the parlour, shall we?'

'I usually sit in the kitchen . . .' Ruby glanced at her sister.

'Oh no, the parlour's much nicer for visitors.'

Pearl gave a little laugh. 'Our Ruby's hardly a visitor, Mum!'

'All the same, we'll sit in the parlour.'

Since when did you start giving the orders in this house? The question nearly tumbled from Ruby's lips. She waited for Pearl to say it instead, but her sister just shrugged helplessly and said, 'As you like. Give us your coat, Ruby.'

Elsie led the way down the stairs and into the front parlour. She made a big show of plumping the cushions in the best armchair for Ruby to sit down.

Ruby watched her throwing extra coal on the fire as if she owned the place.

'Well, this is nice, in't it?' Elsie beamed. 'I was so pleased when our Pearl told me you were coming round. It's time we cleared the air, I reckon.'

'I agree.' Their eyes met across the room, and for a moment she saw a nervous look flash across her mother's face.

'It was lovely to meet your daughters last week,' she said. 'Such wonderful girls, and so pretty, too. And you have another daughter, Pearl says?'

'Ada. She got married last year.'

'I daresay you'll be looking forward to grandchildren?'

'Not for a while. Her husband's away on the minesweepers.'

'Oh, like yours?'

Ruby nodded. 'They're on the same crew.'

'Well, that's nice.'

'I'd hardly call it nice, risking your life in the Arctic Circle.'

Ruby saw her mother's crestfallen look and stopped. She had come here to make peace, she reminded herself. But tiredness had sharpened her tongue.

'Here we are.' Pearl came in, carrying the tray laden with cups and saucers and a Victoria sponge.

Ruby stared at it. 'You've made a cake?'

'Mum did. She followed a recipe from the Ministry of Food.'

'Oh, you shouldn't have brought it in,' Elsie made a great show of looking modest. 'Our Ruby won't want any of that. I'm sure it's only fit for the pig bin.'

'Don't be daft,' Pearl said. 'You should have seen her making it,' she grinned at Ruby. 'She was so proud of herself. She did it especially for you.'

'I don't remember you being so domesticated,' Ruby said.

'Yes, well, people change, don't they?' her mother muttered.

'Yes, they do.' Pearl sent Ruby a meaningful look as she reached for the knife. 'Here, Mum. Why don't you do the honours?'

'Are you sure you trust me with it, after what happened earlier?' Elsie said.

'You mean when you nearly sliced your hand off, opening that tin of corned beef?'

They both laughed. Ruby looked at the two of them, sitting side by side with their matching dresses and carefully styled hair. She couldn't have felt more like an outsider.

They made small talk, like polite strangers, under Pearl's watchful gaze.

'It must be difficult for you, your husband being away for

months on end,' her mother said as she passed her a slice of cake.

'I'm used to him being away on the trawlers.'

'How long have you been married?'

'Twenty-four years. We got married on my eighteenth birthday.'

'Talk about young love!' Her mother looked impressed. 'I bet he's handsome.'

'He is,' Pearl put in. 'He's like a film star. In't that right, Rube?'

Ruby said nothing. Jimmy Maguire was much more than a good-looking man. He was her rock.

She had met him when she was seventeen years old, working as a maid in Kirk Ella during the day and scrubbing floors down at the fish docks by night. Jimmy had recently been discharged from the Army and was learning his trade on the trawlers with his father.

He wasn't like the other dock lads. He liked a laugh and a joke, but he was kind, loving and caring with it. He'd given Ruby a home, a family and the only real stability she had ever known.

'He's a good man,' she said quietly.

'Not like yours, eh?' Elsie cackled to Pearl.

Ruby saw her sister's crestfallen face. 'Frank does his best,' Pearl mumbled.

'Oh, aye? And where is he now?'

'I told you. He's away on business.'

'On business! Sounds to me like you picked a right devil there.'

'And you'd know all about that, wouldn't you?' Ruby jumped to her sister's defence. 'You could certainly pick them too, as I recall.'

Elsie's smile faltered, her lips trembling.

'We could do with a refill, Mum, if you don't mind?' Pearl cut in quickly.

'Of course, love.' Elsie took the pot from her, her gaze lowered.

No sooner had she left the room than Pearl turned on Ruby. 'You promised you'd be nice!' she hissed.

'I was only sticking up for you. Did you hear what she said about your Frank?'

'She didn't mean anything by it.' Pearl glanced worriedly towards the door. 'Did you see her face? She's so upset.'

'She's putting it on.'

'Why do you always say that? She's got feelings, you know.'

'So have I. Or don't I matter any more?'

Pearl was silent for a moment, her mouth tightening. 'I just wish you'd forget everything that happened, that's all.'

'I can't help it. I know you want to brush it all under the carpet, but it in't that easy. I can't forget what she did to us—'

'What did I do?'

Elsie stood in the doorway, the teapot in her hands.

'Nothing, Mum,' Pearl said quickly. 'It's all in the past.'

'Not where our Ruby is concerned, by the sound of it.'

Elsie placed the pot carefully down on the table and sat down. 'Go on, then. What did I do that was so wrong?'

Ruby glanced at her sister's anxious face. 'Pearl's right, it's all in the past. I should just forget about it.'

'You won't though, will you? You're always going to resent me until you've told me what you think of me.' Elsie sat back in her seat. 'Well, go on, then. Let's hear what you've got to say.'

'Mum—'

'No, Pearl. We're here to clear the air, and that's what we're going to do.' Elsie turned to Ruby expectantly. 'What did I do to you that was so wrong?'

Ruby rubbed her hand wearily over her face. Exhaustion had settled into her bones, making her whole body ache.

This was the wrong time, she thought. She needed to choose her words carefully, but she was too tired to think.

'You gave us away,' she said. 'You abandoned your own children for the sake of a man.'

Elsie stared back at her. 'You're right,' she said.

'Ruby, please—' Pearl pleaded, but Elsie lifted her hand to silence her.

'No, your sister's right. I've not been a good mother to either of you. I was weak and foolish, and I let a man come between me and my children.' She turned to face Ruby, the picture of injured dignity. 'I thought Julius would be the answer to all our problems. I wanted you girls to have a real father, someone who would look after you. I had such high hopes of him—' She let her gaze drop. 'But I was wrong. It turned out Julius didn't want to be a father.' She put up her hand to dash away a tear. 'I can't tell you what an awful day that was for me, having to give you up—'

'Then why did you do it?'

Elsie's head shot up. Her eyes were suddenly dry, Ruby noticed. 'What?'

'Why did you get rid of us and not him?'

Her mother's expression turned to panic, eyes flickering like a cornered animal. 'I – I don't understand—'

'I'd never give up my children for any man, and I don't know any other mother who would. But you did. Why didn't you tell him to go instead?'

'I – I—' Her mother's mouth opened and closed, floundering for words.

'I'll tell you why, shall I? Because you didn't really care about us. You might talk about wanting a father for us, but all you really wanted was for him to look after you. You weren't

149

thinking of us, you were only thinking of yourself as usual.'

'I *was* thinking of you! I wanted you to have a better life, with a decent family . . .'

'You dumped us at that orphanage and never even looked back. I don't suppose you gave us a second thought until the day you walked into the WVS and saw me there. And even then you didn't recognise me, did you?'

Pearl looked panic-stricken. 'Ruby—'

'Pearl, you're fooling yourself if you think she cares. She's never cared about anyone but herself.' Weariness made her snap. She could see her sister's worried look, but Ruby felt as if she was rolling down a hill and she couldn't stop. 'As for giving us a better life – I'll tell you what our lives were like, shall I?'

'Ruby, don't—'

'It was like a prison. They separated us, ripped us apart. They put Pearl with the babies and I was only allowed to see her once a day, if I was lucky. I'd lay in the dormitory at night and hear her crying out for me down the other end of the hall.'

She looked at her sister. Pearl was staring down at her hands.

'And they put me to work,' she said. 'Eight years old and I was scrubbing floors and doing laundry day in, day out. Training, they called it. Until I turned fourteen and they could send me out to work as a skivvy. And do you know what I did then? I found a place for Pearl and me. That's all I could think about, getting her away from that place so we could be together. I was more of a mother to her than you ever were!'

The words came out, tumbling over themselves. Years of pent-up bitterness spilling out, burning her throat.

'And where were you while we were struggling? When I

was sixteen years old, working all hours so I could keep a roof over our heads? I daresay you didn't give us a second thought, did you?'

'I did. I thought about you every day . . .'

'I thought about you, too. I used to imagine what it would be like when I saw you again and I could finally tell you what I really thought of you.'

For a moment Elsie stared at her like a cornered animal. Then she did the only thing she could to defend herself. She started to cry.

'Don't, Mum. Don't upset yourself.' Pearl immediately moved to her side, putting her arms around her.

'You're not really falling for this, are you?' Ruby was disgusted. 'It's all an act, Pearl. I've seen her do it a million times, turn on the tears to get herself out of trouble.'

Pearl glared at Ruby over the top of her mother's head. 'I think you'd best go.'

Ruby stared at her aghast. 'What?'

'I mean it, Ruby. You can see how upset she is.'

Ruby looked at her mother's sobbing shoulders, her face buried in Pearl's shoulder. She knew full well that Elsie's eyes would be dry. 'If you believe that you're even more stupid than I thought you were!'

She knew straight away it was the wrong thing to say. Pearl's expression hardened. 'Stupid now, am I?'

'I didn't mean it like that—' Ruby started to say, but Pearl cut her off.

'You've said enough. Just go home, Ruby. You've ruined everything.'

Ruby glanced at her mother. Was it her imagination, or did she see the flicker of a smile in the corner of Elsie's mouth?

Chapter Twenty-Five

'I'm sorry, Mum. I never expected her to behave like that, honestly.'

'It's all right, love. It weren't your fault. Anyway, she was right. Happen I should have tried harder to keep us all together—'

'You mustn't think like that. I know you did your best.'

Elsie reached out and patted her daughter's hand. 'Thanks, love. It means a lot to hear you say that. And you're right, I did do my best. But it in't easy when you're on your own.' She sighed. 'Our Ruby's lucky, she's got a nice home and a husband who looks after her. She don't know what it's like to struggle.'

'I'm disappointed with her, I really am. I've always thought she was so kind-hearted.'

'Now, you mustn't blame your sister. I won't have it.' Elsie paused just long enough, then said, 'I think I should go.'

'Go? Go where?'

'I don't know. Back to that hostel, I suppose, if they in't given my room to some other poor soul by now. Anyway, I'm sure I can find somewhere to rest my head. It in't like I've never been homeless before!' Elsie smiled bracingly.

'I told you, you can stay here for as long as you like.'

'I know, love. But your sister's never going to accept me, she's made that clear enough.' Elsie sighed. 'I'd really hoped we would be together and happy again, but it looks as if that in't what she wants. And I don't want to be any trouble . . .'

'Don't talk like that. I want you to stay. Anyway, this is my home, not Ruby's. She can't tell me who can stay and who can't.'

'That's very kind of you, love. But the last thing I want to do is come between you . . .'

'You in't coming between us. This is all Ruby's doing.'

'You mustn't be hard on your sister. She can't help herself.' Elsie turned her gaze wistfully away. 'It was all I ever wanted, to have my girls back,' she sighed. 'My precious little jewels.'

'It will happen,' Pearl said. 'You'll see, Ruby will come round soon. She's got a soft heart underneath that bossiness. And family means everything to her.'

'I hope you're right, love.' Elsie sighed again.

She looked away, rubbing her hand across her face so that Pearl could not see her expression. Over the years Elsie had become good at hiding her true feelings.

Wretched Ruby, trying to throw a spanner in the works. Elsie had never wanted Pearl to invite her round in the first place. But she was so determined that Ruby and her mother should make their peace, in the end Elsie had no choice but to go along with it or risk looking bad.

But she had always known it would be a waste of time. She was never going to get round Ruby, not in a month of Sundays.

She knew that the minute she had clapped eyes on her in that WVS centre, throwing her weight around and giving orders. She had always been a bossy little thing. Once Elsie had recovered from the shock of seeing her, she had hoped that she might be able to turn the situation to her advantage. But Ruby had made it all too clear she was not going to do her mother any favours.

Luckily she had found an easier mark in her daughter Pearl.

Pearl was like her – easily swayed, fond of a good time and not keen on responsibility. She had always been Elsie's favourite, even when they were bains. Pearl was like a little doll with her fair hair and pretty face. She was always laughing, unlike sullen, red-haired Ruby with her disapproving frown. She was always trying to take charge, putting difficulties in Elsie's way, trying to drag her down. If Elsie had ever felt a twinge of guilt, it was because Ruby had caused it.

She knew Ruby didn't like her, and Elsie didn't care much for her, either. But she had found a nice cushy billet with Pearl and she had no intention of letting Ruby ruin it for her.

And not a moment too soon, either. She was behind with the rent of her rat-infested lodgings and about to be turfed out when the bomb fell on it. The Luftwaffe had beaten the bailiffs to it.

'Another cup of tea, Mum?' Pearl interrupted her thoughts.

As she reached for the teapot, Elsie said, 'Actually, I wouldn't mind a bit of brandy. Your sister's really upset my nerves.' She looked down at her hands trembling in her lap.

Pearl smiled. 'Of course. You sit there, I'll fetch it.'

Pearl left the room and Elsie sat back and smiled to herself. *You've done all right for yourself, girl*, she thought.

All she had to do now was make sure Ruby didn't ruin it for her.

Chapter Twenty-Six

Saturday 5th April 1941

On Saturday morning Edie's old friends Mollie and Jen came to visit from York. Edie went down to meet them from Paragon station, pushing baby Bobby in his pram.

She heard them before she saw them. They came tumbling off the train, squealing with laughter as usual. Edie watched them coming up the platform, dolled up in their fashionable swing coats and matching hats. Seeing them made her wish she had done more with her appearance. But Bobby had been fretful in the night and she had not had the energy to do more than pin up her curls and dab a bit of powder on her nose.

'Edie!' Jen waved madly and ran the length of the platform to greet her. Mollie followed behind, shrieking with excitement as they fell into each other's arms.

'I'm glad to be off that train!' Mollie exclaimed, fanning her face. 'It was so crowded, we were practically nose to nose with strangers all the way.'

'I didn't mind,' Jen said.

'Only because you were talking to that handsome soldier!'

'I was squashed up against him the whole way. It would have been rude to ignore him,' Jen said primly. 'Anyway, it was a waste of time,' she added. 'He spent the whole time telling me about his sweetheart up in Scotland.'

Edie laughed. 'Same old Jen! You in't changed a bit.'

'She's still man-mad, if that's what you mean,' Mollie said.

Jen pulled a face. 'It's all right for you. You've found yourself a husband. I'm still looking.'

Mollie smiled, her gaze falling to the new wedding band that gleamed on her left hand.

'How does it feel to be Mrs Price?' Edie asked.

'Not much different to being Miss Jackson, to be honest.' Mollie shrugged. 'Especially as Joe had to go back to camp straight after the wedding.'

'She's been waiting two weeks for her wedding night!' Jen laughed.

'I'll be waiting a sight longer if the Army gets its way,' Mollie said.

'I'm sorry I couldn't get to the wedding,' Edie said. 'Bobby had a temperature, and I didn't like to leave him.'

'Of course not, I understand. We missed you, though.' Mollie bent over the pram and peered inside. 'How is the little chap now? Better, I hope?'

'Much better, thank you. It was just a cold. But you know how you worry . . .'

She looked at her friends' blank faces. Of course they didn't know. How could they? They weren't mothers. They did not know what it was like to have a tiny human being depending on you for their very life.

Mollie turned back to the pram. 'Oh Edie, he's gorgeous,' she cooed. 'And hasn't he grown! How old is he now?'

'Nearly five months.'

'Really? Has it been that long?' She stroked the curve of his cheek with her finger. 'Look, Jen. In't he a pet?'

'He is,' Jen agreed, smiling down at him. 'And he looks so like his father—' She broke off, blushing.

'You're right, he does look like him.' Edie smiled fondly down at her baby. 'And I don't mind you mentioning Rob, honestly. It's nice to be able to talk about him to people who knew him.'

Part of the reason she had come to Hull was to escape the memories. But sometimes she missed them.

'I don't know about you, but I'm starving.' Jen changed the subject. 'Where are we going to eat?'

They went to the Kardomah. As they passed through the city centre, Edie caught Mollie and Jen's shocked expressions as they looked around them. Apart from a couple of small air raids, York had escaped unscathed, while Hull bore the terrible scars in its ruined buildings and pock-marked streets.

'It must be awful,' Mollie whispered. 'How do you cope?'

'You get used to it. Some people stay at home, but I go to the shelter round the corner most nights. We've all done it up with curtains and lamps and rugs to make it a bit more cosy. We knit and we chat and sometimes we sing – it's quite nice to have a bit of company when the bombs are coming down.'

Once again, she caught her friends' uncomprehending looks. Jen spent most of her nights out dancing with Canadian airmen from nearby Beningbrough Hall.

'How's life at Rowntree's?' she asked, when they had ordered their food.

'You in't missing much.' Mollie grimaced. 'Guess who's been promoted to overlooker?'

'Who?'

'Shirley Peters!'

'No!' Shirley had worked with them on the production line, but she had always considered herself a cut above, just because her father was a supervisor.

'You can just imagine it, can't you? She loves throwing her weight about.'

'I'll bet she does.'

'But she can't get one over on Jen,' Mollie said proudly. 'Tell Edie what you said to her last week.'

Jen told her story and Edie laughed along with Mollie. But as they shared all the gossip about her former workmates, Edie couldn't shake the feeling that they were talking about a group of strangers, not girls she had worked alongside for years.

They shouldn't be here, she thought. Jen and Mollie belonged in York, to her past life, when they worked side by side on the production line, packing shells together.

'It in't the same without you there,' Mollie said.

'We had some good times, didn't we?' Jen sighed. 'I wish you'd come home.'

Edie smiled. 'This is my home now.'

Jen looked around, and Edie could tell what she was thinking.

'Why? There's nowt keeping you here, surely? I don't even know why you moved away in the first place.'

'Jen!' Mollie nudged her sharply. 'You know Edie had her reasons.'

'I did it because of Rob,' Edie said. Hull had been his home before he joined the RAF. And even though Edie had never visited the city before, when he died she felt she wanted to be here to be closer to him.

She had struggled at first, but this was her home now. The Maguires and the Hugginses and all her other neighbours in Jubilee Row had become like family to her.

But she would never be able to explain that to Jen and Mollie. They were looking at her with pity in their eyes, as if they could not imagine why she would ever want to live here.

Their food arrived, and once again Edie changed the subject.

'So tell me all about the wedding,' she urged.

Mollie did not need asking twice. Like a typical newlywed, she was keen to describe her big day, from the ceremony to the reception, the flowers, and her dress. Listening to her made Edie even more sad that she had missed it.

'It sounds lovely,' she said. 'I wish I could have been there.'

'I know,' Mollie sighed. 'It wasn't how we thought it would be, was it?'

They used to spend hours planning their perfect wedding, whiling away the time as they filled fuses on the production line. But real life had not matched up to their daydreams.

'You didn't even tell us you were getting married until after you'd done it,' Jen said to Edie.

'We didn't want any fuss – you know, what with the baby on the way . . .' They all glanced towards the pram, where Bobby slumbered peacefully. 'And we had to do it quickly, as Rob was being sent down south.'

Her friends fell silent, and Edie knew what they were thinking. That was the last time she had seen Rob. A few weeks later, he was killed when his plane was shot down over the English Channel during the evacuation of Dunkirk.

Mollie reached across the table for her hand. 'At least you were married,' she said.

'Aye.' Edie looked down to hide her blushing face. Jen and Mollie did not know the full story of her and Rob's marriage. There were some secrets she could never share.

'And here's me, still on the shelf!' Jen broke the sombre mood.

'Not for want of trying, though,' Mollie smiled.

'Everyone I meet seems to be taken already.' Jen pulled a face. 'I don't suppose you know anyone, do you?' She looked hopefully at Edie.

'Well, I—'

'Of course she doesn't,' Mollie finished for her impatiently.

'Edie's got no interest in chasing men now. She's a widow with a baby. She's got responsibilities, not like us.'

'You make me sound like an old woman!' Edie laughed.

But her friend's words stayed with her long after she had seen them off at the station.

Mollie was right, she thought. Edie wasn't like them any more. They both lived with their families. They did not have to worry about queuing up for food, or scraping together enough money to pay the rent or the gas bill.

She had been so looking forward to seeing them, but she felt curiously empty as she saw them off at the station. Even though they had clung to each other and promised to visit again, she could tell none of them really meant it. Seeing them again made Edie realise how little she had in common with them now.

She's a widow with a baby. She's got responsibilities.

Mollie's words came back to her. Watching her friends hurrying down the platform to catch their train, arms linked, heads together, Edie could not have felt more alone, or more lonely.

When she came out of the station, Edie turned left along Ferensway, passing the vast drifts of shattered masonry and rubble and the ragged remains of what had once been office buildings. The area still swarmed with builders and ARP workers, clearing the debris. They had a long way to go, she thought.

She turned into Spring Bank towards the cemetery on Chanterlands Avenue. She always went to visit Dolly on a Saturday, and today she really felt she needed to see her.

As she pushed the pram around the bend in the path that led to Dolly's grave, Edie saw that someone was there already. Jack Maguire was standing over the grave, his head bowed, broad shoulders hunched. Lucky the terrier sat patiently at his heels, looking up at him.

Edie was about to turn the pram around when Jack called out to her. Edie headed towards him.

'I'm sorry,' she said. 'I didn't mean to disturb you.'

He shook his head. 'You didn't. I was just about to go, anyway.' He looked back at the headstone, as if he could not drag his eyes away from the words written there.

Dorothy Ann Maguire

1908–1940

Beloved wife and mother

Gone too soon

'Are the boys not with you?' Edie asked.

'I left them with Mum. Sometimes I just like to come on my own and spend time with her.' He gazed back at the grave.

'Are you sure you don't want me to go?'

'No, it's fine, honestly.' He nodded to the flowers in Edie's hands. 'Are they for her?'

She looked at the spindly daffodils. 'They in't much, but I was lucky to get them. Flowers are in short supply now everyone's growing fruit and veg. But I like to bring her something.'

She bent to lay the flowers on Dolly's grave. 'I chose the brightest flowers I could find,' she said. 'I know how much she loved bright colours.'

'Aye, she did.'

As she stood up, Lucky circled her legs, sniffing at her ankles. Edie put her hand down to pet his wiry head.

'He thinks you've got a treat for him, greedy little devil,' Jack said.

'I'm afraid not.' Edie smiled down at Lucky, who looked back at her with soulful brown eyes. 'I thought the boys were supposed to be looking after him?'

'They are, but he decided he wanted to come for a walk with me today.' Jack summoned the little dog with a click of his fingers.

'Any luck finding his owner yet?'

'Not so far, but I've asked the ARP wardens to keep asking around.' He tickled the dog's ears, and Lucky rolled on to his back, baring sparse tufts of coarse fur on his belly. 'He's getting a bit attached, to be honest.'

'It looks like the feeling's mutual?'

Jack looked rueful. 'You might be right. I'll be sad to see him go, that's for sure.'

They were both silent for a moment, lost in their thoughts.

'Anyway, I'll leave you to it,' Jack said.

As he went to walk away, Edie said, 'Jack?'

He turned back to her. 'What?'

'Do I seem like an old woman to you?'

He half smiled at the question. 'What's all this about?'

'It's nothing.' Edie shook her head. 'Just something a friend said to me, that's all.'

'Don't sound like much of a friend if they called you an old woman!'

'That's not what they said. It's more how I feel.' Edie sent him a sideways look. 'But you don't want to hear my woes,' she said.

'I've nowt better to do.' He regarded her, his face sympathetic. 'Go on, then. Who are these friends of yours?'

Edie explained about Mollie and Jen coming to visit, and how much she had been looking forward to it, but how it had left her feeling low.

'I saw the way they looked at me, as if they didn't see their friend any more. They just saw a careworn woman who'd got old before her time. And they're right, too. Sometimes when I look in the mirror I don't recognise myself. I'm barely twenty-one and I feel as old as Beattie Scuttle.' Her gaze dropped to her hands. The skin on her fingers and palms had grown thick and calloused from months of net braiding. 'Seeing them again just reminded me of who I used to be. It made me sad to think I've lost that part of my life and I'll never get it back.'

'You could still have fun?' Jack said.

'I think I've forgotten how.' Edie sighed. 'When your brother asked me to go dancing with him, it never even occurred to me to say yes. And now your Iris is courting again, and I just wonder if I'll ever feel like that again . . .'

She caught Jack's frown and felt instantly contrite.

'Listen to me, going on,' she said. 'You don't want to hear me complaining. I've got a lot to be thankful for, I know that. I've got a nice home and good neighbours and a beautiful baby son, and I wouldn't change them for anything. I'm happy with my lot, I really am.' She smiled wanly. 'Take no notice of me, I'm just being daft.'

'I don't think you're daft at all. We all need a bit of light in our lives sometimes.' He looked at her consideringly. 'Happen you should say yes to our John next time he asks you out?'

'I'll think about it.' They looked at each other for a moment. Edie pulled her gaze away first. 'I'd best be getting back,' she murmured.

'Will you do me a favour and take Lucky back to Jubilee Row? I promised I'd walk down to Ferensway and lend a hand.'

'Of course.' Edie nodded. 'The men looked busy when I passed earlier.'

'Aye.' He handed over Lucky's lead. 'Tell Mum I'll be back in an hour or two.'

'I will.'

As he walked away, he turned and called back over his shoulder. 'Edie?'

'Yes?'

He smiled. 'If it means anything, I don't think of Beattie Scuttle when I look at you.'

Chapter Twenty-Seven

Monday 7th April 1941

May Maguire sat at the desk in Pickering's net loft, staring at the telephone.

How she hated that thing. She was always a bag of nerves when she knew she had to use it. She could feel her palms perspiring at the thought of having to pick up the receiver.

All around her, the other women were at their frames, laughing and chatting together. What would they say if they knew fearless Big May Maguire was scared of a telephone?

Sometimes she wished she had never been put in charge. Now, as well as supervising the main net loft, she had to co-ordinate the work of over a thousand braiders scattered throughout the city in ten other depots, as well as the women working at home.

She didn't mind the bookkeeping so much – the manager was always praising her for her meticulous records – but the telephone defeated her. There was just something about it. Today she had to make calls to the old Cod Farm and the Spring Bank depot to make sure they were keeping up with their workload. She would sooner have traipsed all the way up there on foot in the pouring rain than have to call them.

And it didn't help that she had Beattie Scuttle standing over her, going on in her ear the whole time.

'I mean, it's not as if we even know anything about him,' she was saying. 'He could be anyone.'

'Who?' May looked up, distracted.

'That fellow your Iris has taken up with. What do we know about him?'

'Not this again, Beattie. You've talked about nothing else this past two weeks.' May's gaze fell back to the telephone. *Pick it up*, she willed herself. *Just pick it up and get it over with.*

'So what if I have? My Sam's heartbroken. You should see them, carrying on like a pair of lovebirds right next door. Cruel, that's what it is. You know he's bought a gramophone, don't you?'

'Your Sam?'

'Iris's fancy man!' Beattie's thin face twitched. 'They play music at all hours, when decent people are trying to sleep. And when I tried to complain about all the noise they were making, he told me to mind my own business!'

May looked away so Beattie would not see her smile. But she was too late.

'I'm glad you think it's funny,' her friend snapped. 'You won't be laughing when he tells you to mind your own business!'

'He'd better not!'

'You just wait. He's too full of himself, that one.'

May looked at her friend's agitated face. She could not blame Beattie for being upset.

'Look, I feel the same way as you,' she said. 'You know how much I'd like to see Iris and your Sam together. But what can I do about it? She's old enough to make up her own mind . . .'

'Talking about me again?'

They turned towards the door where Iris stood.

'Honestly, I don't know what you found to gossip about while I wasn't here,' she smiled.

Beattie's mouth tightened. 'I'm sure I don't know what you mean.' She stomped off to take her place at the long table with the other women.

166

Iris watched her go. 'She's quiet now, but she had plenty to say for herself when I came in just now,' she said.

'Take no notice of her,' May replied absently.

'Oh, I don't. I've got better things to think about.' She looked back at her mother. 'Are you all right, Mum?'

'I'm fine, thanks. Just got a lot to do this morning.' May's eyes drifted back to the telephone. 'I've got to check up on an order.'

'Tell you what, why don't I give you a hand?' Iris offered. 'Happen I could telephone while you finish off the paper-work? If you're busy, that is?'

Their eyes met across the desk, a look of understanding passing between them.

'That might be helpful,' May said slowly.

She watched her daughter as she sat at the desk, speaking on the telephone to Spring Bank. She seemed so at ease, May knew she would never be like that in a hundred years.

It was good to see Iris smiling again. She had been so tense and skittish when she'd first come home, May had been really worried about her. But now she seemed to be back to her old self, laughing and chatting and singing with the rest of the women.

No one sang or laughed louder than Iris. She was in the thick of all the jokes, joining in with everything. But every so often May thought she caught the flash of unguarded emotion underneath that bright, brittle smile.

And then there was the whole business with Lucy's grave. Iris still refused to visit and May didn't think it was right. But she had given up arguing with her about it, especially now she had Matthew to back her up.

May did not know what to make of Matthew. Like Beattie, she would have much preferred Iris to settle down with a local lad like Sam. Matthew was a Londoner, an outsider, and there was something unsettling about him. But he made Iris happy and that was all May could wish for.

The day ended, and the women went home. May and Beattie were putting on their coats, ready to leave, when Matthew arrived.

He nodded a quick greeting in their direction then closed in on Iris, sweeping her into his arms and kissing her full on the mouth.

Beattie tutted her disapproval and even May had to look away.

'Matthew!' Iris pushed him off. 'Not in front of my mother!' She was laughing when she said it, but her cheeks were scarlet with embarrassment.

'She doesn't mind, do you, Mrs M?' Matthew winked at her.

May ignored the question. 'Come to walk our Iris home, have you?'

'As if she don't know the way herself by now,' Beattie muttered.

'Actually, I've come to take her to the pictures. They're showing *Lucky Partners* at the Carlton.' He turned to Iris. 'I know how much you like Ronald Colman.'

'That's very nice of you,' Iris said. 'But what about the bains?'

'I'm sure your friend Edie would look after them?'

Iris shook her head. 'She's already looked after them twice last week, I can't ask her again.'

'But I've bought the tickets.' There was an edge to his voice that May did not like. She glanced at Beattie and realised she was thinking the same thing.

'Perhaps your mother can help?' Matthew looked at May. 'You wouldn't mind looking after Archie and Kitty, would you?'

'If that's what Iris wants,' May said.

'You'd like that, Iris, wouldn't you?' Matthew said firmly.

Iris looked from one to the other, panic in her eyes. Then, suddenly, her smile was fixed back in place.

'Yes,' she said. 'Yes, I would.'

May knew Beattie would have something to say about it as they walked home. Sure enough, May had barely finished locking up the net loft when Beattie said, 'Well? What did you make of that?'

'Happen a night out will do her good.'

'She's had more than a few nights out lately. A night in with her bains might be better.'

May turned on her, instantly defensive. 'What are you saying, Beattie Scuttle? I hope you in't insinuating my Iris is a bad mother?'

'I in't insinuating anything,' Beattie said. 'I'm saying she's keeping the wrong company. There's something about that Matthew I don't like.'

'That's Iris's business, not ours,' May replied stiffly.

Beattie was right, she thought, as she stuffed the jangling bunch of keys into her bag. There was something about Matthew she did not like, either.

Chapter Twenty-Eight

Friday 11th April 1941

'Ruby, come quick. Your sister's scrapping in the street!'

The potato Ruby had been peeling fell from her hand as she looked up sharply at their neighbour Alice Barnitt in the back doorway. She was breathless, her face alight with excitement.

It was Good Friday and for once all her girls were home. Ruby had been looking forward to a nice peaceful dinner with the family, but Alice's sudden appearance at her back door had put paid to that.

Ruby put down her knife. 'What's she done now?' she sighed.

'I don't know, but you can hear her screaming half down 'Road. She's having a right carry on,' Alice smirked.

'I'd best go and see what she's up to.' Ruby reached for the tea towel to dry her hands. 'Ada, keep your eye on the roast, it should be ready to come out of the oven in ten minutes. Maudie, finish these potatoes. Sybil – where do you think you're going?'

'With you.' Sybil was already shrugging on her coat. 'I wouldn't miss this for the world!'

Ruby could hear her sister long before she reached Wassand Street.

'Take your filthy hands off that, it don't belong to you!' she was screeching.

'You tell him, Pearl,' her mother joined in. 'He's got no right, no right at all.'

Then came a man's voice, rough and brusque. 'You've read the letter. You were told what would happen if you didn't pay up. Now let go, or it'll be worse for you.'

Ruby and Sybil exchanged a horrified look, then both of them started running. As they turned the corner into Wassand Street, Sybil stopped and put her hand to her mouth.

'Oh lord, Auntie Pearl's really done it now!' she giggled.

Furniture was piled up on the pavement. Ruby recognised her sister's battered moquette armchair, and a rolled-up rug. Pearl was having a tug of war with a burly man over a kitchen chair, while Elsie hung from his shoulders like a vicious little monkey, trying to pull him away.

'Turning a defenceless woman out on the street, and at Easter, too. It's unchristian, that's what it is,' Pearl yelled.

'You were warned,' the man said gruffly. He disentangled Elsie from his coat collar and placed her back on the ground.

Ruby hurried down the street towards them. 'What's going on?'

Elsie rolled her eyes. 'Oh, it's you,' she muttered. 'Just what we needed.'

Ruby ignored her, turning to her sister. 'Pearl?'

'What does it look like?' Pearl snapped. 'That nasty cow of a landlady is throwing us out on the street.'

'You should have paid your rent, shouldn't you?' The man dumped the chair on top of the pile and went back into the house.

'Oh, Pearl, don't tell me you've fallen behind again?' Ruby sighed.

'I told you, I had arrears owing. How am I supposed to keep up?'

'What about the money I gave you?'

'That was nearly six weeks ago,' Pearl said sulkily.

'Don't you have a go at her, getting all high and mighty!' Elsie jumped in. 'If you want to make yourself useful, go and stop him putting her out on the street.' She pointed to the man who had emerged from the house, carrying an aspidistra plant in a china pot.

Ruby stepped into his path. 'Excuse me—'

'Don't you start!' He growled at her. 'I've had enough with these two.'

'I don't want a row,' Ruby said. 'I just wondered if there was anything that could be done?'

He nodded to Pearl. 'She could start by paying what she owes.'

'How much is it?'

'According to my records, she's two months behind.'

'Two months!' Ruby stared at Pearl, who folded her arms and looked defiant.

'Why do you think the landlady wants her out?' The man sidestepped Ruby and set the plant down on the kerb. 'She's always been a bad payer, but now she's even worse.' He glared over to where Elsie stood, her arms folded across her chest.

Further down the street, the neighbours were lining up to watch what was going on.

'You can clear off, and all!' Elsie spat at them. 'Go and buy tickets, if you want to see a show!'

Ruby turned back to the bailiff. 'If she paid something towards what she owed, could she stay?'

'You'd have to ask the landlady.'

'If you think we're going to crawl to her—' Elsie started to say, but Ruby held up her hand to silence her.

'What if we paid five pounds towards the arrears? That would help, wouldn't it?'

The man looked at Pearl and then back to Ruby. 'I daresay

it would,' he grunted. 'Mrs Dale in't unreasonable. She didn't want it to come to this. She gave her every chance . . .'

'I'm sure she did,' Ruby said placatingly.

'Anyway,' the man continued in a low voice. 'It wasn't your sister that was causing the trouble.' He glared at Elsie. 'That one was very rude to Mrs Dale, the last time she called round for her money.'

'I didn't like her tone,' Elsie sniffed.

Ruby turned to Sybil. 'Go home and fetch the money your dad sent yesterday,' she said.

'Mum!' Sybil looked shocked.

'Fetch it, Syb. We can't have your aunt out on the street.'

Sybil hurried off down the street, and Ruby said to the man, 'Could you move the furniture back in, please?'

'I'm not sure about that . . .'

'You're going to get your money, I promise.'

The man straightened up, eyeing Pearl severely. 'I really should wait and talk to Mrs Dale . . .'

'And what is my sister supposed to do, live here on the street till after the bank holiday? It'll be dark in a few hours.'

'She should have thought about that before she stopped paying her rent, shouldn't she?'

Ruby looked at her sister's despairing face. As the bailiff headed back to the house, Ruby stepped in front of him, blocking his way.

'I wonder what the Sheriff would have to say about a defenceless woman locked out of her house during the blackout?' she said.

'And who's going to tell him?'

'I will.' Ruby faced him, nose to nose. 'I happen to know Mr Tarran through my work with the WVS. And I also know he'll take a very dim view of this. He's very keen that everyone should have a roof over their heads while all these raids are going on. So if Mrs Dale doesn't want her name dragged through the mud at the corporation, you need to do something about it!'

For a moment they stared at each other, then without a word the man snatched up the aspidistra plant and carried it back inside.

'You be careful with that,' Elsie called after him. 'That pot's worth money!'

Pearl turned to Ruby. 'Thank you,' she said quietly.

'What are you thanking her for?' Elsie said. 'She was only doing what any sister would do. Families should stick together.'

Ruby stared at her mother, lost for words. Then she looked back at her sister. 'I can't keep bailing you out, you know,' she said. 'You've got to sort yourself out, Pearl.'

'I know.' Pearl looked down at her feet.

'Why haven't you been paying your rent?'

'I—' Pearl's gaze strayed to her mother.

'She didn't have it, that's why!' Elsie snapped. 'We've got to eat, in't we? We need gas to cook with, and light to see by, same as everyone else.'

'And I daresay all those new clothes and nights out don't come cheap, either.'

Her mother gasped. 'Do you begrudge your sister treating herself?'

'I do if it means she can't pay her bills.'

'So we have to ask your permission to live our lives now, do we?'

'I don't really care what you do,' Ruby said calmly. 'My only concern is Pearl.'

'Is that right?' Elsie's mouth twisted. 'Well, if you were that concerned you'd help her out a bit more. It in't as if you can't afford it. You'd pay her rent yourself, if you were any kind of sister.'

'And if you were any kind of mother you wouldn't encourage her to get into debt in the first place!'

'Listen to her, talking about you as if you were a child!' Elsie turned to Pearl. 'Don't let her scold you like that, love. You don't have to explain yourself to her or anyone else.' She glared at Ruby. 'I've seen the way you talk to her, always bossing her around and making her feel small. She's a grown woman, you know.'

'Then it's about time she started standing on her own two feet, instead of always coming to me for handouts.'

'She didn't come to you,' Elsie pointed out. 'You were the one who turned up here, throwing your weight around. You in't at the WVS now, bossing everyone about!'

'It was just as well I did turn up, or you two would be spending the night in the gutter. Not that you in't used to it,' Ruby muttered.

Elsie swung round to Pearl, her face white with rage. 'Are you going to stand there and let her talk to me like that?'

Pearl sighed. 'Can't we just stop arguing? All I want to do is move my furniture back inside and forget all this ever happened.'

'She'll never let you forget it happened,' Elsie said. 'That's the point. She'll be reminding you of this forever, making out how daft you are, always telling you how she has to step in and look after you.'

'It's a pity you weren't there to look after both of us,' Ruby snapped.

Elsie stared at her for a moment, her face puckering. Then she burst into noisy tears.

'That's right, have a good cry,' Ruby taunted her. 'You always start sobbing when you know you're in the wrong.'

'Ruby, please,' Pearl begged.

'No, Pearl, I in't having it. She's a bad influence on you.

175

She's dragging you down and you can't even see it.'

Elsie stopped crying, her face twisted with malice. 'Did you hear that? She thinks you're stupid.'

'I think she's being taken in by you,' Ruby shot back. 'And she in't the first, either.'

'Stop it, you two!' Pearl shouted. 'Just stop arguing, you're giving me a headache.' She looked from one to the other. 'If you can't get on then one of you will have to go.'

Ruby turned to her mother. 'You heard her. Pack your bags.'

'I meant you, Rube.'

'Pearl?' Ruby stared at her sister. 'You don't mean that—'

'I do. I've had enough of you and Mum arguing. She's right, you do treat me like a bain sometimes.'

'I'm only looking after you, which is more than she does—'

'And that's another thing. Mum's a guest in my house whether you like it or not. And while you can't be civil to her then it's probably better if we don't see each other.'

Out of the corner of her eye, Ruby caught a glimpse of her mother's smug face, half buried in her handkerchief.

'You don't mean that,' she whispered. 'After everything we've been through together, everything I've done for you—'

'There she goes again, rubbing it in your face,' Elsie put in. 'I told you, she'll never let you forget it.'

'Shut up, you!'

'You see what I mean?' Pearl sighed. 'I can't take it any more, Ruby, I really can't.'

'Mum!'

Ruby looked over her shoulder. Sybil was hurrying down the street towards them, just as the bailiff emerged from the house.

'Have you got the money?' he said.

For a moment no one spoke. Ruby saw Pearl's panic-stricken face as she realised the terrible mistake she had made. But even after all that had been said and done, Ruby could not bring herself to let her sister down.

'Here.' She took the notes from Sybil and handed them over to the man. 'But you can tell Mrs Dale not to expect anything else from me. And that goes for you, too,' Ruby said to Pearl. 'If you want any help in future, you'd best ask your mother. I'm sure she'll be only too happy to oblige!'

Chapter Twenty-Nine

Saturday 12th April 1941

You're a fool, Jack Maguire.

Jack headed home in the early evening, his collar turned up against the first spots of April rain. As he thrust his hands into his coat pockets, his fingers closed around the tickets and he felt a fresh surge of shame.

He should never have bought them. It had seemed like a good idea at the time, a chance to do a good turn for a friend. But he'd had time to think about it all the way across the Humber from New Holland on the ferry, and by the time his boots touched the ground on the Hull side he had convinced himself he had made a dreadful mistake.

It had upset him to see Edie so down the other day. The poor lass didn't have a lot of fun in her life. And she had been so kind to him and the boys since Dolly died, he wanted to do something nice for her in return. So when the senior officer's secretary came round selling tickets for a fundraising dance at Powolny's, Jack had bought two without thinking.

But as soon as he'd handed over the money, he began to have doubts. What if Edie was offended? What if she didn't want to go dancing with him? It was a ridiculous idea, after all, now he thought about it.

He hadn't danced with anyone but Dolly for years. He couldn't imagine another woman in his arms, and he didn't want to.

Then another terrible thought struck him. What if Edie

took it the wrong way, thought he was showing an interest in her, that he liked her as something more than a friend?

He felt the heat rising in his face in spite of the cold wind. That would never happen, he told himself. Edie was like him, still mourning her lost love. Besides, she knew how much he had loved Dolly, how much he missed her.

But would everyone else see it that way? He knew how much the neighbours loved to gossip, and the last thing he wanted to do was set tongues wagging, for Edie's sake as well as his own.

Oh Doll, what shall I do? I've made a right mess of this.

The thought of his wife brought a smile to his face. He already knew what Dolly would say about it.

Let them talk. Who cares what anyone else makes of it, as long as you know the truth.

The thought comforted him. He would give Edie the tickets and hope for the best, he decided. If she turned him down, there would be no hard feelings. And if she said yes – well, he would worry about that when the time came.

Jack sighed. He had set out to help someone, and he had ended up twisting himself in knots. What was it Pop always said? No good deed goes unpunished. Jack had never really understood what it meant until now.

As he walked down the ten-foot he could hear Edie's laughter from next door. When he let himself in through the back gate there she was, over the fence. And she wasn't alone.

'Will you stop messing about? I've got to get this washing in before it gets soaked.'

Edie was pulling clothes off the line and dumping them into the arms of his brother John, who stood behind her.

'And don't drop them,' she warned, 'or I'll make you wash them all again.'

'As if I'd drop your drawers!' John grinned.

'Give me those!' Edie snatched the pair of knickers he was holding up. Then she looked past his shoulder to Jack, standing in the gateway. 'Could you tell your brother to behave?'

'Sorry, Mum's been telling him that for years and it's never done any good.' He looked at John. 'Mind, she's been trying to get him to help with the chores, too, so you're doing better than she is.'

'He in't helping, believe me.'

'What are you doing here, anyway?' Jack asked his brother. 'You in't still mithering the poor girl to go out with you, surely?'

'You might mock, brother, but you mark my words. My persistence will pay off one of these days.'

'I wouldn't bet on it!'

Jack saw the sparkle in Edie's eyes as she looked at his brother. She might pretend to be exasperated, but he could tell she was enjoying the attention. He couldn't remember the last time he had seen her smile like that.

He watched them together for a moment. They made a good-looking couple, he thought. And Edie really seemed to enjoy his company. John was so much closer to her in age, too. If anyone could bring her out of herself, it was his charming, fun-loving brother.

He reached into his pocket. 'Here's something that might help change your mind,' he said.

'What's this?' John took the tickets. Edie looked over his shoulder.

'Tickets to a dance?' she turned to Jack, her expression quizzical.

'It's for a good cause.' Jack shrugged. 'I thought you might be able to make use of them.'

John turned to Edie. 'What do you think? It seems a shame to waste them.'

'Are you sure you don't want them?' Edie asked Jack.

'Who would I go dancing with?'

For a moment their eyes met and held. Jack turned away quickly. 'Anyway, they're yours if you want them,' he muttered.

'Well?' John said.

'That would be very nice,' Edie replied quietly. Jack did not dare raise his gaze, but he knew she was still watching him.

Just then there was a wail from inside the house.

'Someone's hungry,' Edie said. She took the washing from John's arms. 'I'd best go and see to His Lordship.'

Jack watched her as she disappeared into the house, the washing basket tucked under her arm. 'Who'd have thought it, eh?' John's voice interrupted his thoughts. 'I've got to admit, I was starting to think about giving up. You did me a real favour there, showing up with those tickets.'

'You just make sure you look after her,' Jack said.

John smirked. 'Oh, I will.'

'I mean it, John. She's a nice girl, and she's been through a lot. If I hear you've been trying to take advantage—'

'All right, all right, you don't have to go on.' John held up his hands. 'I'll be the perfect gentleman, I swear.'

Jack looked towards the house. 'You see that you are,' he said.

Chapter Thirty

Sunday 13th April 1941

Archie was alone in the air raid shelter. It was cold and damp and he could hardly hear for the roar of aircraft and incessant rattle of shrapnel raining down. He pressed his hands over his ears but he could still feel the ground shaking beneath his feet.

Then he heard another sound. Someone was calling his name. A woman on the other side of the shelter door.

His mother. Her voice was quiet, and yet somehow he heard it over the thunder of the raid. There was something else, too. A child whimpering.

'Mum?' He crossed to the shelter steps, listening at the door.

'Archie? Let me in, love. Please let me in.'

There was a heavy iron bolt across the door. Archie struggled with it but it would not budge.

'I can't get the door open,' he called out to his mother.

'Try, Archie. You've got to help us.'

Archie looked over his shoulder into the shadowy depths of the shelter, but there was no one there to help him. He was completely alone. He scrabbled uselessly at the bolt until his fingers bled, but still it would not move.

And all the while the voice kept calling out to him.

'Please, Archie. You have to help us. You're our only hope. Save us, Archie. Don't let us die.'

'I'm trying, I'm really trying . . .'

Outside, the child's whimpers rose to a terrified scream. Archie gripped the bolt, wrenching it with every last bit of his strength. Miraculously, it gave way and started to shift with a slow, grating movement.

Archie pushed it across and then opened the door, coughing as a cloud of smoky air rushed in, reeking of cordite. He peered through the billowing smoke into the darkness.

'Mum?' he called out.

At first he could not see anyone. Then, as the smoke began to clear, he saw two figures, a woman holding a little girl's hand. They started to walk towards him, wisps of smoke rising from them. As they drew closer, Archie saw the woman's blonde head and realised it was not his mother at all, but his Auntie Dolly. She was wearing a red dress and holding on to his sister Lucy, just as she had been the last time he saw them.

'No,' he moaned. Auntie Dolly smiled at him, a terrible, livid smile.

'You could have saved us, Archie,' she called out to him. 'You were there, you could have saved me and Lucy . . .'

'No!' he cried out. 'No, I couldn't. I couldn't do anything. Leave me alone, I couldn't do anything—'

'Archie? Archie, wake up.'

He opened his eyes and looked around, blinking, trying to get his bearings. He wasn't in the shelter any more, he was in his bed at home, Kitty slumbering peacefully beside him. His mother was looking down at him, her dark curls dishevelled around her sleepy face.

'You were having another nightmare, love,' she said.

A moment later he felt the tell-tale warm wetness spreading beneath him. Archie lay rigid with shame, but his mother seemed to guess what had happened.

'Come on,' she sighed. 'Let's get you cleaned up.'

Archie watched her as she lifted Kitty gently out of bed, then set about stripping off the bedclothes.

'I'm sorry,' he whispered.

'You can't help it. Now, get some dry pyjamas on before you catch cold.'

Archie looked at his mother, desperate for some reassurance. But she kept her face averted as she bundled up the sheets and took them outside.

'Is everything all right?' Matthew stood in the doorway, watching them.

'It's fine. Archie had another nightmare, that's all.'

Matthew's gaze went to the bundle of sheets in her arms, then back to Archie. His eyes were full of contempt.

Archie kept very still, trying to listen to their hushed conversation out on the landing. He could not hear what Matthew said, but he heard his mother whispering, 'He can't help it. He's just a child.'

He crawled back into bed, feeling utterly ashamed. Now Matthew knew and Matthew already didn't think much of him. Archie could see it in his face when he looked at him.

But Archie didn't think much of Matthew, either. Everything had started to change in the month since he had come into their lives, and Archie didn't like it.

There was something going on between him and his mother. There were lots of secret smiles, and whispers, and once Archie had walked into a room and caught them kissing. His mother had jumped as if she'd had an electric shock, but Matthew had just smirked.

Archie didn't know how to feel about it. It was good to see his mother smiling again, but he wished she had chosen someone else to kiss and whisper with.

He did not like Matthew. He didn't like the way he strode about the house as if he owned it. He decided what was best for everyone, and his mother just seemed to go along with it.

Like the photographs of Lucy and their father.

They had just disappeared one day, gone from the mantelpiece. When his mother asked about them, Matthew said, 'I've put them away. You don't need to surround yourself with all those bad memories.'

'But I like them.'

'No, you don't. I see the way you look at them. You're torturing yourself, and you need to stop.'

Archie had looked at his mother, expecting her to stand her ground. No one told Iris Fletcher what to do. But she only shrugged and said, 'I suppose you're right.'

He wished Matthew would go. He had even asked Uncle John when they would be returning to sea.

'Are you trying to get rid of me?' his uncle had laughed.

'Not you,' Archie said. 'Him.'

'What's up, lad? Jealous, are you?' John had ruffled his hair. 'You should be pleased your mother's found someone who makes her happy at last.'

'We were happy before.' But even as he said the words, Archie knew they weren't true.

So he had tried to put on a brave face for his mother's sake. He even did his best to look excited the following morning when Matthew announced they were going to the country for a picnic as it was Easter Sunday.

'In't it a lovely idea?' his mother said brightly as she cut up sandwiches. 'Matthew reckons it will do us all good to get some fresh air.'

Archie looked at Matthew, who was eating his breakfast at the kitchen table. 'What if there's an air raid?' he asked.

'We'll be home long before it gets dark.'

'Can't I stay with Granny May instead?'

His mother opened her mouth to speak, but Matthew got

in first. 'For God's sake!' his voice boomed out. 'Grow up and don't be such a baby. You're coming out with us and you're going to enjoy it.'

Archie looked at his mother. She looked reproachfully at Matthew, but no words came from her lips.

Chapter Thirty-One

They caught the train north out towards Cottingham. As it left the city, the densely packed houses and factories began to spread out to the leafy suburbs and then into open countryside.

'The convalescent home was around here,' Iris said to Matthew. But either he wasn't listening, or he pretended not to hear her. Iris knew he did not like her talking about her time in hospital.

Instead he pointed out the trail of people trudging across fields and down the cinder path alongside the train tracks. Most were families, trailing children behind them. Some had wheelbarrows, others carried packs on their backs.

'They're trekkers,' Iris said. 'Pop told me about them. They camp out in the fields at night and then go back to their homes in the city in the morning.'

'Why?' Matthew asked.

'To avoid the air raids, Pop says.'

Matthew snorted with derision. 'They don't think the planes will find them sleeping in a field?'

'I suppose they reckon they're in less danger than they would be next to a factory or the docks.'

Iris gazed back at the trekkers, making their weary way back to the city. She understood how they felt. She would rather sleep in a field than in her own bed. Since all those poor people in Bean Street were killed, even the shelter did not feel safe any more.

And she wasn't the only one, she thought, looking sideways at Archie. Last night's nightmare had been one of the worst he'd had in ages. She hoped a nice day out in the countryside would take his mind off his troubles.

They got off the train in Cottingham and walked out along a country lane until Matthew decided on the right spot, in the shade of a vast oak tree. He spread out a blanket and Iris set out the picnic. Archie helped her, but he kept squinting up at the sky.

'It's all right,' Iris reassured him quietly. 'The only planes you'll see this time of day are ours.'

She caught Matthew's eye as she said it. His mouth was pursed with disapproval.

'You shouldn't mollycoddle him so much,' he said to her quietly. 'How will he ever toughen up if you keep treating him like a baby? You're doing him no good, you know.'

'He's all right.'

'You call it all right to wet the bed at his age?'

'Shh.' Iris shot an anxious look at Archie. He was sitting a short distance away, playing tea parties with Kitty. Cathy, her favourite doll, lolled between them. 'He'll hear you.'

'So what if he does?'

'You know how embarrassed he gets.'

'There you go again, pussy footing around him, treating him like a baby. He doesn't need you fussing over him. He needs someone to teach him how to be a man.'

Iris looked at her son, patiently holding out an imaginary teacup for his sister to fill. They were so self-contained, the two of them, lost in their own world. Sometimes they seemed like strangers to her.

She couldn't blame them for it. She had let them down,

shut herself away from them for months on end. Was it any wonder they no longer trusted or needed her?

Archie caught her eye and gave her a tentative smile. Poor Archie, he was her son and she did not know how to reach him, how to make him better.

She wasn't sure if Matthew was right about Archie needing a man in his life. She did not know anything any more. Iris had come to trust Matthew's judgement more than she did her own these days. He seemed so sure of himself, so certain about everything. Iris was so full of doubt, it was a blessed relief to sit back and let him make all the decisions.

Matthew sprang to his feet and snatched up the football they had brought with them.

'Come on,' he called out to Archie. 'Let's have a kick about.'

Archie squinted up at him. 'No, thanks.'

'Don't you like football?'

'Of course he does,' Iris put in. 'You love football, don't you, Archie?'

'I don't feel like it,' Archie mumbled.

Matthew sneered. 'You'd rather play with your dolls?'

'Go on, Archie. Just for a minute?' Iris stared desperately at her son, willing him to do as Matthew wanted.

Archie looked back at his mother, and the wretched look in his eyes nearly broke her heart. She opened her mouth to tell him it was all right, he did not have to play if he didn't want to, but Archie was already on his feet, plodding after Matthew across the field

Matthew strode ahead of him, the ball tucked under his arm. Archie looked back at his mother, receding into the distance. She was fussing over Kitty, as if she had already forgotten him.

Finally, Matthew stopped and set the ball down.

'Go on, then,' he said, touching it with his toe. 'Try to tackle me.'

It was a short, dismal game. Archie did his best to enjoy it, but he could not keep up with Matthew's long strides.

'Run faster . . . go round me . . . come on, you've got to do better than that.' Matthew barked orders over his shoulder as he ran in front of him.

And when Archie did finally manage to catch him and get the ball, Matthew tackled him brutally to get it back, tripping him up and shoulder-barging him to the ground.

'You make it too easy for me. You should guard the ball.' He laughed as Archie went sprawling headlong.

As he was picking himself up, Matthew suddenly said, 'I want to talk to you. Man to man.'

Archie sat up, picking grass from his mouth, and waited.

'Do you know how much you're upsetting your mother?'

Archie looked back at his mother. She was sitting with Kitty in her arms, her face turned up to the spring sunshine.

'How old are you?'

'Nine.'

'When I was nine I was helping my father with his milk round. I was up before dawn every morning, in all weathers, driving the cart. I was a man by then, not a little boy like you.' Matthew stood over him, blocking out the sun, tossing the leather ball between his hands. 'Do you know what my father would have done if I'd wet the bed? He would have taken his belt off to me.'

Archie felt his face burning. He looked down at his knees, skinned raw where he had fallen.

'Oh, yes, I know all about it,' Matthew said. 'Your night-mares.' His mouth curled around the word. 'We've all heard you screaming the place down like a baby. And let me tell you this, your mother's had enough of it.'

Archie glanced across the field at his mother. She seemed so far away.

'She'd never say anything herself, but it's true. You're a burden to her.' Matthew shook his head. 'And you wonder why she stayed away at that hospital so long.'

His mother was waving to them, beckoning them back. Dark clouds were rolling in overhead, blotting out the fine spring sunshine.

'We'd best go,' Matthew said shortly. 'But you remember what I said. You'd best buck up your ideas and start acting like a man, or else.'

He put out his hand and grabbed Archie by the wrist, dragging him to his feet. His grip hurt, but Archie did not dare cry out in pain. He felt as if he was being tested, and he did not want to fail.

'There you are,' his mother smiled as they approached. 'Did you have a good game?'

'Very good,' Matthew answered for him. 'We had a nice chat too, didn't we?' He slung his arm around Archie's shoulders, and it was all Archie could do not to flinch.

His mother looked pleased. 'That's nice.' She gathered up the remains of the picnic, packing it away in the basket. 'Come on, we'd better get back to the train before the rain starts.'

All the way home on the train, Archie stared out of the window, not daring to meet Matthew's eye.

Was he really a burden to his mother? He knew she blamed him for what happened to Lucy. No matter how hard he tried, he would never be able to make up for that.

But he had done his best. He guarded Kitty with his life, and he had tried to look after his mother, too, when she came home. But she had kept him at arms' length.

And she had Matthew now. She did not need him any more.

He looked across at her. She sat with Kitty enfolded in her arms, half-asleep, her head resting lightly on Matthew's shoulder.

They looked like the perfect little family, Archie thought. He did not fit it. He was the source of all his mother's heartache, all her problems.

It would have been better for everyone if he was not there.

Chapter Thirty-Two

Thursday 17th April 1941

The skies had been quiet over Easter. After four days without a raid, everyone had begun to hope that perhaps the worst was over. But it was not to be. Just after half past nine on Tuesday night, the all-too-familiar drone of the air raid siren filled the skies.

As if to make up for their absence, the Luftwaffe showed no mercy, dropping three clusters of incendiaries and six parachute mines between Holderness Road and Hedon Road, all the way down to Alexandra Dock.

They could not have wrought more destruction. One of the mines obliterated Ellis Terrace, killing twenty-six people in a shelter. Not a house in the street was left standing. Close by, in Studley Street, another fourteen people died, including a baby girl born only a few hours previously.

After so many months surrounded by death and destruction, Sam had thought he was immune to the heartache. He had grown used to seeing streets and buildings aflame, feeling the searing heat blistering his face and hands, hearing the screams of pain and desolation as people's lives were ripped apart around him. Over and over again, he had witnessed sights no man should ever have to see.

But this, seeing that close-knit little terrace razed to the ground, all those homes and lives destroyed, reminded him too much of home. He could imagine only too well the same fate happening to Jubilee Row.

He had not been able to sleep properly since. Every time he drifted off, he woke with a start minutes later, struggling to breathe from the choking smoke in his lungs.

Was this how his brother Charlie felt, trapped inside a nightmare, doomed to relive the panic and fear forever, he wondered.

This afternoon, Sam had gone to pay his respects to the widow of one of his AFS workmates. His friend George Felton had been fighting a fire in Jennings Street when a parachute mine came down nearby.

He could not forget the despair on the young woman's face. She was twenty-four years old and had just given birth to their second child. She had made Sam tea and thanked him politely as he offered his condolences, but there was an emptiness behind her eyes that told him she had not heard a single word.

When Sam offered her the money he and the other lads at the station had collected, she had just stared at him. Sam had come away feeling angry and ashamed. The poor girl had lost her husband, and her children had lost their father. Why did he ever imagine money could help her pain?

As he headed down Anlaby Road in the gathering dusk, he heard the tinkle of broken glass coming from behind the row of the bombed-out shops, followed by laughter. Sam followed the sound to a patch of waste ground, where half a dozen boys were aiming broken bricks at the burnt remains of a house, smashing what was left of its windows.

'Clear off, you lot!' Sam started towards them and the boys scattered, haring off across the waste ground and disappearing down a side street that led to Hessle Road. All except for the smallest of them, a dark-haired kid in a Fair Isle jersey, who ignored Sam and went on lobbing bricks with fierce concentration.

'Didn't you hear what I said?' Sam strode towards him. 'You ought not to be here, it in't safe—' As he drew closer, he suddenly recognised the boy. 'Archie?'

Archie Fletcher swung round, looking guilty.

'What are you doing, hanging around here?' Sam asked.

'Just larking out.'

Archie went to aim another brick, but Sam grabbed his wrist. 'Oh, no you don't.'

'Let go of me!' Archie twisted to get free.

'Not till you stop chucking bricks about.'

The boy struggled for a moment, then the fight seemed to go out of him and he let the brick fall from his hand.

'That's better.' Sam released his grip. 'What's wrong with you, lad? It in't like you, breaking windows and causing damage.'

'They were all doing it,' Archie muttered sullenly. He glanced in the direction of the alleyway where the other boys had disappeared.

'Yes, but I thought you'd have more sense. What would your mother say?'

'She wouldn't care.'

'I know that in't true.'

'You don't know anything!' Archie glared at him. 'She don't give a damn what I do, as long as I'm not in her way!'

'Now then! Did those lads teach you to curse as well as chuck bricks?'

Archie fell silent, kicking at a broken brick with the toe of his boot.

'Come on,' Sam said. 'You can walk home with me.'

He went to put his hand on Archie's shoulder, but the boy squirmed away from his grasp.

'I in't going home,' he said.

'Why not?'

'Because I don't want to.'

Sam regarded him carefully. Under all his defiance, Archie's eyes were red-rimmed, as if he'd been crying.

'Archie, if there's owt wrong you know you can tell me,' he said. 'Are you in trouble?' Archie did not reply. 'Look, you've got to go home sometime, lad. Your mother will be wondering where you are—'

'I told you, she don't care!' Archie shouted. 'She thinks I'm a—'

'A what?'

Archie stared down at his feet. 'A burden,' he mumbled.

Sam stared at him, shocked. 'Who told you that? Not your mother, I'll bet?' Archie shook his head. 'Who, then?'

Archie did not reply, but his wretched expression said it all.

'Matthew.' Sam muttered the name under his breath. He might have known he would be at the bottom of it.

Sam had been bewildered when he found out about Iris and the sailor from London. What was she thinking, he wondered. One minute she was telling him she did not want a man in her life, and the next she was flaunting Matthew all over the street.

Sam couldn't help being hurt by it. He had done everything Iris had asked, taken a step back, given her all the time she needed.

But as it turned out, she did not need time. She just needed someone else.

Sam was heartbroken, but he had come to terms with his disappointment. His mother was still too angry and bitter to say Iris's name, but Sam had tried to be philosophical about it. After all, he couldn't force Iris to love him. If she had feelings for someone else then there was nothing he could do to change that. He certainly wasn't going to humiliate himself.

But there was something about Matthew he truly disliked. It wasn't just jealousy; Matthew got under his skin. The way he walked down the street, possessively gripping Iris's hand, so full of himself. Sam often heard his voice drifting through the wall that divided their houses. He seemed to have an opinion on everything.

'What else did he say to you?' he asked gently.

'He – he said I should be chopping wood and milking cows and behaving like a man and not a baby.'

'Did he now?'

'I do try.' Archie looked up at him, his eyes brimming with tears. 'I've tried to be brave, but sometimes I just can't help it. I get so scared ...'

Sam pictured himself waking in the night, soaked in sweat. 'We all get scared sometimes, lad.'

'Not Matthew,' Archie said.

Sam thought about Matthew, strutting down the street, laying down the law wherever he went. No one in Jubilee Row had any time for him. The only one who really liked him was Iris.

It was one thing to be arrogant, but it was another to pick on a small boy. Sam Scuttle was not a violent man. But seeing Archie's desolate face, he had never wanted to punch anyone as much as he wanted to strike down Matthew.

'Come on,' he said. 'Let's go home.'

Archie eyed him warily. 'You won't tell Mum what I said, will you?'

'She needs to know.'

'Please, Sam. It will only upset her. And don't say anything to Matthew, either. He'll call me a baby for not fighting my own battles.'

'If Matthew wants a battle he can pick on someone his own size.'

'Please, Sam, I don't want you to say anything. Promise me?'

Sam stared down at the boy's fearful face. 'All right,' he sighed. 'I won't say a word. As long as you promise me you won't hang out with those lads, causing trouble?'

'I won't. I didn't really like them anyway. I just thought . . .'

'You thought it would make you seem more like a man?' Sam guessed. He put his hand on the boy's shoulder. 'Believe me, lad, there's more to being a man than smashing windows and acting like you don't care.'

They walked home in silence. Sam could almost feel the weight of Archie's unhappiness, growing heavier as they approached Jubilee Row.

As they turned the corner, Iris was standing on the doorstep, looking up and down the street, her arms folded. When she saw Archie a smile of relief broke out on her face.

'You see?' Sam said. 'She cares all right, lad.'

'Archie, love, where have you been?' Iris greeted him as they walked towards her. 'Your tea's been on the table ages. And look, you're filthy. What on earth have you been doing?'

'I—'

'He was fighting,' Sam stepped in. 'Some lads got hold of him up on Anlaby Road.'

'Archie!' Iris looked at her son in concern. 'Are you all right?'

'What's all this?' Matthew suddenly appeared behind Iris's shoulder. Seeing his face, it was all Sam could do to stop himself putting his hands around his throat.

'Some lads set about Archie,' Iris explained.

Matthew turned to Archie. 'I hope you gave them what for?'

'Oh, he gave as good as he got,' Sam said. 'Knocked a couple of them down by the time I got to him. And they were big lads, too. I wouldn't have wanted to tackle them myself.'

He caught Archie's quick, grateful look. It was the closest he had come to a smile.

'I'm glad to hear it,' Matthew said. 'Although I must say I'm surprised. I've been trying to teach him some boxing, but he won't fight back.' He aimed a punch at Archie's arm, and he flinched away. 'You see what I mean?'

Sam glanced at Iris and caught her grimace.

'You want to be careful,' he said to Matthew. 'You might end up with a broken jaw one of these days.'

Matthew snorted with derision. 'I think I can hold my own against a kid!'

'I wasn't talking about him,' Sam murmured.

The two men stared at each other for a moment, then Matthew dropped his gaze. 'You heard your mother,' he snapped at Archie. 'Come in and get washed. You've kept us all waiting long enough.'

There was something about the determined set of Archie's narrow little shoulders that almost broke Sam's heart.

'I'll see you, Archie,' he called after him.

Iris waited for them to go, then turned back to Sam. 'Thanks for bringing him home,' she said quietly. Then she added, 'How did he seem to you?'

'What do you mean?'

She glanced back over her shoulder. 'I mean there's nowt I should know, is there?'

Ask your boyfriend, Sam thought. But then he remembered his promise to Archie. 'Nothing you don't know already,' he said.

As he turned to go, Iris said, 'Sam?'

'What?'

'Mum told me about your friend George. I'm so sorry.'

He looked into her warm brown eyes, so full of concern, and he felt himself melt. But before he could say anything,

Matthew's voice rang out from inside the house.

'Iris? Hurry up, tea's getting cold.'

Their eyes met again. Iris gave him a quick, apologetic smile, and then the door closed in his face.

Chapter Thirty-Three

Friday 18th April 1941

'It's our Pearl's birthday today.'

Ruby looked up at Big May over the heap of clothes sal-
vage they were sorting. 'I just saw this and it reminded me.'
She held up a cardigan. 'I've been knitting one for her in red.
It's her favourite colour—'

She felt her voice faltering and quickly turned away, adding
the cardigan to the pile of salvage.

'You mustn't upset yourself, love,' Big May said.

'I in't upset. Happen it will make her think if I forget her
birthday this year. God knows, she's forgotten enough of
mine in the past!'

Big May eyed her sympathetically. 'That in't your way,
though, is it?'

'No, Mum,' Ruby sighed. 'That in't my way at all.'

She knew everyone thought Pearl was a selfish waster,
and Ruby agreed with them. But looking after her sister had
become a way of life for her, and she was lost without it.

'Happen you should go and see her, if you miss her that
much?' Big May suggested.

'Oh, no, I couldn't.' Ruby shook her head. 'She's made it
very clear she wants nothing to do with me.'

'From what I hear, it sounds as if harsh words were spoken
on both sides. People often say things they don't mean in
the heat of an argument. I know I do!' Big May chuckled.
'Lord knows, if we all stopped speaking over it, there'd be no

one in Hessle Road saying a word to each other!'

Ruby picked up a flannel nightgown, examining it for wear. 'Happen I shouldn't have spoken out the way I did,' she said. 'If I'd minded my own business, we wouldn't be in this position.'

'If you'd minded your own business, your sister would have been out on the street,' May reminded her.

'I know.' Seeing her sister's furniture heaped on the pavement had scared Ruby. It made her think of all the times it had happened when she was a child. Pearl was just a baby, too young to remember. But Ruby had grown up seeing her mother dodging the rent man and scrapping with the bailiffs while the neighbours looked on, laughing. The humiliation and uncertainty were burned into her memory.

This was all Elsie's doing, she thought. Pearl might be irresponsible, but Ruby had always managed to keep her sister on the straight and narrow. Now their mother was there, exerting her poisonous influence, Ruby had no chance.

'Go and see her,' Big May urged. 'I can see it's playing on your mind. And I daresay your sister misses you, too.'

'I doubt it,' Ruby said bitterly. 'She probably hasn't even noticed.'

She was hurt at being cast aside so easily. Her family was everything to her, and she had worked hard to keep her and Pearl together. But now Elsie had swept in and taken it all away from her. Ruby was shocked at how easily Pearl had turned on her. She can't have meant very much to Pearl if her sister could cast her aside without a second thought.

'That's where you're wrong,' Big May said. 'If I know Pearl, she's probably just waiting for you to make the first move.'

'Do you think so?'

'I'm sure of it. You know how proud she is.'

Ruby smiled ruefully. 'Stubborn, more like!'

'Exactly. So why don't you take her birthday present round on Monday, use it as an excuse to sort it out?'

Ruby considered it for a moment. Then said she, 'I think I will.'

'Good. Now, happen we can get on with this?' Big May said briskly. 'These clothes won't sort themselves!'

'You're right.' Ruby folded up the nightgown and set it to one side. There was enough good flannel in it to be turned into pillowcases, or a child's pyjamas. 'Thank you, Mum.'

'What for?'

'For talking sense into me.'

'You're talking nonsense now!' Big May brushed off the compliment. But Ruby caught her mother-in-law smiling to herself as she went back to her sorting.

Elsie stood at the window, staring out at the rain and waiting for Pearl to come home. She had sent her daughter out shopping over an hour ago and she hadn't returned yet.

She was probably still sulking, Elsie thought. She had been in a sullen mood all day, and when Elsie had pointed out there was no food in the cupboards yet again, she had thrown a fit and slammed out of the house.

Elsie blamed Ruby for her daughter's bad mood. Pearl had not been the same since their falling-out. She wasn't as interested in going out and spending money or having a laugh, either. Even from a distance, her disapproving eldest daughter still managed to spoil their fun.

Elsie found the secret packet of cigarettes she had stashed inside the aspidistra pot, and lit one up. She thought it would be fun living with her daughter, but Pearl had turned out to be a big disappointment to her. She was selfish and slovenly, and rather than looking after her old mother, she seemed to expect Elsie to help her out. Barely a day seemed to go by without them bickering.

Elsie had complained to her friend Freda about it when they met for a nip of gin in the pub the day before. Freda was an old pal from her music hall days, and they'd had a fine time, reminiscing about the larks they'd got up to.

But poor Freda had properly fallen on hard times, living on gin and her nerves, stuck with a man who treated her like dirt because she had nowhere else to go. Seeing her had reminded Elsie of what her life used to be like. Happen she was better off with Pearl after all, even if her daughter's housekeeping did leave a lot to be desired.

A flash of red hair caught her eye. Elsie peered between the dingy lace curtains to see Ruby coming up the street.

She sighed with irritation and stubbed out her cigarette in the plant pot. She thought they'd seen the last of her, but she should have known Ruby would be hard to shake off.

But then again, she did have a basket over her arm. With any luck she might have brought some food . . .

She feigned surprise when she opened the door to her.

'Oh, hello. I didn't expect to see you.'

'Really? I could have sworn I saw you watching me from the window.'

Elsie's eyes narrowed. So that was how it was going to be, was it? 'What do you want, anyway?'

'I've come to see Pearl.'

'She's gone out.' Elsie nodded to the basket over her daughter's arm. 'What have you got there?'

'It's a birthday present. You do remember it's your daughter's birthday today?'

'Of course I remember. What do you take me for?' Elsie dropped her guilty gaze. No wonder Pearl was in such a bad mood. 'Give it to me and I'll see she gets it.'

She held out her hand but Ruby held on to the basket. 'I wanted to see her myself.'

'I'm not sure she'll want to see you, after what happened last time.' She was pleased to see Ruby's expression falter. 'She took it very hard, you know. Swore she'd never speak to you again.'

'Did she?'

'Aye, she did. And I'll tell you something else. I reckon it will take more than a birthday present to make her forget what happened.'

Ruby gazed down at the basket. She looked so sad, Elsie almost felt sorry for her.

Perhaps she had chosen the wrong daughter, she thought. Ruby would never have let her cupboards get empty. If Elsie had put a bit more effort in with her eldest, she might have been in clover by now.

'Happen I could have a word with her,' she said slowly. 'Try to settle things between you.'

She saw the suspicious look in her daughter's eye. 'Why would you do that?' Ruby asked.

'Because in spite of what you might think, I want us to be a proper family. All three of us together.' She nodded towards the basket. 'Leave that with me, and I'll talk to her. I can't promise anything, mind. You know how stubborn your sister can be.'

She went to reach for the basket, but Ruby held on.

'Happen it might be best if I talked to her myself . . .'

'I told you, she won't want to see you! Now do you want me to help you, or don't you?'

Elsie tugged the basket out of her daughter's hand. This time Ruby handed it over. She looked utterly bereft, Elsie thought.

'I don't suppose I've got much choice, have I?' Ruby murmured.

As Elsie ushered her out of the front door, Ruby said, 'How is she?'

'Pearl? She's all right, I suppose,' Elsie shrugged. 'Why shouldn't she be?'

'I just wondered. She in't used to managing on her own . . .'

'Then it's about time she learned, in't it?'

Ruby sent her a doubtful look. 'You will look after her, won't you? I know she seems a bit hopeless, but she's very fragile.'

'Fragile, my backside!' Elsie snorted. 'If you ask me, she's just lazy. And that's your fault.'

'Me?' Ruby looked bewildered.

'You've smothered her for years, paying her bills and doing everything for her. She's perfectly capable of looking after herself, but she's never had to try, thanks to you.'

'That in't true. You don't know her like I do—'

'I know enough,' Elsie cut her off. 'And if you ask me, you need her more than she needs you!'

She closed the door before Ruby could reply.

Chapter Thirty-Four

Friday 18th April 1941

Pearl plodded down Hessle Road, simmering with discontent. Her arms ached from carrying her heavy shopping, and cold rain dripped down the inside of her collar. She had left in such a hurry that she had forgotten her hat, and her carefully set curls were ruined.

It wasn't fair, she thought. Why did she have to be the one who trailed out in all weathers? It wouldn't hurt her mother to get off her backside and do her share. But Elsie always seemed to have some excuse.

Today it was her arthritis again.

'Been playing me up something terrible for days it has, what with the damp,' she had whined, massaging her knees. But that did not stop her scurrying off to meet her friend Freda in the pub the other day, Pearl thought sourly.

It didn't stop her giving orders, either. She stomped around the house, complaining that her washing hadn't been done and the floors had not been scrubbed. This morning she had stood in the kitchen, throwing open the cupboard doors and pointing to the empty shelves, demanding to know why there was no food in the house.

'There's no money in the house either, in case you hadn't noticed,' Pearl had muttered in reply.

But of course her mother did not offer to contribute. She never lifted a finger or paid a penny, and if Pearl complained about it, Elsie would turn on the tears.

'I wish I had something to offer you,' she would sob. 'You know I'd share my last farthing with you, love.'

But Pearl was beginning to wonder if that was true. She was sure her mother had cigarettes stashed somewhere. She kept smelling smoke in the house, but Elsie always denied it.

She was even more sorry for herself because today was her birthday, and her mother had not even remembered.

Pearl thought about the cake Ruby had made her last year. It had taken so much effort what with all the ingredients being rationed, but somehow Ruby had managed it because she knew how much it would mean to Pearl. She had thrown her a little party, too. Her Frank had been there, and all the Maguires. It was such a special day.

But her mother had not even wished her a happy birthday, let alone baked a cake or written her a card.

It was just beginning to dawn on Pearl how much she relied on her older sister. Like today, for instance. She would not have had to go out shopping, or beg for groceries on tick. Ruby would have made sure her cupboards were full. She often picked up Pearl's rations as well as her own, which saved Pearl standing in dreary queues for hours on end. And sometimes she would drop round with an extra tin of salmon or an onion, or any other treasures she had managed to find. It would never have occurred to her to keep anything for herself, unlike Elsie and her rotten cigarettes.

But it wasn't just her sister's practical help she missed. Pearl needed Ruby's guiding hand. Pearl knew her sister had her best interests at heart. And even though they argued and got exasperated with each other sometimes, Ruby was always there when Pearl needed a shoulder to cry on.

A tear ran down her cheek, mingling with the rain. How she wished she hadn't sent her away. As soon as the words were out of her mouth she had regretted them. She would have gone straight round and made up with her, but her mother had stopped her.

'If there's any apologising to be done, she should be the one to do it,' she had said firmly. 'She's the one who's caused all the trouble.'

And so Pearl had waited. But Ruby did not come.

'She's probably realised she's better off without you hanging on to her coattails,' her mother had said. 'Let's be honest, you were always sponging off her, weren't you?'

It takes one to know one, Pearl thought. But her mother's words had stung, because deep down Pearl knew they were true. She knew Ruby would be there to pick up the pieces, and she had taken advantage of it over the years.

But at least she was trying to do something about it now. She wondered what Ruby would say if she knew Pearl had applied for a job on the buses. She would probably laugh at the thought of her sister as a clippie, collecting fares. But she knew she would be pleased, too, and for the first time in her life, Pearl wanted to do something to make Ruby proud.

It was just a shame her sister would never know about it.

As she let herself in through the front door, Pearl was preparing herself mentally to speak to her mother. This could not go on, she thought. If she was going to be out of the house working, Elsie would have to do more to pull her weight in the house.

As soon as she walked in, she breathed in the unmistakable aroma of cigarette smoke.

She followed the smell down the passage to the kitchen.

'Have you been smoking?' she demanded. 'Only I thought you told me you couldn't afford—' She stopped at the sight of her mother at the stove. 'What are you doing?'

'Making a cup of tea, what does it look like? I thought you'd want one, since it's such rotten weather outside.' Her mother looked over her shoulder at her. 'Poor lass, you're soaked. Here, take off that wet coat before you catch your death.'

Pearl dumped her shopping basket on the floor as her mother fussed around her, pulling off her coat and hanging it carefully.

'You were gone so long, I was starting to worry about you,' she said.

'There was a queue at the Co-op.' Pearl's gaze fell on the carefully wrapped parcel sitting in the middle of the kitchen table. 'What's that?'

'It's for you.'

'For me?'

'A birthday present. Didn't you think I'd remember?' Her mother said teasingly.

'I – I wasn't sure . . .'

'How could I forget, when I've been waiting all these years to give my little girl a gift?'

'Oh, Mum.' Pearl smiled at her, her anger forgotten. 'What is it?'

'You'll have to open it and see, won't you?'

Her mother watched her keenly as she unwrapped the present. Inside was the most beautiful crimson cardigan, soft wool with delicate mother of pearl buttons.

'Do you like it?' Elsie asked.

'It's lovely. And my favourite colour, too. Did you knit it yourself?'

'What do you think?'

'I didn't know you could knit.'

'Aye, well, I'm full of surprises.'

'But when did you find the time? I don't think I've ever seen you with a pair of needles in your hands.'

'It wouldn't have been a surprise if you'd seen me, would it?'

'Yes, but—'

'And I've got you these, too—' Her mother handed over a packet of cigarettes. 'I'm sorry, I sneaked a couple myself. I hope you don't mind?'

'Of course not.' Pearl looked at the cardigan in her hands, still overwhelmed. It was so perfect, she could see the love and care that had gone into every stitch.

'I knew you'd understand.' Her mother nudged her. 'We're two peas in a pod, in't we?'

Pearl looked at her mother. Elsie might have her faults, but at least she was there, unlike her so-called sister.

'Yes, Mum,' she said. 'Like two peas in a pod.'

Chapter Thirty-Five

Friday 25th April 1941

On the day Edie was supposed to be going dancing, Bobby woke up with a temperature and a terrible hacking cough.

'It's probably just a cold,' Mrs Huggins said. 'You'll see, he'll be right as rain by this afternoon.'

But as the day wore on, Bobby seemed to get worse rather than better. His skin was hot and clammy, and his little body was racked with coughing fits that left him fighting for breath.

'What if it's diphtheria?' Edie fretted as she walked up and down the yard, holding Bobby against her shoulder. She hoped the cool, fresh air might do him good.

'Diphtheria, indeed!' Mrs Huggins scoffed from the open back door. 'I told you, it's just a cold. Get some goose grease and brown paper on his chest, that'll sort him out.'

Bobby started coughing again, his tiny chest rising and falling with effort. He stared at Edie with wide, terrified eyes as he struggled to breathe.

Seeing him looking so wretched made up her mind. 'I'm going to fetch the doctor,' she said.

'There's really no need—'

'Leave the lass alone, Patience. She's his mother, she knows what's best.' Mr Huggins's voice came from inside the house. A moment later he appeared in the back doorway beside his wife. 'How about I go and fetch the doctor, love? You can stay and look after the bain.'

Mrs Huggins sighed. 'Please yourselves. But if you ask me, you're both making a lot of fuss and bother over nothing.'

The doctor called half an hour later. Edie could hardly breathe herself as he examined Bobby, listening to his chest and looking down his throat. *Please*, she prayed, *please don't let it be diphtheria*. When she looked across the room, Mrs Huggins had her hands clasped and her eyes closed too.

'Croup,' the doctor declared, when he'd finished his examination. 'Don't worry, my dear, he'll be better in a couple of days. Rest and steam inhalations are what he needs.'

'I told you it wouldn't be serious,' Mrs Huggins grumbled when the doctor had gone. Edie said nothing. She had seen the woman's lips moving in silent prayer, just the same as her own.

With Mrs Huggins's help, they fashioned a steam tent around the baby's cot, made out of two clothes horses strung across with sheets. Mr Huggins found an old spirit stove under the stairs, and made a long funnel out of brown paper to put over the spout of the kettle.

Edie spent the rest of the afternoon by her son's bedside, watching over him as he slumbered, getting up only to heat another pan and replace the steaming water in the kettle. Even though Bobby's breathing was easier, she did not dare take her eyes off the baby for fear of something happening to him.

Outside, the day gave way to darkening twilight. But Edie scarcely noticed the hours pass until Mrs Huggins tapped softly on her door and said, 'John Maguire's here. He says you're supposed to be going dancing with him tonight?'

'Oh lord, I forgot all about that.' Edie stood up, wincing at the stiffness in her cramped limbs. 'I'd best go and talk to him. Can you keep an eye on Bobby for me?'

'Of course.'

Edie hesitated in the doorway, watching as Mrs Huggins took the chair she had just vacated. She hardly dared to leave Bobby, even for a moment.

John waited in the hall below, spruced up in a smart suit, his dark hair slicked. He looked up as Edie came down the stairs, his smile fading as he took in her dishevelled appearance.

'I thought you might have got a bit more dressed up?' he joked.

'Bobby's got croup and I've been looking after him all day.' Edie ran her hand through her hair. The steam had turned it to a mop of damp curls that clung to her shiny, perspiring face.

John frowned. 'Oh no, poor little chap. How is he?'

'Getting better, thank God.'

'I'm pleased to hear it.' John looked at his watch. 'The dance doesn't get started for another half an hour, so you've got plenty of time to get ready—'

'I'm sorry, John. I can't leave Bobby.'

He stared at her blankly. 'But you said he was getting better?'

'He is, but I still want to be with him.'

'Can't Mrs Huggins watch him? You'll only be gone a couple of hours.'

'I want to stay with him myself.'

'But I've been looking forward to it!'

'Happen you could find someone else to take my ticket?'

'Not at such short notice.' John looked as petulant as a spoilt child. 'So that's it, then?' he said.

'I'm sorry, John, I really am,' Edie said.

John opened his mouth to speak, but his reply was interrupted by another coughing fit from upstairs.

'I've got to go,' Edie said.

'Happen we could go out another night—' John's hopeful

voice followed her up the stairs.

'Has he gone?' Mrs Huggins asked, when she returned to the bedroom. Edie nodded. 'That's a shame. You know, you could have gone out if you'd wanted?'

'I wouldn't have enjoyed myself, knowing Bobby wasn't well.'

'No.' Mrs Huggins looked at her thoughtfully. 'No, I don't suppose you would.'

As it turned out, Edie was glad she had decided to stay with the baby. Bobby was very fretful, and would only settle if Edie held him. She spent most of the evening pacing up and down her bedroom with him in her arms, singing to him softly.

'Heaven, I'm in heaven . . .' she sang, her face pressed to his downy head. 'And I seem to find the happiness I seek, when we're out together dancing cheek to cheek . . .' She turned her head to plant a kiss on his plump cheek. 'I could have been dancing cheek to cheek with another man by now, Bobby,' she whispered. 'But here I am, dancing with you instead.'

She was surprised at how little the thought disappointed her.

Chapter Thirty-Six

At half past nine, Edie had settled Bobby back in his cot and was refilling the kettle to boil when the air raid siren moaned.

She listened to Mr and Mrs Huggins downstairs, packing up their belongings and preparing to retreat to the cupboard under the stairs as they usually did during a raid.

'In't you going down to the shelter, love?' Mr Huggins called up to her.

'No, Mr H. Bobby's just got off to sleep and I don't want to disturb him. Besides, it's a bit damp for him down in the shelter.'

'I don't like to think of you up there by yourself. Would you like to come in with us? It's a bit of a squeeze, but I daresay we can make room—'

'Thank you, but we'll be all right. I don't suppose this raid will carry on for long. There hasn't been a bad one for a few days now.'

Edie finished arranging the kettle spout through the gap in the makeshift tent, then sat down beside Bobby's cot. The skies seemed quiet tonight, she thought. She knew she had done the right thing, not going down to the shelter. The damp, cold air would play havoc with Bobby's chest. And by the time she had bundled him up and got him round the corner, the All Clear would probably have sounded.

She rested her arms on the rail of the cot and laid her head down. The quiet sounds of Bobby's snuffly breathing mingled with the sound of the kettle simmering gently on the spirit stove, lulling her. An overpowering weariness came over her, making her limbs heavy and her eyelids gritty for want of sleep. If only she could close them for a moment, she would be all right again ...

'Edie?'

Suddenly there was a hand on her shoulder, shaking her awake. Edie opened her eyes and thought for a moment she was dreaming as Jack Maguire's concerned face swam into focus in front of her.

'Jack?' She blinked up at him.

'I hope you don't mind me barging in, but I saw a chink of light showing at your window. I thought I'd best warn you before our Florence noticed it.'

Edie rubbed her eyes and looked around, still bleary with sleep. 'I must have closed the curtains but forgotten to put the blackouts up.'

She started to her feet but Jack said, 'Let me.'

He crossed to the window and picked up the blackout panel, slotting it in place. 'I knocked but there was no answer,' he said over his shoulder. 'Then I remembered you were supposed to be out with our John tonight.' He sent her a questioning look.

'I couldn't go. Bobby wasn't well.'

'What's wrong with him?'

'Croup, the doctor says.' She looked down at the cot where her son slumbered peacefully at last. 'I didn't like to take him down to the shelter.'

'Aye, you're best out of it.' Jack gazed into the cot. 'How is the little lad now?'

'Getting better, I think. The steam's helping.'

'Aye, it does. Our Freddie had croup when he was a baby.

Dolly turned the house into a Turkish bath!' He smiled at the memory.

A solitary plane passed overhead, and they both tensed.

'Happen you should bring the baby next door?' Jack suggested. 'I'm waiting to see if I'm needed for the rescue party. You could sit downstairs with me?'

From somewhere in the distance came the familiar crump of a bomb landing close by, shaking the floor under their feet.

'Thank you,' Edie said. 'I would feel safer.'

Edie bundled up the baby and they hurried next door. As Jack opened the back door, a terrified whimpering came from behind the kitchen cupboard.

'Lucky? It's all right, lad, you can come out,' Jack called softly. A moment later a scruffy ball of fur emerged, trembling with fear. Jack scooped the little dog up into his arms.

'There, it's all right. I'm here now.' He spoke soothingly, tickling its ears.

'Did the boys not take him to the shelter?' Edie said.

Jack shook his head. 'Florence has put her foot down. She says everyone else is complaining they can't bring their pets, too. Mrs Lassiter wanted to bring her parrot and Florence weren't having that.'

'I in't surprised. Have you heard the language it comes out with?'

Jack grinned. 'That'll be Mr Lassiter's doing!'

He tucked the dog under his arm and went to the stove to put the kettle on. Edie sat down at the kitchen table, Bobby in her arms. Bless him, he was so tired he had barely stirred when she picked him out of his cot.

'Do you want me to set up a steam tent for him?' Jack offered. 'I can fetch the clothes horse from upstairs . . .'

'There's no need. He seems to be sleeping peacefully now.'

She looked around her at the kitchen, sadness welling up

inside her. How many times had she sat here at this very table, sharing a cup of tea with Dolly and Iris while they put the world to rights?

'It doesn't seem the same without her, does it?'

Edie looked up sharply. Jack was watching her over his shoulder.

'How did you know—'

'I think the same thing all the time.'

He made the tea and they sat at the kitchen table to drink it. 'We could sit under the stairs, but I reckon it would be a bit of a squeeze for three of us,' Jack said.

'Don't you mean four?' Edie smiled, as Lucky sprang up on to Jack's knee and huddled in close to him.

Jack looked fondly down at him. 'He's never far from my side.'

'So I see.' Edie paused, then said, 'I don't suppose there's any news of his owner?'

'No.' Jack's smile faded. 'I doubt he made it or he would have come forward by now.' He ruffled the dog's fur. 'I reckon this is your home now, eh?'

'He seems to have settled in very well.'

'Oh aye, he acts as if he owns the place!' Lucky gazed up at Jack with soulful brown eyes. 'Look, he knows we're talking about him. He's a funny little thing, but the boys love him.'

'Just the boys?'

Jack looked rueful. 'I must admit I've got very attached to him.' He stroked the dog's ears, and Lucky licked his face enthusiastically.

'Looks like the feeling's mutual,' Edie said, laughing.

'Aye, he's my pal, all right. He even sleeps at the bottom of the bed at night. Don't know what Dolly would have said about it, mind. She was always adamant she wouldn't have a dog in the house.'

'I can just imagine her, laying down the law,' Edie said.

'She would have hit the roof! And there was no arguing with my Dolly when she'd set her mind against something. Or someone,' he added.

Edie knew exactly what he meant. Dolly Maguire's temper was legendary in Jubilee Row. And if she had a grudge against someone, they knew all about it.

And yet she was also the first one to offer help if anyone needed it.

'She was a good friend,' she said. 'I'll never forget how kind she was to me when I first moved here.' She looked down at Bobby in her arms. 'I don't think I would have coped if she hadn't taken me under her wing.'

'She liked you,' Jack said. 'She admired you, too. She always said you were the bravest lass she knew.'

'Brave? Me?'

'She said it took a lot to up sticks and move to a place where you didn't know a soul. Especially in your condition.'

'After Rob died, I decided I wanted a fresh start.'

'So you came here?'

'This was where Rob was born. I thought I'd feel closer to him here.'

'And do you?'

'Sometimes.' And sometimes she could scarcely remember him. This might be Rob's home town, but they had no memories here together. They had never walked the streets together, or gone to the pictures or a dance hall.

'Does Rob still have family here?'

Edie nodded. 'In Gypsyville.'

'I wonder why you didn't settle there, then. Surely it would have been easier for you to have his family around you?'

Edie twirled the teaspoon between her fingers, thinking carefully about her answer. 'I'd never met them,' she said. 'I hadn't been with Rob long, and I didn't feel as if I could just turn up on their doorstep.'

'But why not? You were their son's widow, the mother of their grandson. Surely they'd welcome you with open arms?'

She looked up at Jack's open, honest face. She was about to come out with her usual excuse, but for some reason she found herself wanting to tell him the truth.

'That's just it. I wasn't.'

Jack frowned. 'I don't understand . . .'

Edie took a deep breath. 'Rob and I weren't married,' she said. She held up the brass ring on her left hand. 'This was just for show. Rob gave it to me the day he left to go south. A promise ring, he called it.'

It was a promise that had turned out to be as empty as all his others.

'But why couldn't he marry you properly?'

'He already had a wife,' she said quietly.

Jack was silent for a moment, looking from her to the baby in her arms and back again.

'I didn't know he was married,' Edie said. 'I wouldn't have given him the time of day if I'd known.'

'When did you find out?'

'Not until it was too late.' She gazed down at Bobby. 'I thought he'd do the right thing by me, but he told me he couldn't.' She swallowed down the old familiar bitterness that rose in her throat. 'He swore he didn't love her. He said he was going to leave her when he came home—'

'But he never did.'

Edie shook her head. She couldn't allow herself to hate Rob for what he had done. He had never set out to hurt her. What had started out as a harmless friendship between a lonely airman and a local girl had turned into something neither of them had imagined.

At least that was how she chose to look at it.

'Did Dolly know?' Jack asked.

Edie shook her head. 'No one knows. I think Mrs Huggins might have guessed, but we've never spoken about it. I've never told anyone else. I promised myself I never would.'

'But you told me?'

She smiled. 'I don't know why.'

'I'm glad you did.'

She allowed herself to look up at him. Jack looked back at her, his dark eyes full of sympathy and understanding.

'So am I,' she said.

Their gazes held until the harsh clang of the alarm bell broke the tension.

'Looks like I'm needed after all.' Jack put down his cup. 'Will you be all right here on your own?'

Edie nodded. 'I'd like to stay, if that's all right?'

'Of course. It might be best if you settled down under the stairs, just to be on the safe side.'

He took his coat and tin hat down from the peg on the back of the door. Edie was suddenly very conscious of him moving around her. They seemed to be giving each other more space than usual, their eyes not meeting.

He didn't look at her at all until he was at the back door. 'Stay safe,' he said.

'You too.'

Their eyes met again. And then he was gone, disappearing into the night.

Chapter Thirty-Seven

Saturday 26th April 1941

A rocking horse hung from the upper floor of a shattered house, in what had once been a child's bedroom.

'Tragic, in't it?' Maggie Cornell said. 'The whole family's gone, according to the warden. A dad and four bains. The youngest was only a baby, too.'

Ruby looked back at the rocking horse from the open hatch of the van. It looked like a much-loved toy. She could imagine a child rocking back and forth, laughing with delight. And now that laughter had been silenced, and no one would ever ride that horse again.

A lump rose in her throat and she had to close her eyes for a moment to steady herself. There was a queue of people waiting at the serving hatch, and they did not want to be greeted by a sad, sobbing mess.

But Maggie was very emotional as she filled the big enamel teapot from the urn.

'To think, there's a woman in hospital who's got no idea her husband and children are dead,' she was saying mournfully. 'How dreadful. Can you imagine it? Poor woman.' She shook her head sorrowfully.

'Could you pass me the fruit cake? I'll get it cut into slices and we'll put it out on display.'

Maggie sent her a curious look as she handed her the tray. 'Imagine losing your whole family,' she said. 'It doesn't bear thinking about, does it? I'll tell you what, I'll be hugging my bains when I get home. That's what it's all about, in't it? Family. That's what's important.'

'Yes, love, what can I get for you?' Ruby turned away to serve the policeman who stood at the hatch. 'A nice cup of tea? And how about a biscuit to go with it? Or would you rather have a sandwich?'

She was aware of Maggie frowning behind her. Ruby wished they hadn't been put together on the van tonight. Maggie always made sure she got all the most tragic stories from the ARP warden, and she was a great one for wallowing in misery. She spent most of her time crying behind the counter. Ruby had tried to explain to her that they were there to do a job and the last thing anyone wanted was more misery. She had told her that the most helpful thing she could do was to put on a brave face and just get on with it.

'How can you just carry on serving tea as if nothing's happened?' she would sniff.

'Because that's why we're here,' Ruby said.

But that did not stop Maggie. Ruby could hear her rummaging for her handkerchief behind her as she handed out cups of tea and coffee.

Besides, the last thing she wanted to do was to think about her family.

It had been a week since she had taken her peace offering round to Pearl's, and she had heard nothing. As the days passed, her hope had started to fade and she was having to face the fact that her sister wanted nothing more to do with her.

I should have waited for her to come home, she thought. *I should never have left without speaking to her myself.* She had even thought about going round again, but her pride would not allow it.

Besides, Big May had advised against it.

'She's already turned her back on you once, you don't need telling twice,' she had said. 'If she wants you, she knows where you live.'

But Ruby could not forget what Elsie had said to her, either. Her harsh words played on her mind.

'Do you think I smother Pearl?' she had asked her mother-in-law.

Big May sent her a shrewd look. 'Where did you get that idea?'

'Just something my m— Elsie said. She reckoned Pearl's never had to grow up because I've always been there to look after her.'

'Aye, well, I hate to admit it, but I reckon she might have a point,' Big May conceded.

'She also said I needed her more than she needed me.'

'And what do you think?'

'I don't know what to think.'

'Well, you do like to be needed,' Big May said tactfully.

Was that what it was, Ruby wondered, as she looked around her. Was that what all this was for, all the volunteering and the organising? She had always thought she was just doing her bit for the war effort, but now she began to wonder if there was something about her that had to be useful and needed.

And perhaps Pearl was just another part of that, like the salvage drive and the fundraising. If she was honest, she did enjoy taking care of her sister, of being the one who swept in and rescued her, instead of allowing her to solve her own problems.

'Penny for your thoughts?' She looked up to see her brother-in-law Jack at the front of the queue. Seeing him gave her a jolt, because his dark good looks always reminded her so much of her dear Jimmy.

'Sorry, I was miles away,' she smiled. 'Cup of tea?'

'Please.' He took off his tin hat and ruffled his dark hair. He looked weary, Ruby noticed.

'You should be having more than a cup of tea,' the man beside him said. 'You should be in hospital.'

She glanced at Jack in dismay. 'What's this?'

'Take no notice,' Jack muttered.

'A gas pipe fractured just now, when we were rescuing a woman from that house over there,' the man explained, ignoring Jack's warning look. 'Jack and another bloke were overcome, but they wouldn't give up trying to get her out.'

'Jack!'

'He's exaggerating,' Jack said.

'The warden wanted them to go to hospital, but they wouldn't go. Bloody fools, if you'll excuse my language.' The man shook his head.

Ruby looked at Jack. 'If your mother found out—'

'You'd best not tell her then, eh?' Jack sent her a long look.

'I suppose not,' Ruby agreed reluctantly.

She poured his tea and gave him a meat paste sandwich to go with it. As he took them, Jack said, 'How are the boys?'

'Safe and sound. Mum took them back to her house after the All Clear.'

'That's good.' Jack looked relieved.

As he was leaving, Ruby said, 'Mum thought she saw Edie and her baby coming out of your house last night after the All Clear sounded. I told her she must have been mistaken?'

'No, that's right,' Jack said through a mouthful of sandwich. 'They took shelter with me last night.'

Ruby watched him striding off, back to the rescue site.

Did they indeed, she thought. Now what was that all about?

Chapter Thirty-Eight

Saturday 26th April 1941

'How did you get on with Edie last night? Did you have a good time at the dance?'

Iris looked over her shoulder at her brother. John lounged against the sink, watching her cook.

'We didn't go.' He reached over and help himself to a piece of leftover meat from the dish. Iris slapped his hand away.

'Don't eat it all, there'll be none left for the Connaught pie.'

'Connaught pie, eh?' John peered into the pan Iris was stirring. 'It looks like you've emptied out the pig bin.'

Iris looked gloomily down at the greyish oat and water mixture bubbling on the hob. It did not look appealing, she had to admit.

'It'll be all right with a bit of cheese sauce on it,' she said. 'Anyway, never mind my cooking. Why didn't you and Edie go dancing?'

'The baby was ailing and she didn't want to leave him. At least that's what she said,' he pulled a face.

'You didn't believe her?'

'Oh, the bain was ailing, all right.' John shrugged. 'But she didn't seem too upset at not going, either.'

Laughter drifted from the yard, where Archie was playing football out in the ten-foot with Charlie Scuttle. Shambling, loose-limbed Charlie was not putting up much of a defence, but they both seemed to be enjoying the game.

It was nice to hear her son laughing again. She glanced at Matthew, who was patching a hole in the fence by the gate. He had his back to them as he hammered a plank of wood into place.

Iris went back to stirring the pot of oats. 'I'm sure she was very disappointed,' she said. 'Anyway, you can always go out some other time, can't you?'

'I'm not sure I'll bother.' John reached for another shred of meat. 'I reckon she's got her eye on someone else, anyway.'

'Never.' Iris put down her spoon and turned to face him. 'Who?'

'Who do you think?'

He went to sneak another piece of meat from the plate but Iris snatched up her spoon and rapped his hand with the back of it, making him yelp. 'Ow, that was hot!'

'Tell me!'

John grinned, a teasing glint in his eye. 'You mean to tell me you don't know?' He shook his head. 'And you call your-self her friend! I spotted it the minute I saw them together.'

'Saw who?' Iris brandished the spoon threateningly. 'Honest to God, John, if you don't tell me this minute, I'll—'

'Our dear brother, of course.'

'Jack?' She laughed. 'You're joking?'

'It's plain as day to me.'

Iris glanced out of the window. Matthew had put down his hammer and gone over to the back gate to talk to Archie and Charlie.

She went back to stirring her pot. 'You must be daft if you think there's anything going on between those two.'

'Not yet,' John conceded. 'But give it a few weeks and I reckon it'll be a different story. I've seen the way her eyes light up when she looks at him.' He picked at the leftover meat and this time Iris did not try to stop him. 'Think about it, Sis,' he said. 'How much time do they spend together? She's always round there, in't she?'

'She helps look after the boys—'

'But why? Why does she go to so much trouble for him?'

'She just wants to help, for Dolly's sake.'

'Yes, but Dolly in't here any more, is she?' John smirked. 'And let's face it, our Jack is quite a catch. Not as good as me, of course, but—'

Iris wasn't listening. She stared down at the glutinous mixture bubbling in the pan, her thoughts elsewhere.

She couldn't believe it. She didn't want to believe it, because she didn't want to think of Edie doing anything so underhand.

But at the same time John's idea made sense. Edie did spend a lot of time with Jack. Iris had always thought her friend was being kind. Now she wondered if she had been secretly scheming to take Dolly's place.

No, it couldn't be, she thought. Not Edie . . .

'She's wasting her time, anyway,' she said. 'Our Jack wouldn't be interested.'

'I wouldn't be too sure about that. You know those tickets he gave me for the dance? I reckon he was planning to ask Edie himself.'

'No!'

'I thought it was a bit strange at the time, but it makes sense now. I mean, who buys tickets to a dance if they don't plan to go?'

Out in the yard Matthew had taken over the game. He stood between Archie and Charlie, pointing up and down the ten-foot, his mouth moving. Iris did not have to hear him to know he would be issuing orders.

'Anyway, I in't too bothered about it.' John shrugged. 'Jack's welcome to her.'

'Hmm.' Iris went closer to the window to listen.

'You're not even trying,' she heard Matthew saying to Archie. 'Look at him. Are you trying to tell me you can't get the ball off him?'

Archie mumbled something under his breath and Matthew's lip curled. 'What's the point in playing if you don't want to win?' he shouted.

'It's good for Archie to have a man about the house, in't it?'

Iris looked at her brother, who had come to look out of the window beside her.

'I suppose so,' she murmured.

Matthew had snatched up the ball and was kicking it down the alley, while Archie and Charlie looked on, bemused.

John was right, she thought. It was good for Archie to have a father figure. Her son might not have taken to him as well as she had hoped, but Matthew said that was only to be expected after all her years of 'mollycoddling', as he put it.

'He'll soon learn to stop being such a baby,' he had assured her.

Now he wouldn't let Iris go to her son if he had a nightmare. And if he wet the bed in the night, Matthew would make him strip the bed and wash the sheets himself. It nearly broke Iris's heart to see her son struggling with the dolly tub in the yard, but Matthew insisted it would teach him a lesson.

Sometimes Iris wondered if he was right to be so tough. But at the same time she needed his confidence and certainty because she had so little of her own. Matthew might not be perfect, but he gave her children a stability she could not provide herself.

'It'll be a pity when he has to go,' John said.

'Go? Go where?'

'Back to sea, of course.' John grinned. 'You didn't think we were going to stay here forever, did you? It won't be long before we're off on another ship. They're crying out for merchant seamen to register.'

'How long before you have to go?'

'I don't know. A few days, perhaps a couple of weeks. It depends who wants us.'

John helped himself to another scrap of meat. 'Anyway, I'd best be off,' he said. 'Mum will be wondering where I am.'

'Are you sure you don't want to stay for your dinner?' She looked at the half-empty dish. 'You've already eaten most of it, anyway.'

John looked at the pan, his mouth twisting. 'Another time,' he said. 'When you've got something worth eating.'

'Cheek! Happen I won't ask you again,' she called after her brother as he strode across the yard.

Iris watched him as he chatted briefly to Matthew in the yard before he headed off down the alley. Of course she had always known that Matthew would leave one day, but the thought of not having his guiding presence filled her with a slight panic.

She went back to her cooking. The Connaught pie had sounded nice when Mrs Buggins made it on *Kitchen Front*, but somehow it did not look quite so appetising in real life.

She was serving it up when Archie suddenly appeared in the back doorway and nearly made her drop the dish.

'Mum, come quick!' he cried. 'Uncle Sam's going to kill Matthew!'

Chapter Thirty-Nine

Iris dropped her spoon and rushed out to the yard after him, wiping her hands on her apron.

She stopped dead at the sight of Sam Scuttle pinning Matthew against the back wall.

'Say that again,' Sam growled. 'Go on, I dare you.'

'What's going on?' Iris asked, but neither of the men noticed her. They were staring at each other, their eyes locked, like fighting dogs. Only Charlie turned her way, wringing his hands, his eyes full of silent appeal. *Do something*, he seemed to say.

'He called Charlie a name,' Archie said. 'Uncle Sam heard him.'

Iris stepped forward. 'Sam, please,' she begged. 'Whatever he said, I'm sure he didn't mean it.'

'I meant every word,' Matthew sneered. 'That brother of yours should be put away. Look at him, he's not right in the—'

Before he had finished the sentence, Sam picked him up by his collar, dangling him like a puppet, his feet inches from the ground.

'Sam!' Iris turned to Archie. 'Go inside,' she ordered. 'You didn't ought to see this.'

Archie stood still, his gaze fixed avidly on Matthew. 'Go inside,' Iris pushed him towards the back door. 'Go and watch your sister.'

Archie went back into the house, but a moment later his face appeared at the scullery window.

Iris turned on the men. 'What do you think you're doing, fighting in front of a bain?'

'He started it,' Matthew snarled at Sam.

'Aye, and I'll finish it, too.'

'I'll finish you!'

'Don't make me laugh! Stick to boxing with little boys, it'll make you feel more of a man.'

'Stop it, both of you!' Iris shouted. 'You're like a couple of kids in the school playground.' She turned to Sam. 'I would have thought better of you.'

'And I would have thought better of you, sticking up for him.' Sam kept his gaze fixed on Matthew. He twisted in his grasp like a worm on the end of a fishing hook.

'Let him go, Sam. Please,' Iris begged.

'He can apologise to my brother first.'

'Apologise? To him?' Matthew hissed from between clenched teeth. 'You must be joking!'

Iris glanced at Charlie. His face was a picture of distress.

'Look at him,' she said to Sam. 'Charlie don't need an apology. He just wants this to stop.'

Sam looked from his brother to Iris and back again. Then, grudgingly, he released his grip on Matthew's collar. Matthew dropped to the ground, gasping for breath.

'Stay away from him in future,' Sam muttered.

'Oh, I will. And I'll be making sure Archie stays away from him, too.'

'That's up to his mother.' Sam looked at Iris. 'What do you say about that? Or does he speak for you now?'

Iris sighed wearily. 'Just leave it, Sam.'

Sam shook his head. 'You're not the woman I knew, Iris Fletcher,' he said sadly. 'The Iris I knew would never have put up with being told what to do. Especially not by the likes of him.'

As he turned to go, Matthew jumped to his feet. Iris caught the movement in the corner of her eye.

'Watch out!'

It all happened very fast after that. Iris stepped between them just as Matthew's fist shot out, catching her a glancing blow to her cheekbone. As she fell, Sam roared with rage, grabbed Matthew and threw him across the yard. He landed with a clatter, sprawled headlong against the dustbin.

'Are you all right?' Sam knelt beside her, his face a picture of concern.

'I – I think so.' Iris put her hand up to cradle her face. 'Nothing broken, anyway.'

'Let me see . . .' Iris winced as Sam's thumb brushed the tender skin on her cheekbone. His face was close to hers, his sea-green eyes full of worry. 'Does that hurt?'

'A bit.' Her gaze slid away, the closeness too much for her.

'It's not grazed but I reckon you'll have a bruise there.'

'She shouldn't have got in the way,' Matthew said sulkily.

Iris saw Sam tense and put her hand out to stop him.

'Don't,' she pleaded. 'Please, Sam.'

Her fingers tightened on the solid muscle of his arm. His skin felt warm beneath his soft flannel shirt. Sam looked down at her hand, then back at her face.

'How could you?' he murmured. 'How could you stick up for him, after what he's done? Can't you see the kind of man he is?'

'It was an accident.'

'And the way he treats your son? Is that an accident too?'

'What about my son?'

Sam glanced towards the house, where Archie's face still

watched them through the window. 'Ask him,' he said in a low voice.

He went to move, but Iris held on to his arm. 'Sam, if you know something, you should tell me.'

'It in't for me to say.' He pulled from her grasp. 'Ask your son.'

Matthew was still sulking about it as they sat down to eat their tea.

'It wasn't my fault you got caught,' he insisted.

'I didn't say it was.'

'You shouldn't have stopped me, anyway. He deserved what was coming to him.'

'He could have killed you,' Iris said wearily.

Matthew snorted. 'I don't think so! I'll have you know I can look after myself.'

Iris thought about Matthew dangling like a puppet from Sam's grip, but said nothing as she passed around the plates.

Matthew turned to Archie. 'I don't want you playing with Charlie Scuttle any more,' he said.

'Why not? He's harmless,' Iris said.

'He's feeble-minded and pathetic,' Matthew declared.

'He's the bravest man I know.'

Matthew laughed. 'Have you seen him? There's nothing brave about that shambling wreck.'

'He can't help it. The war made him ill,' Archie spoke up.

'Only because he wasn't tough enough to take it!'

Iris shot a quick look at Archie. 'That in't fair,' she said quietly. 'Charlie nearly died in the last war—'

But Matthew wasn't listening. 'Charlie Scuttle is not the sort of character Archie should be mixing with,' he insisted through a mouthful of food.

'Better not let Uncle Sam hear you say that,' Archie muttered.

'What did you say?'

Iris jumped in quickly. 'Nothing,' she said, shooting a quick look at her son. 'He didn't say anything. Did you, Archie?'

Archie stared back at her, mutinously silent.

Ask him. Sam's words came back to her.

She did not have the opportunity to speak to her son alone for the rest of the evening. After tea, Matthew insisted that they should all play cards. It was a tense game – as usual. Matthew criticised Iris and Archie for not playing properly and making it too easy for him, then sulked when he did not win.

She finally got her chance as she was getting Kitty ready for bed that night.

'You do like Uncle Matthew, don't you?' she said to Archie as he put on his pyjamas.

He hesitated. 'Yes,' he said finally.

'Are you sure? I know he can be a bit strict sometimes, but—'

'Do *you* like him?' Archie cut her off.

'Of course,' Iris smiled.

'Then so do I.'

Iris watched him as he climbed into bed beside his sister and settled down.

Ask him.

'And you're sure there's nothing you want to tell me?' she tried again, as she pulled the covers up to his chin.

'Such as?'

'I don't know. Anything. I just want you to be happy,' she pleaded.

He looked at her for a long time. 'I am happy, Mum,' he said quietly.

You're wrong, Sam Scuttle, she thought, as she closed the bedroom door softly.

She tried not to think about the fleeting look of sadness in her son's eyes as she had kissed him goodnight.

Chapter Forty

Saturday 3rd May 1941

It was a day Iris had been dreading.

When she opened her eyes that morning and felt the early summer warmth on her face, for a brief moment her heart lifted, thinking it might be a nice day. But then the realisation came, bring with it a flood of sadness and dread.

'It's Lucy's birthday,' she said to Matthew, who was lying beside her. 'She would have been four years old today.'

Matthew said nothing, but his silence spoke volumes.

'I don't know what to do,' Iris said.

'About what?'

'About today. I can't just let it go by, can I?'

'Why not?'

'How can I ignore my daughter's birthday?' She turned her head to stare up at the ceiling. 'I know Mum will expect me to go to the cemetery.'

Her mother had been very quiet on the subject since their last argument. But Big May had organised for the whole family to visit Lucy and Dolly's graves that afternoon, and Iris knew she would not take no for an answer.

'Do you want to go?'

'Since when did that matter to my mother?' She smiled ruefully. 'Anyway, I ought to go, for Archie's sake.'

'Why don't we do something else for him instead?' Matthew sat up in bed. 'We could make a day of it, do something special. How about another picnic? I'm sure Archie would rather do that, wouldn't he?'

Iris looked at him, so eager to please. Matthew really cared about Archie in his own way, she thought.

Ask him. Ask your son.

Sam Scuttle had got it wrong, Iris thought defiantly. Archie liked Matthew, he had told her so himself.

So why did his words keep running through her head?

'I'm sure he would,' she said.

But Archie's face fell when she spoke to him about it at the breakfast table later.

'Granny May says we're going to see Lucy,' he said quietly.

'Yes, but Uncle Matthew and I thought it would be better to go out and remember Lucy by doing something nice?' She silently willed him to agree, conscious that Matthew was listening from behind his newspaper.

'I want to go with Granny May.'

Matthew put down his newspaper with an impatient sigh. 'Your mother and I have decided, and that's what we're doing,' he said.

'But I want to see Lucy!'

'You can't see her, can you? She's dead.'

'Matthew!' Iris turned on him, shocked.

'He needs to accept the truth, Iris.' Matthew leaned across the table towards Archie. 'It's just a headstone, that's all. A slab of cold stone stuck in the ground. That's all that's left of your sister.'

Iris saw Archie's face pale and stepped in quickly. 'That's enough—'

'I don't care!' Archie stood up, pushing his chair back with a noisy clatter. 'I don't care what you say. I want to go and see her. I want to remember Lucy, even if you don't!'

'Archie!'

He turned on her, his face red with anger. 'You never talk about her, I can't even say her name, and I can't even look at her because he's hidden all her pictures!' He jabbed his finger at Matthew. 'But you can't stop me. She's still my sister and it's her birthday and I'm going to see her!'

'You come back here and apologise to your mother right away!' Matthew shouted, but Archie had already gone, slamming out of the room.

Matthew turned to her. 'Are you going to let him speak to you like that?'

'He's upset.'

'That's not the point. He needs to learn some respect.' Matthew glared towards the door, tight-lipped with anger. 'If you ask me, he needs a good belting . . .'

'Matthew, please, just leave it,' Iris begged.

'You're too lenient with that boy.'

'I just don't want any trouble, not today of all days.'

You're not the woman I knew, Iris Fletcher. The Iris I knew would never have put up with being told what to do.

Sam's words came into her mind, taunting her.

He was right, Iris thought. She wasn't that woman any more. That Iris had had fire in her belly. She never doubted herself, or her abilities as a mother. She was like a lioness with her cubs, fierce and strong and independent.

But that Iris had died with her baby girl. Now, when Iris looked at herself in the mirror, she barely recognised herself.

'Not going?' What on earth are you talking about?'

Her mother folded her arms across her broad bosom. She was dressed up in her Sunday best, ready to go to the cemetery. The whole family had gathered, too – Pop, Florence, Ruby and her daughters. Iris could feel the weight of all their disapproval as they stared at her.

Edie was there, too. Iris remembered what her brother had told her about Edie setting her sights on Jack. It seemed as if her friend had already made herself one of the Maguire clan.

'I suppose this is all his idea?' her mother said.

'He's got a name, Mum. And if you must know, Matthew has nothing to do with it. It was my decision.'

Her mother snorted. 'I don't believe it! You don't blow your nose without him saying you can these days.'

'Now then, May. Getting into an argument won't help anyone,' Pop said mildly. He turned to Iris. 'Are you sure, love? Happen it would do you good if you came with us, just this once?'

Iris shook her head. 'I've made up my mind, Pop. You can take Archie.' She looked down at her son beside her, freshly scrubbed and his hair neatly combed. He did not meet her eye. He had barely spoken a word to her since that morning.

She caught Ruby's eye. Even she looked sad and reproachful.

'Pop's right,' Edie spoke up. 'Honestly, you might feel better if you came.' She smiled, her face full of understanding. 'I know you're afraid, but—'

'How do you know what I feel?' Iris cut her off.

'I know because I felt the same after Rob died. I was too scared to let myself grieve for him because I thought the pain would be too much for me. I tried to hold it off, but that only made it worse . . .'

'I don't know what you're talking about,' Iris snapped. 'I don't even know why you're here. You in't part of this family, no matter how much you might think you are!'

Edie's face fell, and Big May stepped in.

'She's here because I invited her,' she said. 'And she might not be part of this family, but at least she cares. She goes to pay her respects to Dolly all the time. Unlike you, who was supposed to be her friend!'

241

'If Edie was such a good friend to Dolly, why is she trying to steal her husband?'

A shocked silence fell. Florence spoke first.

'What are you talking about? What's going on?' She looked from one to the other. 'What on earth does she mean, Edie?'

'I – I don't know,' Edie muttered, but her face had gone from deathly pale to deep crimson.

'Of course you don't!' Iris mocked. 'You mean to tell me you in't set your sights on our Jack? Making out you're so concerned about him and the boys, when all the time you're angling to get closer to him. You couldn't wait to step into Dolly's shoes, could you? I'll bet she was barely cold before you started—'

'That's enough!' Pop raised his voice and everyone shut up because it was so seldom heard. 'Stop it, Iris. You've said more than enough, I reckon.'

'It in't true,' Edie whispered. 'I swear it.'

Big May turned hostile eyes to Iris. 'I hope you're happy with yourself.'

You're not the woman I knew, Iris Fletcher.

Iris looked around her at the numb, shocked faces of her family. Happy was the last thing she felt.

Chapter Forty-One

Monday 5th May 1941

Edie felt as if all eyes were on her as she pushed Bobby's pram up Jubilee Row. Two days after the scene at Big May's house, she still felt as if the whole street was talking about her.

A hot wave of shame washed over her whenever she thought about what Iris had said, and the way they had all looked at her. Florence, Ruby, the twins, all staring at her in shock and revulsion. She did not think she had ever been so humiliated in her life.

The only mercy was that Jack himself had not been there to hear it. Although knowing the Maguires, it would not be long before word reached his ears.

Big May had been very nice about it.

'Take no notice, love,' she had said. 'It's just our Iris being spiteful. No one thinks any less of you.'

But that did not stop Edie feeling mortified. She was even more guilty and ashamed because deep down she was afraid there might be some truth to what Iris had said.

She had not meant it to happen, she hadn't even been aware of it until the night Bobby was taken ill, when she had sheltered at Jack's house. Even then, it was nothing more than the briefest moment, when Edie had looked into his eyes and felt something shift, as if everything was clicking into place, making sense at last. As if this was where she was meant to be.

She had pushed it to one side, told herself she was wrong

to feel that way. But then she had seen the look of startled recognition in Jack's face and it dawned on her that he might feel the same.

Or perhaps it had just been wishful thinking. Either way Edie could not dare think about it.

Iris was right, she should be ashamed of herself. What kind of friend would ever do such a thing? Even if she had never set out for it to happen, it was still wrong. That much was written on the Maguires' faces as they looked at her on that dreadful day.

She had been too embarrassed to leave the house all weekend. It was only Mrs Huggins's nagging that convinced her to venture out in the middle of a dreary Monday afternoon.

'Do you want me to make you those new curtains, or not?' she had demanded. 'Only if you do you're going to have to go into town and buy some material. I can't sew them out of thin air.'

So Edie had sneaked out of the house, looking this way and that, scurrying past Pearce's shop with her head down in case one of the Maguires happened to be in there, passing the time of day with Viv Pearce. She did not dare look up until she had gone all the way down Anlaby Road.

She was supposed to be going to Hammond's to look for the curtain material but she was fearful of running into Sybil or Maudie so she made her way up Ferensway and headed for Thornton Varley's on Prospect Street instead.

She managed to find a cheap and cheerful offcut to the measurements Mrs Huggins had given her. She was coming out of the shop with the parcel tucked under her arm when she spotted the tall, dark figure of Jack Maguire on the other side of the street.

She froze on the pavement opposite, her heart hammering

in her throat. It was as if her worst fear had somehow summoned him out of nowhere.

Edie turned away quickly, her head down, ready to hurry back into the shop. But a moment later he called out, 'Edie?'

She turned slowly to face him. He was waving to her from across the road. A bus rumbled past, obscuring him from view and for a moment Edie was tempted to run, but the next minute he was crossing the road towards her.

'I thought it was you.' He was smiling, but there were lines of strain around his eyes. 'Been shopping, have you?'

'Mrs Huggins is making me some new kitchen curtains.'

'Ah.' An awkward silence fell between them. Was this how it was going to be from now on, Edie wondered. She had never been tongue-tied with Jack before, but now she felt as nervous as –

As a girl in the first flush of love. She let her gaze drop, worried her feelings might show on her face.

'I've been on an errand myself,' Jack said. 'I had to take Lucky back to his owner.'

'No!' Edie glanced at Jack's feet, as if she might see the little dog sitting there as usual, his tail wagging eagerly.

'The ARP Warden came round last night. It turns out his owner lost his house and ended up moving in with his daughter and her family over in Holderness Road. No wonder we couldn't find him.' His mouth twisted. 'It was just by chance he was talking to one of the wardens over there and mentioned he'd lost his dog.'

'I expect he was happy to see him again?'

'Aye, they both were. Turns out the dog's name's Toby, so that's another mystery solved.' He looked down at the lead dangling from his hand. He was still smiling, but Edie could see the emotions he was doing his best to hide.

'How are the boys taking it?'

'Better than me, I reckon.' He shrugged. 'It's daft, in't it? I've spent all this time looking for the little lad's owner, and now he's been found, I didn't want to part with him. Still, I always knew we wouldn't have him forever.'

Edie looked up into his face and felt her heart break. He was smiling, but there was something so desperately vulnerable about him, it was all she could do not to put her arms around him and comfort him.

She dragged her gaze away, suddenly awkward. Jack did the same. 'Well, I won't keep you,' he said.

But as she went to walk away, he suddenly called after her, 'I don't suppose—'

'What?'

He hesitated. 'I don't suppose you'd like to come round later? Happen you could have a bit of tea with me and the boys? I know it sounds daft, but I could do with the company . . .'

It was an innocent offer, one she wouldn't have thought twice about before, but now it seemed charged with meaning. His dark eyes were fixed on hers, full of intent. In that moment Edie knew that she wasn't mistaken, that he had felt the same shift she had. It was like an electrical charge crackling between them.

He wasn't just asking her round for tea. He was reaching his hand out to her, inviting her to take that first step into an unknown future with him. And she knew if she said yes there would be no going back for either of them.

'I'm sorry Jack, I can't. I promised Mrs Huggins I'd play cards with her while Mr Huggins is on Home Guard drill,' she said.

The light of hope faded from Jack's eyes. 'I understand.' He gave her a resigned smile. 'It was a daft idea, wasn't it?'

Edie watched him walk away, his hands thrust in his pockets, broad shoulders hunched. She fought the urge to run after him.

No, she thought. *No, it wasn't a daft idea at all.*

Chapter Forty-Two

Wednesday 7th May 1941

'Hurry up, or we'll miss the first feature!'

'I'm nearly ready.' As Iris put her lipstick on in the mirror, she caught Matthew's amused reflection behind her.

'I don't know why you bother putting on make-up just to sit in the dark!' He turned to Archie. 'I'll never understand women, will you?'

Archie did not reply. He was packing up a bag with his sister's belongings. Kitty watched him with big solemn eyes, her favourite doll, Cathy, tucked firmly under her arm.

Iris clicked the top back on her lipstick. 'I can do that,' she said, reaching for the bag. But Archie held on to it firmly.

'I'd rather do it myself, then I know she's got everything.'

They stared at each other for a moment, and Iris saw the look of stony dislike in her son's face. She let go of the bag.

'You will be all right while we're gone, won't you?' she said.

'Of course he'll be all right,' Matthew answered for him. 'He can take care of himself and his sister. Can't you, Archie?'

Archie ignored him again. Iris caught Matthew's darkening frown and said, 'Archie? Uncle Matthew was speaking to you.'

Archie turned to Iris. 'Why can't we go to Granny May's?'

'I thought it would be nice for you to stay with Auntie Ruby instead. You'll have more fun with Sybil and Maudie.' She smiled brightly.

'I'd rather go to Granny May's.'

'Well, you can't.' Matthew stepped in again. 'You heard your mother, now stop whining like a baby.'

'I in't a baby,' Archie muttered.

'Then stop acting like one.'

Iris saw the look of resentment that passed between them, and stepped in quickly. 'That's enough,' she said to her son. 'Now fetch your things, and I'll walk you both up to Auntie Ruby's.'

'I can take Kitty by myself,' Archie said, scowling at Matthew. 'I in't a baby.'

'I wish you wouldn't speak to him like that,' she said to Matthew as they made their way up Anlaby Road, heading towards the city.

'Like what?'

'Telling him off all the time, calling him a baby. It upsets him.'

'He should grow a thicker skin, then.'

'I mean it, Matthew. I don't like it.'

Matthew looked sideways at her. 'You've never said anything before?'

'I'm saying it now.'

He fell sulkily silent. Iris wondered if she had offended him again and for once she was amazed to find that she did not really care.

She was tired of keeping the peace between him and Archie. More often than not she took Matthew's side and now she could see it was driving a wedge between her and her son.

She could not forget the way Archie had turned his cheek away when she had tried to kiss him goodbye. Sometimes when she looked at him, he seemed so lonely and sad, all she wanted to do was hug him.

But it wasn't all Matthew's fault. She was the one who had brought him into their home, she had handed over control to him. If things had turned sour, then she only had herself to blame.

She blamed herself for a lot of things, one way or another. Like the fact that she was hardly speaking to her family. She had not seen her mother for nearly a week, not since her outburst at Edie. Now she was too embarrassed to face them all. She knew the rest of the family had not forgiven her. Even Ruby had barely been able to bring herself to speak, let alone smile, when Iris asked her to look after the children. But being Ruby, of course she did not refuse. Angry as she was she would never turn down the chance to help someone.

She gazed up at the moon, like a bright new penny against the black velvet sky, and a shudder ran through her.

'Another bomber's moon.' Matthew spoke her thought aloud.

'Don't.' She looked around at the street, dark and quiet at eight o'clock in the evening. 'Happen we shouldn't have come out tonight, after all? What if there's a raid?'

'We'll be all right.'

'It's Archie and Kitty I'm worried about.'

'Your sister-in-law will look after them.'

'Yes, but I should be there . . .'

'They seem to manage quite well without you. Anyway, we can't waste the tickets,' Matthew went on. 'And you know how much I've been looking forward to seeing this film.' He put his arm around her. 'It's just a moon,' he said. 'Nothing to worry about.'

His casual comment stayed with her all through the film. While everyone else was laughing at the mad antics of the Crazy Gang on the screen, Iris could not stop thinking about what Matthew had said.

They seem to manage quite well without you.

She thought about Archie, carefully packing his sister's bag, insisting on doing it himself. When Kitty fell or hurt herself, it was her brother she always ran to, not Iris.

She thought of the dull resignation she saw in Archie's eyes, as if he expected nothing from her. She wasn't surprised. She had been away for such a long time, and the children had had to learn to rely on themselves and each other.

But it was more than that. She sent Matthew a sideways look in the darkness of the cinema. He was laughing loudly, his eyes fixed on the screen, oblivious to her.

She had brought him into her home, allowed him to take over, to make the decisions she should have been making. All because she was too frightened to take responsibility herself.

It had to change, she thought. *She* had to change.

The main feature was coming to an end, and the Crazy Gang was just about to defeat the Nazis and come home triumphant, when the picture flickered and Bud Flanagan's grinning face disappeared from the screen. The audience groaned in protest as a moment later the manager appeared, announcing that the air raid warning had just sounded. He told everyone to gather in the foyer where they would be guided to the nearest public shelter.

'That's a swizz,' Matthew complained. 'The film had nearly finished, too.'

'They must be expecting a bad one, otherwise they would have just put a message up on the screen,' Iris said, looking around her nervously. The rest of the audience were already filing along the rows.

She was right. As they made their way down the sweeping staircase, they could see the darkened foyer was crowded with people. Their voices mingled with an ominous rumbling from outside, like a thunderstorm crashing overhead.

'What on earth—'

'Wait. Don't go.' Iris hung back but Matthew was already pushing his way through the crowd towards the double doors.

'I wouldn't go out there just yet, mate.' The uniformed commissionaire stopped him as he went to push open the door. 'It's hell out there. The whole city's on fire, I reckon.'

A crash came, shaking the building. Everyone screamed and dropped to the floor.

Everyone except Iris. She stood staring at the flickering orange sky that even managed to penetrate through the blackout curtains.

She jumped as Matthew grasped her arm in the darkness. 'We'll stay here a minute, then we'll get to the shelter,' he said. 'There should be space in the one round the corner—'

'I want to go home.'

'Are you mad? You heard what that man said. The whole city is on fire.'

'I need to get back to the children.'

'You'll get yourself killed.'

'I don't care, I've got to go.' She remembered Archie's solemn little face, the way he looked at her. She had let him down more than once. But she wasn't going to do it again.

'Do as you please,' Matthew said. 'But I'm not coming with you.'

Iris stared at him. 'Fine,' she said. 'I'll go by myself.'

As she reached the door the commissionaire put out a hand to stop her.

'Just a minute, Missus—' he started to say but Iris side-stepped him.

'Let her go,' Matthew said. 'She'll be back soon enough. I know what you're like in an air raid. You get terrified at the slightest bang. You won't last five minutes out there . . .'

His taunting voice followed her as she pushed open the doors.

It was like walking into hell.

All around her, the city was burning. Everywhere she looked, Iris could see fire engulfing buildings, flames licking from rooftops. The sky blazed orange, bright as day. The air was hot, thick with dust and heat and bitter, stinging smoke.

And the noise – people screaming, sobbing, calling out to each other, the peal of bells as the fire appliances rushed past, so many of them, heading in all directions at once. The roar of planes, the dull explosions, the answering retort of the anti-aircraft fire. The crackle of fire and the creaks and groans and rumble as buildings collapsed and toppled around her. It was as if the whole city was being consumed before her eyes.

She stood for a moment, too transfixed by fear and horror to move, staring at the blazing building that had once been Hammond's department store. Flames licked from the rows of windows, consuming the domed roof where Iris had once gone dancing.

It couldn't be, she thought. It was all some terrible nightmare. In a minute she would open her eyes, and—

'Oi, Missus! Get some shelter.'

Iris turned around. A man was waving to her from a few yards away. Through the thick smoke she could make out the tin hat and overcoat of an ARP warden.

'Get some shelter!' His voice rose over the din. 'It in't safe to be stood out here—'

There was a bang and a blinding flash and suddenly he was gone. Iris stared at the space where he had been. He had disappeared as if by some horrible magic.

She looked back at the cinema doors.

You won't last five minutes out there.

Then she started to run.

Chapter Forty-Three

The water was ankle-deep in the shelter.

At the far end, John was singing 'One Man Went to Mow' to the children, his voice lost beneath the thunder of the falling bombs. Beattie Scuttle was weeping, her shoulders shifting silently. Families huddled together in corners, putting on brave faces, many praying silently.

May Maguire was saying a few prayers herself, even though she was not a religious woman. She was praying for her children, who had all turned out for their various duties as soon as the raid started, whether they were rostered or not. Jack had gone to join his ARP rescue team, Ruby had put on her green uniform and set off to open up the WVS emergency shelter on Anlaby Road, while Ada had gone to the nearest First Aid Post to see what help she could offer there.

'Be careful,' May had said to her daughter Florence as she donned her tin hat and boots.

Florence had smiled and said, 'You too, Mum,' and the pair had shared a rare moment of affection before she, too, disappeared into the night.

The shelter door opened and Sybil came tumbling down the steps, Kitty in her arms. Archie followed, carrying the bag. Maudie was behind them.

Kitty was wailing at the top of her voice.

'We've got to go back,' Archie was saying.

'I in't going back out there, thanks very much!' Sybil

dumped Kitty into her sister's arms and straightened her hat. 'What a night!' she gasped. 'Tell you what, I'm glad I in't on fire watching duty tonight. What do you say, Maudie?'

May looked from one to the other. 'Where's our Iris?'

'Gone to the pictures.'

'Why didn't she ask me to look after the bains?'

'I don't know, do I?' Sybil shrugged.

'I daresay she didn't like to, after what happened the other day,' Maudie put in. 'Now what?' she turned to Archie, who was tugging on her sleeve.

'We have to fetch it,' he said.

'What's all this?' May looked from Archie to Sybil and back again.

'They left Cathy behind,' Archie shot his cousins a baleful look. 'Kitty won't settle without her.'

'Half the city's on fire, and you want me to go out there and rescue a doll?'

'But Kitty needs—'

'Syb's right,' May cut him off. 'It's too dangerous to go out there, love.' She held out her arms. 'Here, give the bain to me. I'll try to settle her.'

Archie looked on, biting his lip, as Maudie handed the wailing Kitty into her arms.

'She won't settle,' he muttered. 'Not without her doll.'

No sooner had he said it than a tremendous bang came from outside. The ground rocked and the walls seemed to swell, then all the lights went out, plunging them into darkness.

For a moment everyone was shocked into silence, except for Kitty, who howled even louder. Then Beattie Scuttle started sobbing again, and somewhere in the darkness a voice began muttering the Lord's Prayer.

Dust showered May's face and she brushed it away.

'I don't think anyone's going anywhere for a while, lad,' she said.

Archie knew his grandmother was frightened. She was doing her best not to show it, but he could hear it in her voice. He had never known her show fear about anything before, and that only made him more scared.

Everyone was afraid. The adults were all singing and cheering on the anti-aircraft guns and telling each other jokes to hide it, but then they would pray, or cry, or whisper to each other that it was the worst raid they had experienced so far.

'It's been going on for hours. I'd be surprised if there's anything left by tomorrow,' he heard Mrs Lassiter saying in the darkness.

Archie lay curled up on one of the ledges next to Kitty, covered in Pop's old coat. The scratchy wool reeked of stale tobacco and horses, but somehow the smell comforted him.

It seemed to comfort Kitty, too. She had finally cried herself to sleep, much to everyone's relief.

'You see?' his grandmother said. 'I told you she would settle in the end.'

But Archie could hear his sister's tiny whimpers in the darkness, and he knew it would not be long before she woke up again.

At least she had managed to sleep. Archie did not know how many hours he had lain awake, staring into the darkness, worrying.

Where was his mother?

He wished he had not been so rotten to her before she left. But he was still angry at her for ignoring Lucy's birthday, and for being rude to Auntie Edie, and for letting Matthew ruin everything.

Beattie Scuttle was crying in the darkness. She had been

crying on and off for hours, longer than Kitty even.

'I don't know what's going to happen to our Charlie,' she sobbed to Archie's grandmother. 'He's going to be killed, I know he is. I wish he'd come to the shelter with me instead of wandering about out there.'

His mother was wandering about out there. Would she be killed, Archie wondered? Perhaps she was already dead, gone in a second like Lucy and Auntie Dolly.

Gradually, everyone fell silent. It was hard to tell in the darkness if they had fallen asleep or if they were just lost in their own thoughts. It felt as if it was just Archie lying awake, listening to the thudding and crashing from outside, his heart racing.

He can take care of himself and his sister. Can't you, Archie?

The responsibility settled on him like a huge weight, crushing his chest and making it hard to breathe. He had to look after his sister; he had no choice. His mother wasn't there and even if she was, Archie didn't think she really cared about looking after them any more.

But could he do it? He had failed before. He had not taken proper care of Lucy and look what had happened to her. Now Lucy was dead and his mother hated him for it.

'Mum?' Kitty stirred beside him.

'Shh, it's all right.' Archie put his arm around her, holding her close. 'Go back to sleep.'

But Kitty was already awake, wriggling from his grasp. 'I want Mum!'

'She'll be here soon. Go back to sleep, and when you wake up she'll be here.'

'Cathy?'

Archie's heart sank. 'Go to sleep, Kit,' he pleaded. 'You don't want to wake everyone up, do you?'

'Cathy! I want Cathy.'

'Shh! Let me think for a minute.' Archie sat up and rubbed his eyes.

He can take care of himself and his sister. Can't you, Archie?

This was his chance to redeem himself, he thought. He would not let anyone down this time. He would look after Kitty and perhaps his mother would learn to love him again.

He listened carefully. The crashing from outside seemed to have subsided, or perhaps he had just grown used to it.

He looked towards his grandmother. He couldn't be sure if she was asleep or not, but it did not matter. No one would see him leave in the dense darkness.

'I'll fetch your doll, all right? But you've got to be quiet until I get back. Promise me?'

Kitty nodded, her wide eyes still wet with tears. 'Cathy,' she whimpered.

'Go back to sleep.' Archie planted a kiss on her forehead and scrambled down from the ledge. 'And when you wake up I'll be back with Cathy and everything will be all right, I promise.'

Chapter Forty-Four

'What do you mean, he in't here?'

Iris shone her torch in Sybil's face. It was all she could do not to grab her niece by the throat and shake her. 'Where is he, if he in't with you?'

'We don't know.' Sybil looked shaken. 'He was here, I swear. He was sleeping over there with Kitty. Then all the lights went out, and the next minute he was gone.'

'Gone? Gone where?' Iris swung her torch around the shelter, the dim beam illuminating rows of pale, scared faces. The air was thick with dust and the stench of stale sweat, urine and fear.

It had taken her so long to get here, she had lost track of time. It seemed as if she had been fighting her way through the burning streets for hours, past buildings billowing black smoke and flame. Time and time again she had to turn back because streets were on fire, or blocked by drifts of smoking masonry or destroyed by giant craters. All the while wardens and policemen tried to stop her, warned her to find shelter. But Iris ignored them and pressed on. All she could think about were her children and how she needed to be with them.

And now she was finally here, and Archie was gone, and she was so exhausted by fear she almost could not take it in.

'I think he might have gone back to our house,' Maudie spoke up. 'Kitty was upset because we'd left her doll behind. Archie wanted us to go back to fetch it.'

Iris looked from one to the other. 'No!' The word escaped as a low moan from her throat. 'No, no, no . . .'

Pop put his hand on her arm. 'Try to stay calm, love—'

'My son's out there!' Iris shook him off. Panic seized her brain, stopping her breath in her chest. She turned on Sybil, savage with fury. 'How could you? How could you let him go?'

'I'm sorry, Auntie Iris.'

'Why didn't you watch him?'

'I did.'

'So how come he's gone? How come he's out there, on his own—'

Her voice cracked and Pop stepped in. 'Now then, blaming each other in't going to help anything.' He turned to Iris. 'The wardens are out looking for him. They'll find him, don't worry.'

'Have you seen it, Pop?' Iris pointed towards the door. 'The whole city's burning. There's a string of fire from here to St Andrew's Dock.' Someone whimpered with fear in the darkness. 'Do you really think they'll be looking for a little boy with all that going on?'

She looked around at the blank, helpless faces staring back at her. 'Well, I in't going to stand around waiting.' She snatched up her bag and headed for the door.

'Where are you going?' Pop said.

'To look for my son, where do you think?'

'You can't go, it's too dangerous.'

'You think I don't know that? I've just walked two hours through a burning city.'

'Iris, please—' Pop tried to hold her back but Iris wrenched free.

'Let me go, I've got to find Archie.'

'Leave her, Pop,' her mother said quietly. 'Let her do what she's got to do.'

Iris looked back over her shoulder at her mother. In the dim torchlight, May's tired face seemed to have aged twenty years. But her eyes were full of understanding. She knew what Iris had to do to make things right.

But the shelter warden, Harry Pearce, had other ideas. As Iris went to leave he stepped in front of the door, blocking her way.

'I'm sorry, Iris, I can't let you go,' he said.

Iris gritted her teeth, fighting to stay calm. 'Let me through, Harry.'

'It's for your own good.'

'I swear to God, Harry, if you don't step aside right now I'll knock you flat!'

Harry hesitated for a moment, his round face flushing deep crimson in the torchlight. Then he opened the door and stepped aside to let her through.

'I hope you find him.' His words followed Iris as she scrambled up the steps.

Outside the air was hot and thick with smoke. Iris covered her mouth with her handkerchief but the acrid fumes stung her eyes as she inched her way across Hessle Road. The blazing buildings on either side of the road had joined to make one long avenue of towering flame. The heat scorched her face, but Iris pushed on across the road. All she could think about was finding Archie.

There was an ARP warden on the corner of Jubilee Row.

'Sorry, love, you can't come down here,' he said.

'Why? What's happened?' Iris craned her neck to see past him. At the far end of the road she could make out a fire pump and a rising plume of smoke.

'Incendiary,' the warden said. 'They put it out but it's a

terrible mess. Managed to burn right through the roof and the bedrooms.'

'Which house?'

'Eh?'

'Which house was it? Tell me!'

'Far end, on the left. Here, you can't go down there, I said—'

But Iris had already dodged past him and was running down the street, screaming out Archie's name.

She stopped dead at the smouldering remains of Ruby's house. The front windows had been blown out, and the net curtains snagged on the jagged broken glass. Fire had eaten away at the roof and two firemen trained their hoses on the blackened brickwork of the upper floor, sending arcs of water into the night sky.

'Archie!' Iris ran towards the house. She heard the firemen call out to her as she sprinted past, but the next moment a pair of strong arms encircled her, lifting her off her feet.

'Let me go!' Iris struggled and kicked to escape, but the fireman held her fast.

'Iris, it's me.'

She went still at the sound of Sam's voice. Then she started again, trying to wrestle out of his grip.

'Let me go. I've got to find Archie—'

'*Archie's* here?' Sam relaxed his grasp and her feet touched the ground. Straight away she took off, running towards the house.

Sam caught up with her as she reached the front door, pulling her back.

'Don't, it's too dangerous.'

'I don't care.'

'I've told the warden. He's sending for the rescue party.'

'What if they don't get here in time? What if he's—'

Iris glanced fearfully towards the house. She tried to twist from Sam's grasp but he held on to her firmly.

'Listen to me.' Sam turned her to face him. 'They're going to get him out, Iris. I promise you.'

The next moment the fight had gone out of her and she was sobbing in his arms.

'They'll get him out,' he said, his breath warm against her hair. 'They'll find him, Iris, I promise. Look, here they come now ...'

Iris looked up to see three figures running down the street towards her, dressed in heavy coats and tin hats. They carried coils of thick rope and torches, and one had a sledgehammer over his shoulder.

She recognised one of them and her heart lifted with hope.

'Jack!' She ran towards her brother. 'Oh Jack, thank God it's you!'

He dropped the rope and caught her in his arms. 'Iris, what are you doing here?' He looked from her to Sam, realisation dawning. 'They said a boy was trapped. It in't—'

'Find him, Jack,' Iris begged. 'Bring him back to me.'

Jack glanced towards the house, then back at her. 'I will,' he promised.

As he walked away, Sam called after him, 'Is there anything I can do?'

Jack nodded towards Iris. 'Look after her,' he said tersely, then turned and followed the other men.

And then came the wait. Sam stayed at her side, but Iris was barely aware of him as she paced restlessly back and forth.

'I should never have left him,' she said. 'If I'd stayed in tonight he would have been safe.'

'You weren't to know.'

'I should have been there,' she insisted. 'I'm his mother, I should have been there to protect him. But I let him down. Just like I let Lucy down.'

She dragged her gaze back to the house. She would change all that, if she got the chance. *Please God*, she prayed, *please let him be safe so I can make it up to him.*

Sam put his arm around her and she leaned against him, glad of his quiet strength as the storm rumbled and raged around them.

They were still standing there when a tall, shambling figure headed through the smoke towards them.

'Charlie!' Sam greeted his brother with a frown of concern. 'What are you doing here?'

Charlie ignored his brother, turning to Iris with a questioning look. She opened her mouth to speak, but no words came.

'Archie's missing,' Sam said. He glanced towards Ruby's house. Charlie followed his brother's gaze, and his expression changed to a look of alarm.

'Jack's in there now,' Sam said. 'They're going to get him out.'

Charlie looked back towards the house, and for a moment Iris saw the flicker of uncertainty in his eyes.

'What?' she said. 'What is it, Charlie?'

'Nowt,' Sam said quickly. 'He's just worried for you, that's all.'

Charlie hesitated a moment, then he nodded and his hand moved tentatively to rest on Iris's shoulder, his eyes full of gentle sympathy.

Dread uncurled itself in Iris's stomach. She knew Charlie's expertise as a tunneler and his brush with death had given him a kind of sixth sense. But before she had a chance to ask him, Sam suddenly said, 'Someone's coming out of the house!'

Iris's heart shot into her throat. 'Is it Jack? Has he got Archie?'

But it wasn't Jack. The man was hurrying towards them, his head down so she could not read his face. As he approached, Iris noticed he was holding something in his hand, but she couldn't make it out.

She gripped Sam's hand, her whole body tensing. Then the man looked up and she saw he was smiling.

'Jack's found him,' he said. 'He's alive.'

'Oh, thank God!' Iris's legs buckled underneath her, and she would have fallen if Sam hadn't been there to hold her up. 'Is he all right?'

The man nodded. 'Part of the chimney collapsed and he got trapped underneath the rubble.'

'Oh God!'

'It's all right, Jack reckons there are no bones broken. But the smoke weakened him, which is why he couldn't free himself. Jack's getting him out now. He gave me this for you . . .'

Iris took the filthy, battered doll he was holding out to her, and felt herself breaking inside. Cathy was sopping wet and reeked of smoke, but she was safe. And so was her son.

Beside her, Charlie let out a sudden gasp, like an underwater swimmer coming up for air. Sam turned to his brother.

'What is it? What's wrong?' he asked, but Charlie did not seem to hear him. His terrified gaze was fixed on the far end of the street, as if he could see something no one else could.

'Charlie?' Iris reached for him but he flinched away.

A moment later, there was a cry from outside Ruby's house.

They all turned to look, except Charlie, who looked down, covering his face. A low, animal groan came from deep in his throat. It was the first sound Iris had heard him make in years.

'What the—?' the man started to say, but Sam held up his hand.

'Look! The house!'

'Oh, Christ, it's going.'

The brickwork seemed to groan and shift, as if it was stirring from sleep. Suddenly people were shouting, running, calling out to each other. But Iris could only watch as, with an agonisingly slow rumble of collapsing brickwork, the house crumpled in on itself with a grinding crash, sending a cloud of bright sparks up into the smoky air.

Chapter Forty-Five

'What time is it, do you think?'

'I don't know. Must be nearly dawn, I reckon.'

'Surely not. Has it really been that long?'

'It feels like longer to me.'

'You'd think they'd bring some lights down, wouldn't you?'

'Is it still going on, do you think?'

As if in answer to the question, a resounding crash shook the walls of the shelter, showering them all with dust.

'Blimey,' someone joked feebly, 'You'd think the Nazis would have run out of bombs by now!'

'Sounds to me like they've been home and fetched some more!'

Edie listened to the comments going back and forth around her. Everyone was doing their best to keep themselves cheerful, but she could hear the strain in their voices.

They had been sitting in darkness for hours, water lapping around their ankles and shrapnel clattering down on the concrete roof above them, listening to the thunder of the raid outside. There had been a terrible moment earlier when smoke started to fill the shelter and everyone started to panic. But Harry Pearce had ventured outside and discovered it was just a telegraph pole on fire close by. He'd quickly summoned another warden and together they had put out the flames with a stirrup pump.

'Good old Harry!' Mr Lassiter chuckled when the warden

came down the steps to a hero's welcome. 'Remember when he tried to show us how to use one last year? I said to the wife then, "I bet he makes a right cod's of it when the time comes." But you didn't, did you? Good on you, lad.'

'He must have been practising since then!' Alice Barnitt said.

Edie smiled sadly. She remembered the demonstration at the school hall, when Harry and Florence had nearly burned the place down and Sam Scuttle had had to come to the rescue.

It all seemed like such a long time ago now. They were still at war, but there had been no air raids over the city, and no one had taken Harry's demonstration seriously.

And now look at them, buried in a shelter, terrified, while German planes rained fire on their city.

She glanced across at Big May. She could just make out the outline of her bulky body in the darkness, sitting between Pop and Beattie Scuttle. Kitty was curled up in her lap.

Usually Edie would have been sitting with them, listening to the older women talking. But she was still too embarrassed to face them, so she kept a careful distance on the other side of the shelter.

'Iris should be back by now.' Sybil finally dared to speak aloud the thought that had been in all their minds. 'Do you think she's all right?'

No one answered.

'It's my fault, in't it?' Sybil whimpered. Again, no one spoke.

The water that covered the floor of the shelter had seeped into Edie's shoes. She took them off and put them up on one of the ledges to dry out.

Poor Iris, she thought. There might be a rift between them, but Edie still felt for her. She could only imagine what she was going through.

She looked at Bobby, sleeping soundly in his pram, oblivious to everything going on around him. She was lucky he was so young and unaffected by it all. The poor baby had been born into war, he had never known a time when there were no air raids or shelters or bombs crashing down.

She tried to imagine how she would feel if he was older and had got lost out there on the bombed-out streets. She knew that like Iris, she would be out there looking for him. It would be nothing to risk her life because her life would not be worth living if anything happened to her son.

The door to the shelter opened and another ARP warden came down the steps, the beams from his torch illuminating the darkness. They all watched as he paused at the foot of the steps to speak to Harry Pearce.

'What are they talking about?' Beattie wanted to know.

'I daresay we'll find out sooner or later,' Pop said.

'Happen he's brought some lamps with him,' Mr Lassiter said. 'I'm sick of sitting here in the pitch black.'

'You're welcome to go outside,' one of the other neighbours said. 'I daresay it's nice and bright out there.'

The men finished talking and Harry pointed over to the corner where the Maguires had congregated. The ARP warden swung his torch, briefly illuminating Big May's face. Her features were stiff with terror, Edie noticed.

'Mr and Mrs Maguire?'

'That's us.' Pop stood up, shielding his wife. 'What's to do?'

The whole shelter fell silent, watching their conversation.

'I hope Iris is all right,' Sybil whispered. Edie kept her gaze fixed on Big May's face, trying to work out from her expression what might have happened. But while Pop nodded and spoke to the warden, May Maguire's face was like a mask, giving nothing away.

As the ARP warden left the shelter, climbing the steps,

Edie saw Big May gathering herself, her broad shoulders straightening. She also saw the worried glance she exchanged with her husband before he spoke.

'We've had a bit of news,' he announced.

'Is it Archie?' Sybil jumped in. 'Has he been found? Please say they're all right.'

'Shh!' Maudie nudged her. 'Let Pop speak.'

'Aye, he's been found, all right,' Pop said. 'But it in't as straightforward as that.'

'Is he all right?' Maudie whispered.

Pop paused, drawing in a deep breath. 'He's trapped inside a burned-out building,' he said. 'They're trying to rescue them now.'

'What?'

'No!'

'Oh God!' A chorus of dismay rippled around the shelter. Edie said nothing. Dread dripped like ice down her spine.

'Them.' She didn't realise she had spoken out loud until all eyes swivelled in her direction.

'You said "them". Who else is trapped?'

Everyone looked back at Pop.

'Is it Iris?' Sybil said.

But Edie somehow already knew the answer. It was like a warning, singing in her blood, even before Pop said, 'Our Jack had gone in to save him when the place collapsed.'

'Can they get them out?' Maudie said.

Edie saw the look that passed between Pop and May. 'They're doing their best. They've called in the rest of the rescue party to help.' He glanced towards the corner of the shelter, where Freddie and George were sleeping. 'Not a word to his lads until we know for sure what's happening, all right?'

Everyone murmured their agreement.

'Is there anything we can do?' Edie said.

May turned her head to look at her for the first time, and Edie thought she saw the shadow of a smile.

'Just wait, lass,' she said sadly. 'Wait and pray.'

'Why are they wasting so much time talking? Don't they know every second counts?'

'They're just trying to work out the best way of getting to them.'

'They've been standing there for ages!'

'It's only been a couple of minutes, Iris,' Sam said patiently. 'They're doing all they can.'

'Well, it in't enough!' Iris paced restlessly back and forth across the street, oblivious to the rumble of the bombs and the flashes that lit up the sky. 'I can't just stand here waiting, I'm going to find out what's going on.'

'Iris, wait—'

'I can't wait, Sam. Not any more. My son and my brother are in there and I'm going to get them out even if I have to dig them out with my own bare hands!'

'And then what will happen to you?' Sam snapped.

'I don't care!' Emotion clogged her throat. 'Do you think I give a damn what happens to me? Do you?'

'No, but I do,' Sam said softly.

Charlie got to his feet. He had been sitting so quietly, Iris had nearly forgotten he was there until he stood up and walked towards the rescue party.

'Where are you going?' Sam called after him, but Charlie ignored him. He walked with a heavy, shambling gait, his head down.

'Charlie?' Sam hurried after him and tried to grab his arm, but Charlie shrugged him off and walked over to the men. Sam followed him.

Iris watched the scene from a distance. Charlie was

pointing towards the shattered remains of the house, making sketchy movements with his hands. Sam was talking to the rescue workers. He looked as if he was translating, but whatever he was saying, he did not look happy about it.

When Charlie bent down to pick up the coiled rope at his feet, it slowly began to dawn on Iris why Sam was looking so serious.

'No,' she whispered. 'No, he can't.'

She crossed the street just in time to hear Sam saying, 'Listen to him, for God's sake. He knows what he's talking about.'

'What's happening?' Iris looked at Charlie, who was tying a rope around his waist. 'He can't mean to go in there, surely?'

'It looks like it,' Sam said. 'He reckons he can go in through next door. The way it came down, he says there's bound to be a crack or something in the adjoining wall. He can tunnel his way through from there.'

The men exchanged uneasy looks. 'It's risky.' The head of the party looked doubtfully at Charlie. 'Do you reckon he can do it?'

'If he says he can.' Sam nodded. 'My brother knows more about tunnels than the rest of us ever will.'

'But he'll be terrified.' Iris turned to Charlie. He did not look terrified. He didn't even look like Charlie Scuttle any more. Not the pale, frightened man who refused to venture down the steps to the air raid shelter, at any rate. There was a grim determination to him as he donned a tin hat and jammed a hammer into his belt. When he looked at Iris, she could almost see the grinning young man she vaguely remembered as a child, the boy who had carried her on his shoulders as he marched off to war with the other lads.

'Are you sure, Charlie?' she said.

Charlie reached out and squeezed her hand reassuringly. Then he turned and nodded to the other men and slowly began to pick his way through the rubble.

Chapter Forty-Six

Thursday 8th May 1941

Ruby was washing baby bottles at the sink when the All Clear sounded just after half past eight.

She stopped, lifting her head as the familiar drone filled the air outside. She did not think she would ever hear such a welcome sound.

'Thank the lord for that,' she heard Maggie Cornell cry out. 'I was beginning to think it would never end.'

'They must have run out of things to hit,' Olive Oxley replied gloomily.

It had been a long, exhausting night. As soon as the siren sounded the previous evening, Ruby had telephoned the ARP office for instructions, and had been told to open up the rest centre on Anlaby Road.

The other women were already waiting for her when she arrived. Ruby was impressed at the turnout; even the likes of Maggie and Olive, who had not been on the roster for that night, had come to lend a hand.

As it happened, they needed all the help they could get. Throughout the night people poured through their doors, looking for sanctuary, advice and comfort. ARP workers and policemen dropped in all night, along with terrified neighbours just looking for a cup of tea and a friendly face.

Some had lost everything. Ruby and the other women set up camp beds for them, gave them food and drink and fresh clothes to wear. They had even taken in the injured when the local First Aid Post got hit.

As fast as people came in, they were billeted out. But there were so many of them, it was a struggle to find them a place to stay. Emergency hostels quickly filled up as it became clear that the whole city had been affected. Soon Ruby was making frantic telephone calls to people's distant relatives and even casual acquaintances, only to find that they, too, had been bombed out and were looking for a place to stay.

On top of that, they still had to keep the refreshment vans stocked and out on the street, as well as supplying endless urns of tea to the rescue parties.

Sometime in the middle of it all, Ruby was too busy to notice when, a policeman came in for a cup of tea and happened to mention that they had seen a fire burning in Jubilee Row.

Everyone looked at Ruby, who was on the telephone, trying to find emergency accommodation for a family of six and a canary.

'That's where you live, in't it?' Maggie Cornell said.

'Yes.' Ruby kept her head down, ticking off addresses on the list in front of her.

'Do you want to go home?' Alice Peachey said.

'Why?'

Alice glanced at the other women. 'I just thought you might want to check on your family . . .'

'I'm sure I'll hear soon enough if there's owt wrong. Besides, there's too much work to do here.' Thankfully the telephone rang before Alice could say any more. Ruby snatched up the receiver. 'Hello? And you can take all six? That's wonderful, thank you. I'm very grateful. And did I mention the canary?'

Once the All Clear had sounded, there was even more to

do. Telegrams started arriving, sent on from the town clerks' office and the ARP, from concerned friends and relatives. Others turned up in person from all corners of the city, desperate to track down missing loved ones.

Families who had been billeted for the night returned, looking for help with clothes, ration books, missing paperwork.

One poor woman came in to identify her husband's body, and Ruby had to break it to her that it had been moved up to Spring Bank.

'But I went there first and they told me he was here!' The poor woman looked utterly exhausted and near to tears.

'I'm dreadfully sorry,' was all Ruby could offer in response. She had never felt so helpless, even though she was doing the best she could.

And all the time the telephone rang with yet more requests for help. The newly opened Communal Feeding Centre on Prospect Street had been damaged, and volunteers needed to go down to the Emergency Cooking Depot and help prepare five hundred meals. Water mains had been hit all over the city, and the ARP were calling for urns of water to be delivered. Firemen who had been working all night at the Rank Flour Mill needed a mobile canteen.

'Honestly, what do they take us for?' Maggie said, exasperated. 'We've been working all night!'

'The WVS never says no, remember?'

'That's as may be, but I'd like to get home to my bains.'

Ruby looked at the woman's weary, worried face. 'I can take the van out by myself,' she said.

Hope lit up Maggie's face, then she shook her head. 'Miss Brekke wouldn't like it.'

'Miss Brekke in't here, is she?' Ruby patted her shoulder. 'You get off and have a rest.'

'Not much chance of that!' Maggie grimaced. 'My mother's

just telephoned to say her chimney came down in the night and now the parlour's full of soot!'

It wasn't until Ruby set foot outside the Rest Centre, carrying a box of supplies to the van, that it finally hit her how truly bad the previous night's raid had been.

Tears sprang to her eyes as she looked around, trying to take it all in. She set down the box and stared at the tortured landscape of cratered streets and wrecked buildings, some of them still wrapped in flames. Water from broken mains gushed up through the street, which was lifted and split as if an earthquake had hit it.

She barely recognised the city. The whole skyline had changed overnight. There were no straight lines or tidy shapes left; every outline was jagged and broken, every building askew. The street before her had been reduced to a blazing shambles, with roofless, smoking buildings and bent, decapitated lamp posts. The trolleybus wires had come down, draped like cotton across the piles of smoking rubble.

'Mum?'

She swung round. Her daughter Maudie stood behind her, wrapped in a heavy coat in spite of the sunlit May morning.

Ruby took one look at her pale, distraught face and she felt herself crumple. 'What is it? What's happened? Is someone hurt?'

'Is there somewhere we can go?' Maudie said. 'I need to talk to you . . .'

Chapter Forty-Seven

Iris and Sam sat in the hospital corridor, side by side, neither of them speaking. Doctors and nurses hurried back and forth, but no one spared them a glance as they sat in silence, lost in their own thoughts.

'You don't have to stay, if you want to be with Charlie?' Iris broke the silence.

'The nurse says he's still sleeping. I'll wait till Ma gets here before we wake him up. Unless you'd rather be on your own?' He sent her a sideways look.

She looked down at his hand, entwined in hers. It was still grimy with soot, the back flecked with red where sparks had burned him.

'No,' she said.

His fingers tightened around hers, strong and reassuring, just as he had been through those long hours of the night.

It was strange, she thought. Under the mantle of darkness she had found it so easy to talk to him. But their closeness had faded with the dawn, and now they were as mute as strangers.

'They'll be all right, you know,' Sam said.

'I hope so.'

She looked down at the doll, lying in her lap. Cathy's hair was thick and matted with dust, her dress filthy and torn. She had been clinging to it all night like a lifeline.

Beattie came round the corner, all in a fluster. Iris

automatically let go of Sam's hand, but Beattie barely looked her way as she made straight for her son.

'How is he?' she wanted to know.

'He's resting.'

'Resting? What does that mean?' Beattie's voice sharpened. 'He's all right, in't he?'

'Yes, Ma. A bit battered, but he's fine.'

Beattie's narrow shoulders relaxed. 'Is it true what they said about him? That he's a hero?'

'He is, Ma.'

Iris listened quietly as Sam told his story. She felt as if she had already lived through every painful moment a thousand times.

It had taken hours for Charlie to tunnel his way through the crumbling masonry, in a space barely wider than his shoulders, edging inch by inch for fear that the whole lot would fall in on him. All the while Iris had waited, clutching Sam's hand, desperately willing him on and trying not to think that if he reached Jack and Archie at all, he might already be too late.

For a long time there was silence. And then, just as Iris was letting go of her last shred of hope, one of the rescuers came running over and said, 'He can hear them. They're half buried, but they're alive. The little lad's asking for water!'

Iris had fallen into Sam's arms, sobbing with relief. But then there followed another agonising few hours as Charlie had to shore up the narrow tunnel enough to drag Archie through, Jack pushing him from behind as best he could.

Iris's heart had nearly burst when she saw Charlie emerge, coughing and choking from the dust in his lungs, carrying the limp little figure over his shoulder.

Beattie listened to her son's story in amazement. 'Charlie?' she murmured. 'Our Charlie did that?'

Sam nodded. 'And he insisted on going back in with the rest of the rescue team to help clear the debris that was trapping Jack so he could get out too.'

'He saved them,' Iris added quietly. 'He's a hero, Beattie.'

'Aye.' Beattie allowed herself a little smile of pride. 'I always knew he was.' Then she turned to Iris and said, 'How are Jack and the bain?'

'We're still waiting for news.' Iris lowered her gaze. Getting them out was one thing, but it was only half the battle. Archie had been overcome by the smoke, and even though Jack had managed to get them both to safety under a table when the house began to collapse, they had still suffered broken and dislocated limbs.

'They'll be all right, lass.'

How can you say that? Iris wanted to snap. But then she saw the kindness and sympathy in Beattie's eyes. She was only trying to help, she thought.

'I know,' she said quietly.

'Happen we should go and see if our Charlie's awake, now you're here?' Sam seemed to notice her struggling and stepped in quickly.

No sooner had he gone than Iris missed him. She couldn't bear to be alone with her thoughts. Even when she and Sam weren't speaking, she still took strength from him just being there.

She suddenly remembered Matthew, and was shocked that she had not thought of him at all. He had been so far from her mind she didn't even stop to wonder if he'd got home safely the previous night.

She was glad he wasn't here with her. He would probably tell her to stop crying, or to pull herself together, or something. He would certainly not put his arms around her and hold her while she sobbed.

He was not the right man for her, she realised. She had thought of him as a tower of quiet strength, but now she could see that he lacked compassion. Whether it was just the way he was, or the result of losing his family, Iris did not know. But she understood that he saw any kind of emotion as a weakness, to be pushed down or ignored completely.

She had thought that was what she needed, too. But last night had shown her that it was not.

And it was definitely not what her son needed.

Chapter Forty-Eight

A nurse hurried by with an armful of linen, and Iris stopped her.

'Please, is there any news about my son?' she asked. 'He was brought in last night.'

The nurse glanced up the corridor with a frown, put out at being stopped in her tracks. 'So were a lot of people. We're very busy, as you can tell—'

'I know, Nurse, but if you wouldn't mind checking? Their names are Jack Maguire and Archie Fletcher—'

'Maguire?' The nurse looked at her closely. 'Do you mean Ada's uncle?'

Iris smiled. 'Do you know Ada?'

'Of course, we're often on duty together.' The nurse patted her arm. 'I'll have a word with the ward sister and find out what's going on,' she said.

'Would you? I'd be ever so grateful.'

The nurse hurried off with her linen and Iris went to the window to look out. They had taken Archie and Jack to the Sutton Annexe on the eastern edge of the city, the closest hospital since the Infirmary took a hit at the end of March.

They had all been so shocked when the hospital was lost, along with the Shell Mex building on Ferensway. It had seemed like the end of the world at the time.

Now, looking out of the window, she knew what the end of the world really looked like.

Last night had been a nightmare, but to see the smouldering remains of the city in the daylight was even more shocking.

Everything was gone. Hammond's, Thornton Varley's, Bladons, were all reduced to smoking rubble and a tangle of twisted girders. Clouds of black smoke rose from buildings that still burned hours later.

There were no buses, so Iris had had to go through the city on foot, retracing the terrifying journey she had made the night before. On King Edward Street, the tower of the Prudential Assurance Building rose defiantly through the fog of smoke and dust, but it was battered and badly listing. All around it were huge gaps where once proud buildings had stood. Prospect Street was a line of ruins, with the beautiful church roofless and smoking.

She heard footsteps behind her and turned, thinking it was the nurse coming back. But instead she found herself face to face with Edie Copeland.

Edie stopped dead when she saw her. The two women regarded each other warily down the length of the corridor.

'May told me to come,' Edie blurted out defiantly. 'She had to stay at home and look after Kitty, so she sent me to find out how he was. But they won't tell me anything because I in't family . . .'

Iris saw the raw despair in the girl's eyes. Whatever feelings Edie had for Jack were real, she thought.

'I don't know much either,' she said. 'I've asked the nurse to go and find out. The last I was told, they'd put his broken leg in traction and they were waiting for him to wake up so they could check him for concussion.'

Edie winced. 'And what about Archie?'

Iris shook her head. 'He hasn't woken up either. They're worried the smoke might have damaged his lungs.'

'Oh, Iris, I'm so sorry.'

This time the sympathy was too much for her and all the grief and fear she had been holding in came out in a huge sob.

'Come here, love.' Edie put her arms around her, hugging her close.

'I don't want to lose him, Edie,' Iris wept into her friend's shoulder. 'I don't think I could bear it, not after Lucy . . .'

'I know, pet. I know.' Edie stroked her hair. 'It'll be all right, I know it will. You won't lose him. He's a tough little lad, your Archie.'

'I wish I could believe that.' She pulled away from Edie, sniffing back her tears. 'I'm sorry,' she said. 'I don't know why you're being so nice to me, after all the horrible things I said to you.'

'That doesn't matter,' Edie said. 'None of it matters any more.'

'But it does,' Iris insisted. 'You're my friend, and I was cruel to you.'

'We all lash out when we're upset.'

'I didn't do it because I was upset. I did it because you were right and I didn't want to admit it.' She wiped her eyes on her sleeve. 'You touched a nerve when you said I was too afraid to grieve. The truth is, I miss Lucy and Dolly so much, I can't even let myself think about them, in case . . .'

'In case it's too much for you?' Edie finished. Iris looked into her friend's face, so full of understanding. 'I felt like that about Rob. I couldn't even allow myself to remember the happy times, because I was so afraid I wouldn't be able to cope. I can't even imagine how it must have been for you, losing your baby—'

'It broke me,' Iris said quietly. Just saying it out loud felt like a weight lifting from her shoulders. 'That was why I couldn't come home for so long. I didn't know how I'd ever manage, surrounded by all those memories . . .'

It had been hard enough in the hospital. Day after day, she had felt herself descending into that deep well of sadness, and she knew when it happened she would never be able to climb out.

'So you tried to run away from them instead?' Edie nodded, understanding.

'It was just easier to cut myself off,' Iris said.

Matthew had become part of that. He encouraged her, made her feel as if she was following the right path, that if she kept pushing down the grief and pretending it was not there then she would get through it.

But there was another reason why she had attached herself to him so determinedly. She was afraid to risk her heart again. She knew her feelings for Matthew would never run too deep. If she lost him she would never feel the same crippling despair that she feared so much.

She understood now that it was the reason she had kept Sam and her son at arms' length. She was too scared to let them close in case she lost them.

'I've been such a fool,' she mumbled. 'I've pushed away everyone I've ever cared about.'

'Lucky thing we in't that easy to get rid of, eh?' Edie said, putting her arm through Iris's.

Iris looked at her friend. 'How do you get over the pain?' she asked.

Edie's smile faded. 'You don't,' she said quietly. 'But you do learn to live with it.'

'And you learn to love again?'

Edie caught her eye and blushed deeply. 'I don't—' she started to say, but Iris interrupted her.

'You can stop pretending, Edie. I know I'm right about you and our Jack. You've fallen for him, in't you?'

Edie turned away guiltily. 'I know it's all wrong, but I can't help it,' her words came out in a rush. 'I didn't mean it to happen, honestly. Nothing was further from my mind. I truly didn't think I'd ever feel that way about anyone after Rob—'

'And how does my brother feel?' Iris asked.

'I don't know. I – I think he feels the same.' A deep blush rose in Edie's face. 'But I know nothing can come of it,' she added quickly.

'Why not?'

'Because Dolly was my friend . . .'

'Dolly's gone, love,' Iris said gently. 'And besides, if Jack was going to find someone else, don't you think she'd want it to be someone she liked?'

Edie looked hopeful. 'So you think she'd approve?'

'Well, I don't know about that,' Iris laughed. 'Knowing Dolly, she'd probably slap your face for you!'

'I reckon she would, too!' Edie smiled sheepishly.

'But she wouldn't like the idea of her Jack being lonely. And if you make each other happy . . .' she shrugged.

'What about your family? I don't know what your mum would say about it. They've all been so good to me, I don't want her to disapprove.'

'Edie Copeland, will you listen to yourself?' Iris turned on her. 'Fretting away about this and that. Blimey, lass, if this war's taught us anything, it's that life's too short to waste worrying about what other folk think. If life gives you a second chance at happiness, you've got to grab it while you can. Besides,' she added, 'you think Mum doesn't already know about you and Jack? Believe me, my mother's got a sixth sense when it comes to her children. And if she sent you here, then I reckon that means you've got her blessing.'

'Do you really think so?'

Before Iris had a chance to reply, the nurse came down the corridor.

'Mrs Fletcher?' she said. 'Your son's awake, if you'd like to see him?'

Archie was groggily aware of someone moving around him. He heard the rattle of metal rings as a curtain was swished aside, then the sound of water being poured from a jug. When he breathed in, he could smell carbolic soap.

He opened his eyes, squinting in the sunlight that poured in through the window. At first he thought the woman at his bedside might be his cousin Ada in her starched apron and striped uniform, but this nurse was much older. She smiled down at him, her face kind and motherly.

'Good morning,' she greeted him. 'How are you feeling, my dear?'

'My chest hurts.' He didn't recognise the strange, gruff voice that came out of his mouth. He breathed in and felt a burning sensation between his shoulder blades.

'I'll talk to Sister about getting you something for the pain. Here, try this—' The nurse offered him the glass of water from his bedside. Archie shook his head, but she insisted. 'Go on, it will help you.'

As Archie sipped the water, his gaze moved past the nurse to the empty chair beside his bed.

'Where did she go?' he asked.

'Who?'

Archie looked at the empty chair. It must have been a dream, he thought. And yet he remembered everything, every single detail . . .

He looked up at the nurse, who was watching him with a curious expression. 'Who was here?' she repeated.

Archie looked away quickly. 'My mum,' he mumbled. 'I thought she was here.'

The nurse smiled. 'Your mother's been waiting outside all night,' she said. Then she cocked her head and added, 'I think I hear her coming now.'

Footsteps hurried down the ward, the curtain was wrenched aside and suddenly there she was, standing at the foot of his bed.

She did not look like his mother. She seemed older, more haggard. Her dark hair hung in untidy strands around her dirt-streaked face. Her eyes were wild and bloodshot, her mouth twisted in a grimace. A blackened object dangled from her grimy hand. Archie looked down and saw it was Cathy, his sister's doll.

He couldn't help himself. He started to tremble, and the next minute he was sobbing uncontrollably.

'Oh, Archie!' The doll fell to the floor and his mother ran to him, throwing her arms around him and pulling him close.

Was this still a dream, Archie wondered. But then he felt his mother's heart beating against his, smelt the scent of her, and he knew it was real. It was the first time his mother had really held him properly since before Lucy died.

'Careful,' he heard the nurse saying. 'He's already dislocated his shoulder once.'

His mother released him, but she sat on the edge of his bed, as close as she could get, holding on to his hand.

'You had us all worried,' she said.

'I'm sorry.'

'It doesn't matter now. You're here, and that's all I care about.' She reached out and Archie tried not to flinch as she stroked a strand of hair from his face. 'What do you remember?'

'I – I'm not sure.' His glance flicked to the chair beside the bed. He couldn't tell what was real and what wasn't any more. 'I was in the house, and it was full of smoke, and I couldn't find my way out. But I wasn't frightened. All I wanted to do was lie down and go to sleep. But then Uncle Jack was there, and I didn't recognise him at first because the smoke was so thick and he had a scarf over his mouth, hiding his face. He told me we had to get out.' His words tumbled out in a rush as the memories came flooding back. 'We were trying to find our way to the back door but then there was a big noise from upstairs, and Uncle Jack shoved me under the table and dived in on top of me, and then I didn't remember anything else until I heard Uncle Jack saying they'd come to get us.' He hesitated, trying to make sense of the muddle inside his head. 'Uncle Jack said it was Charlie who'd come to rescue us, but I know that can't be right . . .'

'It was,' his mother said. 'Charlie burrowed his way in to get you.'

'So it was him at the other end of the tunnel?' Archie was thoughtful for a moment, taking it in. If that was true, then perhaps the rest of the story was true, too? 'I know it sounds daft, but I heard him speaking to me. He asked me if I wanted a drink, and then he reached through the tunnel and passed some water to me.' He remembered the long arm stretching through, his grimy fingertips barely reaching, curled around the metal flask. 'But I must have imagined that bit, because I know Charlie don't talk.'

His mother smiled. 'After last night, nothing Charlie Scuttle did would surprise me any more.' She looked at him thoughtfully. 'Do you remember anything else?'

Once again, Archie glanced at the chair beside the bed. He didn't want to tell her the rest of what he had seen. He wasn't sure how she would take it, and she was being so nice to him, he didn't want to upset her.

He shook his head. 'Nothing.'

He looked at the blackened body of the doll lying on the floor. 'I'm sorry I caused so much trouble,' he mumbled. 'I only wanted to fetch the doll for Kitty. Granny May said I wasn't to go, but Kitty was crying so much, and I knew you'd be angry with me if I didn't look after her—'

'Why would you think I'd be angry with you?'

He glanced at her briefly, then flicked his gaze away. 'You're angry with me for not looking after Lucy.'

For a long time his mother did not speak. When Archie finally risked another look at her, he was shocked to see her weeping silently, her head bowed, shoulders heaving.

He couldn't remember the last time he'd seen her cry. Archie rushed to comfort her, desperate to find the right words to make things right again. 'I'm sorry, Mum, I didn't mean to upset you. I shouldn't have mentioned Lucy, I know you don't like to talk about her—'

'Oh, Archie.' His mother looked up, her face wet with tears. 'What have I done to you?'

And then she started crying again, her head buried in her hands. Archie stared at her, uncomprehending.

'I'm sorry,' he said again, anxious to stem her tears. 'I know I let you down, but I tried my best—'

'I'm the one who let you down. You and your sisters.' She looked up at him, her face puffy from crying. 'I was too wrapped up in myself to see how much you were suffering. I wasn't the mother you needed me to be.'

Archie stared at her, trying to take it in. 'You don't hate me?'

'How could I ever hate you? I love you and Kitty with all my heart.' Her mouth trembled. 'And to think I could have lost you . . .'

You nearly did. He looked to the empty chair and thought

about the woman who had been sitting there when he woke up in the night. If he closed his eyes he could still see her there, her blonde curls illuminated by the dim night light. She wasn't angry as she had been when he had seen her in his dreams. This time she was like her old self, smiling and warm.

'You daft bugger, Archie,' she had scolded him. 'You know you could have been killed, don't you? You'd best not do it again.'

'I won't.'

She had sat there for a long time, just watching him. Then, finally, she had stood up. Archie immediately felt a surge of panic. 'You're not leaving me?'

'I've got to go, lad.'

'Can't I go with you?'

She stroked his hair. Her touch was light, but he could feel the warmth of her hand. 'Silly boy, you've got to stay here. Your mum loves you.'

As she turned to go, he said, 'Is Lucy with you?'

'What do you think?' Auntie Dolly winked over her shoulder at him, and then she was gone. Archie had listened for the sound of her high heels tapping down the ward, but there was only silence. And then he had drifted off to sleep again.

And now his mother was here, clutching his hand and sobbing and telling him over and over again how sorry she was, and how much she wished she could have made things different.

'I'd turn back the clock if I could,' she wept. 'But all I can do is promise to change, to make things better—'

Your mum loves you. Auntie Dolly's words echoed in his head.

'I don't want you to change,' he said. 'You're my mum.'

'And you're my whole world.'

His mother hugged him again. And this time when the nurse stepped in and told her to stop she didn't listen, much to Archie's relief.

Chapter Forty-Nine

Friday 9th May 1941

Pearl came home from her shift on the buses exhausted. The last two nights' air raids had played merry hell with the route, and she'd had to deal with a lot of irate customers whose journey had taken them on some unexpected twists and turns.

'You didn't tell me you were only going as far as Baker Street,' one of them grumbled. 'I'm going to have to walk now.'

'Don't complain to me. Have a word with old Hitler, if you're not satisfied,' Pearl had retorted. 'And by the way, you're lucky to even have a bus after last night.'

All the bickering had left her worn out, and she was looking forward to sitting down and soaking her feet in a bowl of warm water and some Epsom salts. Her ugly corporation shoes pinched her feet far more than her high heels.

Her mother was in a state of high agitation when Pearl got home. As usual, there was no sign of an evening meal.

'You've not made a start on tea, then?' Pearl remarked. 'Honestly, it wouldn't kill you to stick on a pan of potatoes.'

'Sit down, I've got some news.' Her mother's faded blue eyes shone with excitement.

'What is it? Have you come up on the football pools?'

'Our Ruby's been bombed.'

'Never?' Pearl sank down on to the kitchen chair. 'Is she all right?'

'Oh, she's fine, so I gather. But her house is a right state. I walked round there and had a look for myself. There's nowt left of it, just a heap of dust and bricks and broken timber.' She crossed the kitchen to put the kettle on. 'Incendiary, so the ARP warden reckons. It was the only house in the street to get hit, too. Can you believe it?'

'Poor Ruby.'

'Oh, don't go feeling sorry for her. I daresay she's insured.'

'I daresay she is, but it's still a terrible thing to happen. That little house meant everything to her.'

'How the mighty are fallen, eh?'

Pearl stared at her mother. 'You don't have to look so happy about it.'

'I'm only saying, she could do with being taken down a peg or two.' Elsie banged the kettle down on the hob. 'She's always been one for lording it over everyone else, just because she's got a nice house and a husband that provides for her. Happen it'll do her good to find out what it feels like to lose everything.' Her face was bitter. 'I hope that lot at the Emergency Centre are just as high-handed to her when she's got nothing.'

'Our Ruby's never been high-handed in her life,' Pearl said.

'No? Look at the way she's treated you all these years. You've told me yourself how she treats you like a child, always telling you how to live your life.'

'She's only ever tried to help me, just like she helps everyone.'

It came as a revelation to her. Elsie was right, there had been times when Pearl resented her sister. Ruby always seemed to be right, and her constant advice grated on Pearl's nerves. But Pearl understood that her sister had only ever wanted to look after her.

'She never done anything for me.'

That was so typical of her mother, Pearl thought. She was

beginning to realise that Elsie only ever saw people for what she could get out of them.

We're like two peas in a pod.

'She might have if you'd been around all these years,' she said quietly.

Elsie looked shaken for a moment, her hand fiddling with the locket at her throat. Then she turned away sharply.

'I'll make a start on tea, shall I?' she mumbled.

'I'll do it.' Pearl rose wearily to her feet.

She couldn't stop thinking about Ruby. As she dropped peeled potatoes into the pan of water, she thought about all the times she had arrived at her sister's house without warning and expected to be fed. Ruby had never complained or turned her away. She had always welcomed her warmly and made sure there was enough food for her, even if she had to go without herself.

She had gone without so many times for her sake, Pearl thought. She remembered when they'd first left the orphanage. On her own, Ruby could have found a nice live-in job and not had to worry. But instead she had skivvied all day and cleaned down at the fish docks all night, just so she could put a roof over both their heads.

It had only been one dingy room in lodgings, but Ruby took real pride in it. She'd mended the torn curtains and lined the mantelpiece with cheap ornaments to make the place look cheerful. She beat the dust out of the rugs and aired the mattress to get rid of the bugs.

'Our first proper home,' she had said to Pearl. 'Just you and me.'

Pearl's smile faded. Had she been grateful for it? No. She had complained bitterly about the mice behind the skirting board, and the draught that rattled the window panes, and the fact that Ruby had separated her from all her friends at the orphanage. It hadn't even dawned on her what a terrible time she would have had there on her own if Ruby had chosen to abandon her.

But Ruby would never abandon her.

'I'm going to see her,' she announced.

'Eh? What for?'

'She's my sister. I might be able to help her.'

'You? Help?' Elsie laughed harshly. 'What could *you* do?'

'I don't know . . .' Pearl felt her confidence faltering.

'You've never helped anyone in your life. Take, take, take, that's all you've ever done.'

'I must get that from you, then.'

They glared at each other across the kitchen. Then Elsie said, 'She won't need you, anyway. She's got her family to look after her.'

'I *am* family.'

'Not any more,' Elsie cackled. 'You've well and truly burned your bridges there, my girl.'

'And whose fault is that?'

'Oh, don't go blaming me. You're always blaming other people for your own failings. You want to take a good look at yourself, instead of—'

'Where did you get that?' Pearl interrupted.

'What?'

'That locket you keep fiddling with. Where did you get it?'

'It's mine.'

'I've never seen you wear it before. Let me see it.'

'No!'

Elsie tried to move away but Pearl was too quick for her. She grabbed her mother by her narrow shoulders, swinging her round to face her so she could examine the chain around her neck.

It was only a cheap locket, the gold plate rubbed and faded

through wear. But there was a distinctive red stone in the middle of it that Pearl recognised immediately.

'That's Ruby's necklace,' she murmured.

'No, it in't.'

'It is, I'd know it anywhere. Where did you get it?'

Her mother's face twitched, and Pearl could see her mind working, trying to twist out another lie.

'If you must know, I found it when I went to see the house,' she said finally. 'But it's not how it looks,' she added quickly. 'I was keeping it for her. I salvaged it because I thought it might mean something to her.'

'Is that why you're wearing it round your neck?' Pearl was so angry, it was all she could do not to snatch it from her mother's scrawny throat. 'Give it to me.' She held out her hand.

'You don't understand.' Elsie's eyes filled with tears. 'I wanted to give it to her myself. I thought if I could do something nice for her, it might help make amends—'

'Don't make me laugh! You were going to keep it for yourself. Or pawn it.'

Elsie's tears dried instantly, her face hardening. 'So what if I was?' she said defensively. 'She's lost everything, she in't going to miss it, is she? It might fetch a few bob at the pop shop. Think what we could do with the money,' she said. 'We could treat ourselves. Happen you could get a new dress?'

Pearl stared at her mother, horrified. 'You'd rob your own daughter?'

'Why not? You've been doing it for years.'

They faced each other across the kitchen.

'I want you to leave,' Pearl said.

Elsie looked panic-stricken. 'You don't mean that.'

'I do, Mum. I want you to go.'

'You mean you'd put your own mother out on the streets?

What if there's another raid like last night or the one before? I wouldn't stand a chance.'

You'd be all right, Pearl thought. Elsie Finch was like one of those bed bugs that Ruby had tried so hard to get rid of from their lodging room. She would survive anything.

'You can stay till the morning, then you need to find somewhere else to live.'

'And where will I go?'

'Happen one of your friends can take you in? How about that one you go off drinking with while I'm at work all day?'

'All right, then, if that's the way you want it. I was thinking about moving on, anyway. You don't take care of me properly.' Elsie glared at her, her eyes narrowing with spite. 'But don't imagine that sister of yours will welcome you back with open arms. She's probably realised she's better off without you, just like I have!'

Chapter Fifty

'I've cleared a space in the wardrobe for you,' Florence said. 'And I've emptied the chest of drawers so you can put your things in there.'

'We don't have any things,' Ruby reminded her quietly.

'Oh. Oh no, of course not.' Florence blushed deeply. 'I'm sorry, I didn't think . . .'

Sybil started to cry, and Florence stared at her in dismay.

'I'll leave you to it, then.' She beat a hasty retreat from the bedroom, leaving Ruby and her two daughters alone.

'Come on, Syb, buck up.' Maudie put her arm around her sobbing sister. 'We've just got to make the best of it.'

Ruby knew she should comfort them, or at least say something to make them both feel better, but did not have the will to do anything. She could only sit there on the edge of Florence's bed, lost and numb. It was as if all the energy had drained out of her. Her body felt like a coal sack, too heavy to move. She could not even summon the will to pick up the cup of tea that was going cold on the nightstand in front of her.

It had been a long, exhausting day. She had spent most of it in various corporation offices, trying to sort out emergency ration books, insurance claims and various other bits of paperwork.

She had found herself sitting across the desk from a WVS volunteer just like herself. She looked so smart in her bottle green uniform, bristling with efficiency.

'You mean to tell me you don't have anything at all?' She stared at Ruby blankly. 'No bank books? Nothing?' Ruby shook her head. 'Well, this makes things very difficult. Most people keep their valuables in a bag and take them to the shelter.'

'I wasn't in the shelter when my house burned down. I was at the Emergency Centre, helping other people.'

That shut her up. Ruby wondered if this was how she had come across to all those other poor souls. She always thought she was being helpful, but with this woman she felt like just another name on the list, to be processed and pushed out of the door as quickly as possible.

Sitting there, among all the other helpless, homeless people in her borrowed clothes, Ruby wanted to cry. But her last shred of pride would not allow it.

John called up the stairs to say that tea was ready. When they went downstairs, Big May was bustling about, draining vegetables and taking a pot out of the oven.

'Here, let me help—' Ruby went to take the colander from her, but her mother-in-law waved her away.

'You sit yourself down, love.'

'But I always help.' Ruby looked around at Florence laying the table.

'Not this time. You've had a shock and you need to rest.'

'I in't an invalid,' Ruby muttered, but no one listened to her.

She sat down at the table with the others, her stomach roiling in protest at the plate of steaming yellow pease pudding John set down in front of her.

'I'm really not hungry,' she tried to say, but once again no one seemed to hear her. It was as if she had somehow become invisible, her voice ignored. In a matter of hours, she had gone from Ruby Maguire, the woman everyone depended on, to no one.

But that did not stop them discussing her. Ruby toyed with the food on her plate as she listened to the conversation going on around her.

'I had a word with my friend down at the corporation,' Pop was saying. 'He reckons it will be a while before they can start rebuilding the house.'

'We don't need to talk about that,' May said quickly. 'Ruby and the girls are welcome to stay here for as long as they like.'

'Aye, I know that. But she's going to want a place of her own.'

'Happen they could rent somewhere?' Florence suggested.

'She'll be lucky,' John said. 'I reckon there'll be a lot of people looking for places.'

'You're right.' Pop gestured to Ruby with his fork. 'You'll need to get your name down as soon as you can, lass.'

'Has anyone thought about telling our Jimmy? He'll want to know . . .'

Ruby looked from one to the other, letting it all wash over her. She felt as helpless as when she was a child in the orphanage, standing there with her arm around Pearl's shoulders, listening to the adults discussing what was to be done with them. She had always promised herself she would never be at the mercy of other people's charity again, and yet here she was.

'I was thinking, happen she could move into our Jack's house?' Florence was saying. 'He'll need someone to look after the lads while he's in hospital?'

Ruby stared down at her plate. She knew she should feel grateful that at least she had a roof over her head, but instead she felt broken and ashamed.

'Why don't you ask her what she wants?'

Ruby looked up sharply at the sound of her sister's voice. Pearl stood in the kitchen doorway, watching them.

Big May glared at her. 'How did you get in here?'

'Through the front door.'

'Nice of you to just walk in. People usually wait to be invited, in case you didn't know. Anyway, this is family business.'

'I am family.' Pearl folded her arms. 'I'm Ruby's family.'

'No one asked you to come.'

'And yet here I am.' Pearl met Ruby's eye defiantly across the room. 'And not a minute too soon, from the way you lot are going on.' She turned around to face them. 'Have you heard yourselves, talking about our lass as if she wasn't here?'

'No one asked you for your opinion,' Big May grumbled.

'No, and no one's asked Ruby either,' Pearl looked around at them all. 'You're all so sure you know what's best for her, yet no one's even bothered to ask her what she wants.'

'We're only trying to help,' Pop said reasonably.

'I'm sure you are,' Pearl said. 'But you don't know my sister.'

'And you do, I suppose?' Big May scoffed.

'I know she don't like to feel helpless. And I know she don't need people making decisions for her, no matter how well-meaning they are.'

May turned to Ruby. 'So what do you want to do?' she asked.

'I—' Ruby glanced back at her sister. Pearl nodded, silently encouraging her. Ruby took a deep breath.

'I want to go home,' she said.

They stood side by side, staring in silence at the broad drift of rubble that had once been her home.

Every so often, her gaze would alight on a familiar object amid the debris. The mirror that had been a wedding present, its glass now shattered in its twisted frame. A charred shred of fabric from the patchwork quilt she had made. The edge of the tin bath buried under a fallen wall.

302

All her treasured belongings, cruelly exposed to the world. 'It's all gone,' she said.

'You'll get it all back.'

'How? Look at it, Pearl. It's ruined. Everything's lost ...' Emotion choked her voice. 'How can I replace years and years of work, of memories?'

'You've still got your memories, in't you? And as for this,' she looked back at the ruined house. 'It's just bricks and mortar. A family's what makes a home, and yours are all safe, thank God.'

She bent down and picked up an object wedged under a lump of fallen brickwork. 'Here,' she said. 'Look at this.'

It was an old photograph, taken when the twins were babies. The glass was cracked and the edges of the photograph were scorched, but she could still make out their faces. Her and Jimmy, both looking so proud and happy, each holding a baby while Ada stood between them, smiling shyly at the camera.

'It's what's in that picture that's important,' Pearl said softly. 'And you've still got all that.'

'It's about all I've got.' Ruby smiled ruefully.

'It's all you need. For now. And as for the rest – you'll make a home for them. Just like you did for me.'

Ruby looked at her sister in surprise. 'Oh, Pearl.'

'Don't,' Pearl warned. 'Don't get soft with me, or we'll both be bawling like bains.' She reached into her pocket and handed her something. 'I nearly forgot. I've got this for you ...'

Ruby stared down at the locket nestling in her palm. The tiny stone winked deep crimson in the fading evening light. 'My Jimmy gave me this for our first anniversary.'

A ruby for my Ruby, he'd said.

'Where did you get it?'

Pearl shrugged. 'I found it.'

Ruby looked sideways at her sister. She had a feeling there was more to the story than Pearl was telling her.

'Thank you,' she said.

'I daresay we could find a few other bits, too, if we searched for them?'

Harry Pearce was standing guard over the wrecked house, but he allowed Ruby and Pearl to hunt for salvage. Most of the pieces they found were broken and burnt beyond recognition, or soaked by the firemen's hoses. Ruby found it very painful to see her treasured possessions ruined, and would have given up, but Pearl insisted they should keep looking. In the end they managed to retrieve quite a few pieces, including some pots and pans, a few bits of jewellery and even some clothes.

Ruby found herself smiling as Pearl struck a pose in one of Sybil's favourite hats, damp but still intact. She looked so daft standing on top of a mountain of broken bricks, a soggy feather dripping onto the end of her nose.

'I'm glad you made me do this,' she said as they carried her belongings across the street, a clock under one arm, a charred photograph album under the other.

'I'd like to help you, if I can.' Pearl was suddenly seriously. 'You've looked after me all these years. I reckon it's about time I did the same for you. If you'll let me?'

Ruby was about to say no, that she could manage very well by herself. Then she saw the hopeful look on her sister's face.

'I'd like that too,' she said.

Chapter Fifty-One

Saturday 7th June 1941

On a damp Saturday morning in June, Jack Maguire came home from hospital.

George and Freddie had been running back and forth down the street all morning, going to the corner every few minutes to look for Pop's rully.

'Bless them,' Big May said, smiling fondly through the window at them. 'They're so excited to have their dad back at last.'

They're not the only ones, Edie thought. She hadn't been able to sleep a wink the night before, thinking about it.

How would it be when he came home, she wondered. Their friendship – she still did not dare allow herself to call it more than that – had blossomed while he was in hospital. She had visited Jack as often as she could, sometimes sneaking in when his mother and the rest of the family weren't there, and other times using the excuse of taking the boys to visit their father. And when she could not visit, they had written each other long letters.

Jack had been all for being open with his family about their relationship.

'Why shouldn't we tell them? We in't done anything wrong,' he'd said.

But Edie had begged him to keep it a secret until he came home. 'At least then if they disapproved we could face them together,' she'd said.

'Why should they disapprove? My mother already loves you like one of her own. If anything, she'll probably think I'm not good enough for you!'

Edie watched Big May as she picked an ornament off the kitchen mantelpiece, polished it on her sleeve then put it back. The two of them had been cleaning the house all morning, scrubbing and dusting to get it ready for Jack's return.

Jack was right, Big May had taken Edie in to her family. But would she still feel the same when she found out she had fallen in love with her son? May Maguire might have a heart as big as the Humber, but she was also fiercely protective of her children.

'It will be good to have him home,' May's voice broke into Edie's troubled thoughts. 'It's just a shame that no sooner has one come home than the other is going.' She shook her head.

'I know, May.' It had come as no shock to anyone when Iris had announced she was taking Archie and Kitty to live in the country for a few months. 'But it's what she wants.'

'It'll do them all good, I daresay.' Big May smiled sadly. 'Anyway, one day when all this is over we'll all be together again. Even our Jimmy, God willing.' She crossed herself and glanced skywards. 'It's like in that song – "We'll meet again, don't know where, don't know when."'

'Shall I put the kettle on?' Edie offered.

'Yes please, love.'

As Edie filled it at the sink, Big May said, 'It's good of you to give me a hand with the cleaning. You didn't have to do it.'

'I don't mind. I'm happy to help.'

'I'm sure Jack will appreciate it, too.'

Their eyes met briefly, Edie looked away, blushing.

Iris swore her mother knew what was going on, but Edie wasn't so sure. Now she wondered if she should have done as Jack wanted and come clean right from the start. She didn't want Big May to think that she was deceitful, hiding things from her.

She sighed as she turned off the tap. She had got herself in a right muddle with it all.

'He's here!' George and Freddie tumbled into the room, their eyes shining with excitement.

'Where? Outside?' Big May wiped her hands on her apron.

'They're just coming down 'Road now.'

Edie was thrown into such confusion she dropped the kettle with a crash, splashing water everywhere.

'Someone's nervous,' Big May remarked, as Edie quickly grabbed a mop to soak up the puddle.

They came out of the house just as Pop's rully turned into the street, hooves clopping and harness jingling. Edie and May waited by the front door while Freddie and George tore down the street to greet them, running alongside the cart as it made its way down the terrace.

Jack was perched on top, next to his father. He looked pale and lean after nearly a month in hospital, but he smiled as he waved to the neighbours who came out of their houses to see him.

'Whoa, Bertha. We're here, girl.' Pop pulled up the rully and George ran to grab Bertha's harness while Freddie fetched her nosebag from the back of the cart. Not that Bertha was in a hurry to get away. After the long, slow plod down from Sutton all she wanted to do was rest and chomp on her oats.

'Welcome home, lad,' Big May greeted her son,

'Hollo, Mum.' Jack handed his wooden crutch down to his father, then manoeuvred himself to get down off the rully. Edie saw him struggling and without thinking she stepped forward and reached for his hand to help him. He stepped down, wincing with effort.

'Does it hurt?' Edie asked anxiously.

'Put it this way, I in't going to be doing the can-can in a hurry!' He grinned, still holding on to her hand. Edie tried to draw away but he held on, his gaze holding hers.

Big May coughed, breaking the moment. Edie pulled her hand from Jack's grasp, blushing guiltily.

Pop dragged the bag from the back of the rully. 'I'll take this inside, shall I?' He started towards the house but May said, 'Let the lads take it. We'll go home and leave them to settle in.'

'Eh?' Pop looked at her, frowning. 'What are you on about, woman? You've been up since dawn waiting for him.'

'Aye, but we don't want to overcrowd him when he's just got home, do we?'

Edie saw Pop's baffled look. 'I'll go—' she said. May shook her head.

'I reckon you're the one he wants to see, don't you?' she said with a wink.

Their eyes met and Edie saw the look of understanding on Big May's face. She had her blessing.

A huge wave of relief washed over her, and for the first time she allowed herself to relax. Perhaps it would be all right, after all?

'Thanks for the lift, Pop,' Jack said as they waved them off. 'I'll be joining you for a pint in the Fishermen's Rest later.'

'I'll hold you to that, lad,' Pop grinned.

As they headed into the house, Jack looked over his shoulder to the spot at the end of the terrace where Ruby's house had stood. Work had not yet started on it, and a drift of debris, broken timbers, roof slates and masonry still filled the gap.

'The corporation are going to start clearing it soon, so Pop says,' Edie said.

Jack nodded, but did not say a word. As he dragged his

gaze away, Edie saw the look of pain in his eyes. His physical injuries might be mending, but she knew there were other scars that might never heal.

'Come inside, Dad!' Freddie urged, grabbing his hand and pulling him towards the house. 'We've got a surprise for you.'

His brother turned on him. 'Freddie! You're not meant to say anything.'

'I didn't say what it was, did I?'

Jack looked at Edie. 'What's all this, then?'

'You'd best come and see.'

He followed her into the house, the boys rushing ahead of him. 'So what's this big surprise—' He stopped dead as a small, sandy brown missile shot down the passageway from the kitchen and launched itself into his arms. 'Lucky!'

'Oh no!' Edie cried. 'I thought I'd tied him up in the back yard!'

'He's even worse at surprises than Freddie!' George said.

Lucky's carefully tied bow had come loose around his neck but he did not seem to care as he licked Jack's face enthusiastically.

'Someone's pleased to see me!' Jack laughed. 'How did this come about?'

'Edie got him back!' Freddie said.

'You make it sound like I stole him!' Edie said, seeing Jack's eyebrows rise. 'His owner came round a few days ago,' she explained. 'He said the dog hadn't settled at his daughter's and she wanted him out. Apparently he barked and whined all night, and he chased her cat out of the house.'

'Did you do that?' Jack ruffled Lucky's coarse fur. 'Look at him. Like butter wouldn't melt.'

'He probably only did it because he wanted to come home to us,' George said.

'Anyway, she told her father he couldn't keep him, so he

called round to ask if you could give him a home.' She lowered her gaze. 'I hope you didn't mind that I said yes?'

'I would have minded more if you hadn't.' Jack looked into the dog's soulful eyes, and Lucky gazed adoringly back. 'So you're properly one of the family now, lad?'

'It's a shame for the old man, though,' George said.

'Aye, you're right. Still, happen he can come round and visit him sometimes?'

'I already told him he could,' Edie said, blushing.

'Great minds think alike.'

'But what shall we call him?' Freddie said. 'Should he be Lucky, or should we call him Toby now?'

'Lucky.' Jack met Edie's eye over the top of the dog's head. 'There in't too many people who get second chances at happiness, are there?'

Edie smiled back. 'Definitely Lucky,' she said. 'Very lucky indeed.'

Chapter Fifty-Two

Monday 9th June 1941

'Watch out!'

Ruby put her hand out, bracing herself against the dashboard as the van hit another deep crater in the road. Muddy spray flew up and there was a crash of china from the back.

'Stop screaming, you're making me nervous.' Pearl leaned over the steering wheel to peer through the mud-spattered windscreen.

'I'm making *you* nervous?'

'You're an even worse passenger than you are a driver, and that's saying something.'

Ruby winced as Pearl took the corner too quickly then screeched to a halt at the barrier across the road. There was another crash from the back.

'You didn't lock those cupboards properly, did you?' Ruby said.

'I thought you were meant to do it.' Pearl looked over her shoulder as she reversed the van up the narrow street, narrowly missing a man on a bicycle.

Ruby watched him shaking his fist at them through the rear-view mirror. 'Are you sure I shouldn't drive?'

'No, thank you.' Pearl looked offended. 'Anyway, I'm a better driver than you are. I'll have you know the police instructor said I was nearly perfect.'

'You must have been flirting with him.'

'Happen I was.' Her sister turned to wink at her. 'Old habits die hard, eh?'

'Look out!' Ruby gripped the edges of her seat as a coal cart swerved out of their way. 'Please try to keep your eyes on the road and your hands on the wheel.'

'That's just what I said to the police instructor!' Pearl roared with laughter and Ruby had to join in. Her sister was incorrigible but she was also very entertaining.

She took a sideways glance at her sister. Sometimes it seemed like a dream that Pearl was with her. She looked so smart in her bottle green WVS uniform, although being Pearl of course she had taken up the skirt and fitted the jacket so it showed off her curves.

'If I'm going to be a do-gooder, at least I can look good doing it,' she had said.

Miss Brekke the District Organiser was not in the least bit impressed, but she did not say anything because Pearl was such a hard worker and very popular, especially with the men in the ARP rescue parties. Ruby also suspected she was a bit intimidated by Pearl, who wasn't afraid to answer her back.

Pearl caught her looking and said, 'What are you staring at?'

'Nothing,' Ruby smiled. 'I was just thinking how nice this is, that's all.'

'Driving through the rain on a Monday morning to serve tea to soldiers, you mean? Yes, it's my idea of heaven.' Pearl smiled wryly. 'What with this and the buses, I never seem to be out of a bloody uniform these days!'

Ruby would never have imagined her sister getting a job, let alone sticking to it. But she was astonished at how much Pearl had changed over the past few weeks.

The blitz had turned both their lives upside down. Ruby had lost not just her home that night, but her self-respect and her identity with it. She was completely and utterly lost, but amazingly it was Pearl who had helped her find herself again. She had been a real tower of strength to Ruby, bringing her and the girls to live with her, shopping and cooking for them, doing their washing and looking after the house. She patiently listened and offered a shoulder to cry on when Ruby needed it, but she also stopped her wallowing in her own misery.

It was Pearl who had gently bullied Ruby into going back to the WVS when she felt too embarrassed to face everyone. She had even started volunteering herself so she could be at her sister's side if she needed her.

In a way, losing her house had been a blessing in disguise for all of them, Ruby thought. It had given Pearl a chance to show her strength, and it had given Ruby a chance to be vulnerable for once.

'Don't be soppy, you know I can't stand it.' Pearl snapped her back to the present. 'Tell me where we're supposed to be going again? I've lost my way with all these roads closed.'

'I've got it here somewhere . . .' Ruby rifled through the papers on her lap for the directions they had been given. She was just trying to make out Miss Brekke's elaborate handwriting when Pearl suddenly jammed on the brakes again, throwing them both forward as the van screeched to a halt.

'Did you see that?' Pearl sounded breathless.

'What? Oh God, don't tell me you've run another cat over?'

'It was our mother.'

'What? Where?' Ruby craned to look over her shoulder.

'Look, over there. Walking away from us on the other side of the street.'

'I can only see that well-to-do couple – oh!'

As the couple crossed the street, Ruby caught a glimpse of the woman's sharp profile, the narrow little mouth. But her shabby fur coat had been replaced by a gleaming sable, and her bleached blond hair was hidden under an elaborately feathered hat.

She strolled on the arm of a tall, distinguished-looking gentleman in a smart suit.

'It *is* her,' Ruby marvelled. 'But who's that she's with?'

'I don't know. But it looks like she's found herself a rich one!' Pearl shook her head. 'You've got to admire her, in't you? Whatever happens, she always falls on her feet.'

'I'm glad,' Ruby said. 'I didn't like to think of her on her own.'

'She'll never be on her own,' Pearl said. 'Not while there's someone daft enough to pay her bills for her.'

She looked so bitter about it, Ruby felt sorry for her. They did not discuss their mother, but Ruby knew Pearl was hurt at how her mother had used her. Even after she'd gone, Pearl discovered Elsie had helped herself to the wages Pearl had squirreled away in a shoe box at the bottom of her wardrobe.

'Anyway, let's talk about something else,' Pearl said briskly. 'What do you fancy for your tea tonight? I heard a rumour the butcher has some ox tongue.'

'If he has, I expect it'll all be gone by the time we get back,' Ruby said gloomily. 'Tell you what, I'll go shopping later. If I can't get the tongue I can always cook sausages and mash—'

'I can cook,' Pearl interrupted her. 'It's my turn, remember?'

Ruby hesitated. Once she might have taken charge, but things had changed. 'If you like,' she said.

'Although ...' Pearl slanted a sideways look at her. 'I wouldn't mind a few bob to go shopping for food, if you can spare it?'

Ruby grinned. At least some things never changed.

And she was very glad about that.

Chapter Fifty-Three

Monday 9th June 1941

The rain had cleared by the time Pop finished loading up the rully and pulled the tarpaulin over the bags in the back.

'Better to be safe than sorry,' he said, squinting up at the grey sky. 'It's quite a way to Cottingham and it looks like it might pour again before we get there.'

'Anyone would think you were moving away forever, the amount of stuff you're taking,' May said.

Iris smiled as she watched Pop fixing the tailgate in place. 'I'll be back, don't you worry.'

'Are you sure about that?'

'I'll be back, Mum.' Iris laid her hand on her mother's arm. 'It's only for the summer. We'll come home for when Archie starts school again in September.'

'Listen to what she says, May,' Beattie put in. 'She won't stay there. We're fishing folk, we in't made for the country.'

Her mother looked troubled. 'I just don't like the thought of you staying with strangers, that's all.'

'They're not exactly strangers. I went to school with Lilian, remember?'

'I remember her,' Beattie said. 'Very whiny girl, as I recall.'

Iris glanced at her neighbour. She did not understand why Beattie was even there, apart from the fact that she liked to stick her nose into everything. She had dragged Charlie out of the house to see Iris off.

Iris had hoped that Sam might be there too, but Beattie said he was still at work.

'I liked her,' Iris said firmly. 'And she was good enough to invite us to stay.'

They had stayed in touch after they'd left school and got married. Lilian had wed a farmer and moved out of the city, and she had come to visit Iris a couple of times while she was in hospital since it was close by the farm. When she had heard what had happened to poor Archie, she had written to Iris straight away to invite them to stay.

'It sounds ideal,' Iris said to her mother. 'They've got a nice little cottage on their land for us, and the bains will love it. Archie can help out on the farm, too. And you never know, I might even try my hand at being a land girl myself!'

'Happen you're right,' her mother agreed grudgingly. 'The fresh air will do the bains good. Especially him,' she glanced over at Archie.

Not just the fresh air, Iris thought. Even now, knowing they were going to leave, Archie was the happiest she had seen him in a very long time. The weight of the world had gone from his shoulders.

'If you ask me, Archie's been a lot happier since *he* went,' Beattie said. 'Mind, so have the rest of us,' she added, tight-lipped.

There was no need to ask who she meant. Matthew and John had finally found a ship and returned to sea two weeks earlier.

There had been no tearful goodbyes, and no promises to see each other again. It was as if they both knew that their relationship had come to its end that night in May. But Iris did not regret the short time they had spent together. If she had not been with Matthew, she might never have realised what was truly important to her. She would have been running lost forever.

'You will come back and visit before September, won't you?' her mother asked.

'Of course I will.'

'Cheer up, May,' Beattie nudged her. 'Your Ruby will be moving in to look after the house, so you'll have her close by again.'

Her mother frowned. 'I don't know about that,' she grumbled. 'We've hardly seen her since she moved in with her sister. They're thick as thieves now.' She sighed. 'It seems like this whole family is growing apart.'

'At least our Jack's home,' Iris said. 'And you never know, it might not be long before Edie and Bobby join the family.'

That drew a smile to her mother's face. 'Wouldn't that be lovely?' she said.

'Aye, it would,' Iris said, and she meant it. It was wonderful that Edie and Jack had found each other after they'd both been through so much heartache. She could not think of anyone better suited to her brother.

'Here's my Sam now,' Beattie said.

Iris swung round. Sam Scuttle was hurrying down the street towards them, still in his fireman's uniform and heavy boots. Archie ran down the street to meet him.

'I had to stay on past the end of my shift,' Sam said. 'I thought I'd missed you.'

'Surely you didn't run all the way from the station?' Iris said.

Colour tinged his cheeks. 'Just to see you? Don't flatter yourself.' He turned to the children. 'But I couldn't let this pair go without saying goodbye.'

He swept Kitty up in his arms, swinging her high into the air. She squealed with delight.

'So you won't miss me, then?' Iris said.

'I daresay we'll get used to the peace and quiet.' He looked sideways at her.

The next moment Sam had turned away from her, hoisting Archie up so they were eye to eye. 'I reckon you'll be as tall as me next time I see you.'

'Don't be daft, I won't be away that long!'

'I hope not.' He glanced at Iris. 'I suppose it depends if your mother gets a taste for country air.'

'Not a chance. I'll probably be on the first train back if a cow gives me a funny look.'

They grinned at each other. This was how they had been over the past month, laughing and joking together. Whatever else was happening under the surface, it seemed as if neither of them dared to make the first move.

She wished she could find the right words to tell him how she felt about him, but somehow they wouldn't come.

Charlie cleared his throat and tapped his brother on the shoulder. Sam turned to look at him. 'What is it?'

Charlie gestured to Iris, then to him. Iris watched as he and Sam carried on what seemed to be a very animated, but totally silent, conversation. It reminded her of the argument she had witnessed on the night Charlie had braved the tunnel to rescue Archie and Jack.

'What's going on?' She asked Beattie.

'Search me,' she shrugged. 'But I've seen them go on like this for hours.'

Finally, Sam turned away from his brother.

'Well?' Iris asked.

Sam glanced back at Charlie, then without warning he stepped forward, trapped Iris's face between his hands and kissed her firmly on the lips.

Before she had a chance to react he released her. 'Happy

now?' he said over his shoulder to his brother.

Charlie grinned and gave them a thumbs up.

'About time, too,' her mother declared.

'I'll say,' Beattie agreed. 'For a lad who never speaks, you certainly managed to talk some sense into your brother,' she said to Charlie.

Iris and Sam smiled sheepishly at each other.

'I suppose you could always come and visit us?' she said.

'I suppose I could.'

'Just for the bains, obviously.'

'Why else would I traipse all the way out to Cottingham?'

Pop sighed. 'Well, this is all very nice, but we really need to get going if we want to get there before the rain starts again.'

Iris climbed up on the rully next to Pop, and Sam hoisted the children up to her. As her father jingled the reins and the cart lurched forward, Iris looked back over her shoulder at Sam and the others. She waved to her mother, Beattie and Charlie, but it was Sam she fixed her gaze on until they turned the corner and he was out of sight.

They carried on for a while in silence, the only sound the steady clop of Bertha's hooves. As they passed through the city, Iris could hardly bear to look at the blackened ruins of the buildings. When she looked at her father, she noticed he also kept his gaze downwards, fixed firmly on Bertha's rolling flanks.

'You're doing the right thing, getting away,' he said gruffly. 'You don't want to stay here. It in't good for them,' he glanced down at Archie and Kitty, tucked in between them.

'I'm not sure Mum agrees.'

'You know what she's like. She always frets when her bains are away from home. But happen you won't stay away so long this time, eh?'

'We'll be back before you know it,' Iris said. She touched

her fingers to her lips, where she could still feel the imprint of Sam's kiss.

'You come back when you're ready,' Pop said. 'You need to get yourself and your family right first. This will all be here waiting for you when you come back. And so will that lad,' he added, guessing her thoughts. 'Lord knows, he's been waiting long—'

'Stop the cart.'

'Why?' He glanced back at the back of the cart. 'Surely you can't have forgotten owt?'

'I need to go back.'

Pop sighed. 'I told you, Sam will wait for you—'

'It's not Sam. There's someone else I need to see first. To say goodbye.' *Someone I should have said goodbye to a long time ago*, she thought. It had taken a while, but at last she felt ready.

Pop looked at her for a long time. Then he nodded wisely and pulled on Bertha's reins to turn the cart.

'Wait,' Iris said. 'I haven't told you where we're going.'

'Oh, I know where we're going,' he said. 'We're going to see Lucy.'

Acknowledgements

2020 was a funny old year, and certainly a strange time to write a book. But writing about families struggling to cope with their own fears for their survival really put the pandemic in perspective for me.

Due to lockdown, I missed my regular trips to Hull History Centre. Luckily I had copious research notes to keep me going, and I'd like to thank the very helpful City Archives staff for that. I'd also like to thank Leo Whisstock of the RNPS Society for his help in tracking down a suitable land-based job for Jack and thus saving me a huge plot problem.

In the absence of physical research I had to rely on books for much of my information. I was very lucky to get my hands on two wonderful accounts of the Hull Blitz – *City On Fire* by Nick Cooper and *A City In Flames* by Esther Baker. And thanks to the amazing British Newspaper Archive, I was also able to read first-hand accounts of the air raids in the *Hull Daily Mail*, which really helped with fitting all the dates and times together. Any errors are entirely mine, and strictly in the interests of telling a better story!

My wonderful editor Katie Brown left while I was writing the book, and I would like to thank her for her all her help and enthusiasm in getting the Yorkshire Blitz series going in the first place. She has been replaced by the equally wonderful Rachel Neely. Hopefully by the time this book comes out we will have been able to meet properly!

Thanks also to the publicity, marketing and sales teams at Orion, who have worked so hard on my behalf. And to my amazing agent, Caroline Sheldon, who has been such a tower of strength, albeit from a distance. I'm looking forward to a lunch in London at the first opportunity!

Last but not least, thank you to my family – Ken, Harriet, Lewis and baby Seb. Especially Harriet, who is my first reader and my fiercest critic. I'm so pleased to say she loved this one, even if I did fail to give the red cardigan a satisfactory ending ...

Credits

Orion Fiction would like to thank everyone who worked on the publication of *A Sister's Wish*.

Agent
Caroline Sheldon

Editor
Rachel Neely

Copy-editor
Ilona Jasiewicz

Proofreader
Melissa Smith

Editorial Management
Clarissa Sutherland
Charlie Panayiotou
Jane Hughes
Claire Boyle
Jake Alderson

Audio
Paul Stark
Amber Bates

Contracts
Anne Goddard
Paul Bulos
Jake Alderson

Design
Lucie Stericker
Debbie Holmes
Joanna Ridley
Nick May
Clare Sivell
Helen Ewing

Production
Claire Keep
Fiona McIntosh

Publicity
Alainna Hadjigeorgiou

Marketing
Brittany Sankey

Sales

Jen Wilson
Victoria Laws
Esther Waters
Lucy Brem
Frances Doyle
Ben Goddard
Georgina Cutler
Jack Hallam
Ellie Kyrke-Smith
Inês Figuiera
Barbara Ronan
Andrew Hally
Dominic Smith
Deborah Deyong
Lauren Buck
Maggy Park
Linda McGregor
Sinead White
Jemimah James
Rachael Jones
Jack Dennison
Nigel Andrews
Ian Williamson
Julia Benson
Declan Kyle
Robert Mackenzie
Imogen Clarke
Megan Smith
Charlotte Clay
Rebecca Cobbold

Finance

Jennifer Muchan
Jasdip Nandra
Rabale Mustafa
Ibukun Ademefun
Levancia Clarendon
Tom Costello

Operations

Jo Jacobs
Sharon Willis
Lisa Pryde

Rights

Susan Howe
Richard King
Krystyna Kujawinska
Jessica Purdue
Louise Henderson